SHIFT

THE BLACK MOUNTAIN PACK BOOK 1

LANA SKY

Shift

Shift By Lana Sky

Copyright © 2022 by Lana Sky
All rights reserved.

Cover Design and Interior Formatting by Charity Chimni
Editing by Charity Chimni

ACKNOWLEDGMENTS

Thanks so much to everyone who supported this draft along the way, including the many beta readers who provided encouragement! Please keep in mind that this story includes dark, graphic, and explicit content matter that may not be suitable for readers under the age of 18—or for readers who are uncomfortable with the following subject matter: age-gap relationships, explicit sex, mentions of abuse, and graphic depictions of violence.

*L*oren Connors faced the world beyond the battered screen door with the same hope she had every morning since moving in ten months ago. Was it too much to ask if today could be…

A little less shitty?

As always, the optimism didn't last. Seconds into her trek to the bus stop, a familiar dread ran down her spine, heralding a truth that seemed as inevitable as the rain promised by the purple clouds swirling above. Today would be just like the rest—another shitstorm she'd have to trudge through in a worn pair of sneakers.

The shoes were a sticking point, weighing on her mind with every step. Last night, she'd hoped to convince her father to buy new ones. A pair of boots, perhaps? It was the least he could do. Considering that she'd destroyed her sneakers performing the job that should have been his—delivering newspapers to their outlying part of town.

She planned to spring the request on him last night after dinner, when he was well into his second beer. Winter was approaching fast, and the bottoms of her *Kicks* were already reinforced with more duct tape than the original soles.

To be fair, the attempt almost succeeded. She cooked dinner like usual and even managed to stay out of his way afterward.

But then...

She got too close. Close enough for him to smell *it* on her —the intoxicating scent of fresh air and horses. Instantly, he knew she had been *there*.

Game over.

Instead of new shoes, that bit of disobedience earned her a blow to the chest that still ached beneath her sweater. Her sole consolation was that he didn't hit her in the face, where the resulting bruise would signal that all was not well within the crumbling walls of the Connors' household.

Devising excuses to explain the multiple injuries had become a game of sorts during the few months she lived with him. Today she'd need a reason to skip gym, where the thin T-shirt wouldn't be enough to disguise this newest injury.

Her period, maybe? Or had she used that excuse last week? Lost in thought, she didn't notice a hot pink sports car pulling up alongside her until one of the occupants called out.

"Hey, Connors." The driver, a beautiful blond by the name of Naomi, cackled maliciously. "Need a ride?"

Loren didn't bother replying. Like a turtle recoiling in its shell, she had her own tricks to avoid detection—keep walking and mentally count the steps remaining between her and the bus stop.

One. Two. Three.

"Naomi," a minion stage-whispered from the convertible's back seat. "You know she's like, *mute.*"

Loren felt her lips quirk into a faint smile. As far as the student body at New Walsh Academy was concerned, she had spoken all of ten words since she'd moved there. Namely to teachers, and never without vigorous prompting on their part.

The rumored consensus was she was cripplingly shy, or a little "touched." Mute. The real explanation was a lot simpler. It was so much easier to live a lie in silence. There was a selfish motivation, too. If she *hadn't* clammed up all those years ago, the sound of her own screaming might have driven her insane. Still, she should have had enough sense to hide her emotions this time—her smile was too wide, and Naomi's green eyes cut to her maliciously.

"You think this is funny?" The tires of that expensive sports car squealed as Naomi slammed her foot on the brake. "I think I prefer your dumb blank stare to that shitty little smirk."

"Hey..." The second minion spoke up. "Naomi, I don't want to be late again—"

The blond shrugged off the protest. "Just a second."

With her head held high, she climbed from the driver's seat to block Loren's path.

"You think you're so much better than us, Connors?" she demanded, hands on her perfectly slender hips. "Ever since you moved here, you've been a stuck-up little bitch, walking around with your nose in the air. Hello? I'm talking to you—"

Loren barely heard her. She was too busy eyeing the girl's beautiful pair of faux-kidskin boots. Obviously, she didn't have to beg *her* father for new shoes.

"Hey!" A pair of manicured fingers appeared beneath her nose, snapping impatiently. "I'm talking to you, Connors. Do. You. Think you're better than us?"

Naomi gestured to her so-called friends, who all seemed like bleached-blond copies.

Loren shook her head and kept walking.

Five.

Six.

Seven—

"Not so fast."

A hand latched onto her forearm, wrenching her around. She staggered to find her balance, and a sharp pain lanced through the sole of her foot. *Oh no.* Some of the duct tape must have worn through.

Distracted, she missed the manicured hand swiping at her face. *Wham!* The blow dislodged her woolen cap, and her hair fell loose, tangling around her shoulders.

"Did you hear me?" Naomi demanded. "Or are you *deaf,* too?"

Blank, Loren scolded herself, fighting to smother her shock. *Be empty. Make your face a mask—that's it. Never let them in. Never let them see.*

Once she regained control of her breathing, she stooped for her hat. The second her fingers contacted the wool, the heel of a thigh-high white boot descended to crush them.

Loren gasped before she could reel it in.

Mistake, a part of her scolded. *Big mistake.*

"So, she *does* speak!" Naomi cackled with glee and snatched for her forearm next.

Dragged to her feet, Loren lost her grip on her bag, spilling books and materials over the sidewalk. "No! Don't!" she croaked, this time consciously.

Unbothered, Naomi stooped for her bag and rifled through it.

"Oh, what?" she taunted. "Don't want us to see what the little mouse is always hiding?"

She overturned the bag, dumping out the contents.

Loren winced as her homework scattered on the wind, but nothing tugged at her heart more than the plastic baggie full of carrots that landed in the street. Or the apple that dented against the damp ground.

"Is that her lunch?" Someone giggled from the car's back seat.

No. Most of the time, she went hungry, though some days Mona, the lunch lady, tossed her a banana from the lunch line if she looked pathetic enough.

The carrots, carefully rescued from the back of the fridge among the many cases of beer, had been a gift meant for the only friends she had. And Naomi gleefully stomped them into mush without a second thought.

"Guess you'll just have to go without, hun," a blond from the convertible suggested.

Don't cry, Loren told herself, blinking against that warning sting prickling the backs of her eyes. Still, her heart lurched as Naomi turned her attention to the discarded apple.

"Stop!" The plea broke loose, hoarse and broken. She raced forward, but Naomi kicked the apple out of her reach.

"Hold the bitch back," Naomi demanded, and, like well-trained dogs, her two minions scrambled from the back seat to do her bidding.

One snatched a chunk of Loren's hair and used it as a leash to keep her restrained, while the other kicked the fruit into the street.

"Aw, look," the culprit taunted. "She looks like she's going to cry."

Loren tried to keep the tears at bay but failed. Unbidden, they coated her cheeks in bursts of warmth. Sorrow wasn't the source—just guilt and rage. It had been so *hard* to scavenge those meager offerings. If her father knew that she had stolen the carrots, he'd…

Kill her.

"Aww, lighten up, Connors," Naomi urged cheerfully. "It's not like any guy will give you the time of day, even if you went on a diet."

They all laughed, but Loren flinched, subconsciously huddling tighter within the confines of her sweater. Attention from anyone was the last thing she wanted.

The only plus side to having little money to spend on clothes was that the few things she *did* own were nondescript and shapeless. The perfect armor to go unnoticed. The sweater she wore now was four sizes too big and hung to her knees, perfectly obscuring the pair of black leggings that had cost fifty cents at *Goodwill*.

"Ah, look, Naomi," the second minion remarked on a laugh. "She's blushing."

"Maybe she already has a boyfriend?" the girl clutching her hair wondered with a playful yank.

"As *if*," Naomi countered. "Who would date a freak like her? I wouldn't walk around so high and mighty if I came from a shithole like little Loren here. My dad knows the police chief from Ridgerton."

Loren flinched at the name. It was a town a few hours north, and the focal point of most of her nightmares.

"I heard them talking about a case that occurred under my father's friend's jurisdiction. A certain case involving a woman who killed herself one day, leaving her daughter to be shipped off to an uncle who lived in town. From the outside looking in, everything had appeared okay at first. Until neighbors started hearing the screaming at night—"

No. Fear gripped Loren's lungs, painfully squeezing out whatever air they contained. *No.* She *wouldn't* go back there. Not to that house, or that room—*God,* not that room. Not to the stifling scent of cheap cologne, or the darkness, and pain…

"Naomi…" Minion number one took a step back. "This isn't funny. Knock it off."

"Why?" the blond demanded. "I was just getting to the *best* part. Apparently, this Uncle *Bart*—"

"Stop!" The other minion was shouting now, disobeying the unspoken cardinal rule of being one of Naomi's "friends."

Like sheep, Loren thought around a hysterical snicker. Naomi liked her friends like a shepherd liked his sheep. But Uncle Bart hadn't liked it when she talked back, either.

He didn't like it at all.

"No," Naomi hissed.

Then she crouched before Loren so that they were nose to nose.

"They say a neighbor finally called a cop one night," she continued. "Apparently, the girl wouldn't speak. She just went to school one day and *stopped talking*. Clammed up. When they searched that house, the things they found there... Some on the force still talk about it to this day."

Loren knew damn well what they had found. A room. One so small it seemed more like a closet. In fact, it *was* a closet. Clothes had been kept there—sometimes, lying there at night, she could almost smell the mothballs.

Of course, what had caught everyone's attention had probably been the chains. Long, they had stretched from a man-made post drilled into the wall. The perfect length for her to use the bathroom at night whenever her cell happened to be unlocked.

"The conditions were so bad that they relocated the girl to a different city rather than find a foster family in Ridgerton. With a father who hadn't even wanted her in the first place." Naomi's voice was cold. Like the detached voice of a narrator on the evening news.

And the girl, whose name has not been released, was removed from the home. Rescued...

Only not really.

"*Still* think you're better than me, Connors?" Naomi snarled. "Still think that, huh?"

"Naomi! We're leaving," Minions one and two announced, backing away as swiftly as their nice shoes could carry them. "We can *walk* to school."

"Fine. Leave then," Naomi snapped. "But don't think this changes anything. You're *nothing*, Loren Connors."

But that was the whole point. She *was* nothing—hell, she strived to be nothing.

"But, hey," Naomi added with a cruel smile of mocking perfection. "Like mother like daughter—"

Snap!

It was something internal. Some intangible muscle right *there* in the pit of her stomach that cracked at the comparison. Like daughter, like...

Mother.

Her mother had been beautiful, happy, young, carefree—before life and sorrow beat her down. Loaded her with pain that she couldn't bear. Couldn't escape, except for one way out...

In the pit of her soul, Loren knew that she wasn't like her mother.

She wasn't brave.

She was weak. Too weak to fight. Too weak to die.

Until now.

Her vision went red. *Insanity*, Loren thought. She had just gone insane.

Lost her damn mind.

She once read in a book that one of the signs of schizophrenia was alternate perceptions of reality. You saw things that weren't there. Heard things…

But Loren doubted that description included launching yourself at your enemy with your hands drawn like claws.

And, she was pretty confident that when most people succumbed to schizophrenia, they didn't growl. They didn't bare their teeth like fangs and…snarl.

At least, for the first time in her life, as she raked her nails along the perfect skin of Naomi Tanner's face, the blood on her fingers wasn't her own.

2

L oren!

Loren Connors!

Someone was calling her name—though the ringing in her ears could be another symptom of insanity. She'd already hit the trifecta of potential red flags. Hearing voices. Losing control of her limbs. Feeling so much rage, she could *explode*.

For the first time in her life, Loren Connors didn't want to hide. She wanted to…

Kill. The impulse wasn't coherent—more like a writhing mass of urges, she felt all at once. A need to draw blood, attack…bite? Experimentally, she snapped at the air. Oh hell, yeah, she wanted to bite, but something firmer. Her teeth ached with a sudden need that had her glancing down, through a haze of red.

She wanted flesh…

"LOREN CONNORS!" The bellowed shout resonated like a gut punch.

As her vision cleared, several realizations confronted her at once. The foremost being that she was straddling Naomi Tanner. Not only that, but...

God, she had both hands around the girl's slender throat— so tightly Naomi's green eyes bulged from their sockets.

And blood splattered her chin. In tiny rivulets, it stemmed from three violet marks streaked across the side of Naomi's fashionably tanned cheek.

Oh no, Loren thought, horrified. *Did I do that?*

"Get the fuck off me!" Naomi lashed out. With the strength that came from years of training as the head cheerleader, the blond easily shoved her off. Not before giving her a kick to the stomach as a parting gift.

But, Loren was forced to realize that *she*—a girl with barely enough muscle on her wiry frame to fill a teaspoon—had knocked Naomi down in the first place.

And choked her.

Wide-eyed, Loren gaped at her own hands. They couldn't belong to her, not mousy Loren Connors. Someone else. *Something* else.

"Oh, I am so pressing charges, you stupid bitch!"

"That's enough, Ms. Tanner." The voice was too deep to belong to one of the minions. Or a woman. It was masculine, richer than any baritone she'd ever heard.

"Did you see what she fucking did? Well, aren't you going to *do* something?"

It was only then that Loren noticed the man nearby, standing behind the open door of a police squad car. He was tall, imposingly so, with stern features and piercing gray eyes. Eyes that bore into hers as he spoke a command solely directed her way.

"Get back." To her ears, it sounded like a stern suggestion, but inside her head…

It was an order.

Heart pounding, Loren scrambled backward until she sat fully in the mud, a good five feet from Naomi.

"God! She scratched me!" the blond shrieked, cupping the side of her face. "Should I go to the hospital? Get a damn rabies shot or something?"

"I'm sure you'll be fine, Ms. Tanner," the officer replied. Once again, his tone resonated with double-meaning. Less concerned and more…mocking? "Though, if you want, I can call ahead to the hospital to let them know you'll be coming in."

"Thanks," the blond muttered as she flashed Loren a glare that could melt steel. Then she entered her car and took off.

The officer waited until that pink vehicle finally turned the corner before returning his attention to Loren. Tense with anticipation, she braced for a scolding.

Care to explain? It was what her father said when she did something wrong. Before she could respond, he always followed up the question with a blow. A kick. A punch.

Instead, the officer inspected her with an intensity presumably reserved for only the most dangerous criminals. He started with her head, roving his gaze down her body, almost as if searching for something. *For any weakness,* a part of her suspected.

"You could be in a lot of trouble, Ms. Connors," he said finally. His voice was no less booming, reducing her to a cowering puddle. It wasn't only his tone causing such a reaction.

From her position on the ground, he seemed massive, undeniably handsome—but in her world, beauty meant danger.

He had a face that could have been chiseled from stone, with stern cheekbones, pink lips, and a smattering of black stubble along his jaw—a jaw currently set in a firm line.

"Especially if Naomi Tanner does decide to press those charges," he continued. "Her father is the head of the city council."

Loren felt her bottom lip tremble. Then, hot and fast, more tears spilled down her cheeks. All she could do was brace her blood-stained fingers against the muddy earth and try to keep her composure.

Sobbing would help nothing. Neither would begging, but both impulses were all she seemed capable of at the moment.

"I'm sorry," she rasped. "I'm so sorry. I didn't mean—I mean I...I didn't...I just." She was rambling. After years without carrying on a full conversation, even forming a coherent sentence took effort. "I'm sorry. I'm sorry. I'm sorry—"

"Here."

In the space of a second, the officer cleared the distance between them, holding her backpack by its filthy strap. He was trying to be helpful; she could tell that much. He had no idea that the sight of him, towering above, reminded her of someone else.

"I'm sorry!" She threw herself face-forward into the icy muck, hands over her head to ward off the blow she knew was coming. Instead of the threat of physical violence, the only sound she heard was...

Thunk. Peeking through a fringe of hair, she realized the noise was that of her math book being dropped into her bag by the officer. He did the same with her scattered pencils and notebook. Then he extended a calloused hand in her direction.

"Can you stand up?" Once again, what sounded like a harmless question resonated in her bones far differently.

Stand up. Her limbs lurched into motion before her brain processed the action. As she inspected herself from the neck down, she couldn't suppress a groan at the sight of her clothes. Her tights were caked in mud. So was the bottom of her sweater.

If she went to school like this, they'd send her home. Or worse, call her father. Either prospect was so terrifying she didn't hear the officer speak until he shouted.

"Loren, did you hear me?"

She jumped, too shaken to wonder just how he knew her name. Though…as she eyed the planes of that strong face, she realized that she knew *him.*

Officer McGoven. *That asshole McGoven,* according to her father. The very same officer who came by whenever he and his drinking buddies got too rowdy and alarmed the neighbors.

He had never seen *her,* of course. She would watch him through her bedroom window and wonder how one man could possess so much patience.

Never once did he raise his voice, even when her father and his cohorts would threaten violence. He seemed unshakable, someone worthy to carry a badge—a rare quality in her opinion.

From far away, she'd gotten a good idea of his bulk, but up close, he was downright intimidating. She'd never met anyone with eyes like his. They gleamed silver in contrast to his dark hair, which looked slicked back as if by a lazy hand.

Tanned skin the exact shade of pure honey softened the effect somewhat, keeping him from seeming frightening. Just stern. She wondered at his heritage—Native American, mixed with a bit of European to explain the eye color?

It was the same guess she figured most people made whenever they looked at her, with her dark hair, pale skin, and wide hazel eyes.

"If you would like to get a change of clothes, I can give you a ride to school," he offered. "It looks like you missed the bus."

Oh no. Loren realized it must have passed by during the scuffle with Naomi, and her heart sank. His offer aside, walking was her only choice. She loathed deceiving an officer, but she rationalized it the way she always did—lying wasn't a sin if survival was on the line.

"I…I don't have any clean clothes," she told him. "And it's laundry day. I'll be fine on my own." As the words left her mouth, the man gave her an odd look that made her stomach flip. Like he knew she was lying. Regardless, for once in her life, she couldn't seem to shut up. "Our washing machine is broken, too. My father hasn't gone to the laundry mat yet. I'll be fine once I get to school—"

"You should wash up," he repeated. His voice was so strange, seeping into her brain and battling the logical part of her that resisted. *You should listen,* a part of her urged. *It's fine. Go with him…*

"F-forgot my key," she lied again.

He cocked his head. Then he returned to his patrol car, still holding her backpack hostage. "Get in. My place isn't far from here. You can wash up there, and I'll have you at school before the bell rings."

Loren tried to keep the panic from her voice—she was all out of lies. "R-Really, I'm fine."

"I insist." His tone left no room for argument. "Get in."

Like a puppet on a string, she lurched forward. Step by tortured step, she approached his vehicle.

"You can sit up front," McGoven suggested. Already, he had climbed into the driver's seat and leaned over to push the passenger-side door open.

Aware of her filthy appearance, Loren perched herself on the seat's very edge.

"Sorry," she whispered in anticipation of causing a stain on the spotless upholstery. "I...I can clean it."

Officer McGoven didn't say a word—but Loren didn't miss just how tightly he gripped the steering wheel.

He's going to turn you in, a part of her insisted. *They'll see the bruises. They'll call Youth Services.*

Or, no, they wouldn't. She was already eighteen, aged out of the system. If they thought that her father wasn't a fit guardian, they'd place her in a shelter. Or out on the street. Alone.

The thought spurred her to keep talking, desperate to find an excuse that would stick. Most people never tried this hard—her silence always scared them off.

"I'm fine, honestly. I don't know what happened. Please, I'll apologize to Naomi. I don't mind walking, either. It's not that far."

Officer McGoven said nothing, purely focused on driving.

In defeat, she stared fearfully from the window, bracing for the moment they would pull up to the police station. Instead, he abruptly turned down a dirt road that led into a swath of country surrounding the town like an insulating blanket.

He headed north, leaving the town proper, and Loren's pulse quickened. She knew these wide-open fields only a stone's throw from her father's backyard. She also knew the area was quiet and mostly deserted. A "no one around to hear you scream" type of wilderness. Warily, she eyed Officer McGoven with a different perspective.

What if he wasn't as honorable and upstanding a citizen as she thought?

"I can't let you go to school looking like that," he explained as if sensing her fear. His tone was sufficiently gentle, nothing like the coarse bellow he used before. "And I would be entertaining truancy if I allowed you to skip. Let me do my good deed for the day, just this once."

Is that all you want to do? Loren might have asked that if she were the brave, bold sort of person used to questioning police officers. Someone who might be terrified of the fate that could await her out in the middle of nowhere, with only the wind to snatch away her screams.

As it was, she just felt…

Tired. Dodging her father's fists took most of her energy these days. The threat of being murdered didn't even faze her anymore. At least she wouldn't have to go home and hide her soiled clothes.

It might have helped if he resembled the monsters she was used to. Dejectedly, she observed him more closely, convinced the honorable spiel was just an act. What secrets lurked behind those gray eyes?

Or, perhaps, in plain sight—he had a tattoo on his neck, barely visible from beneath a fringe of black hair and the collar of his jacket. Tendrils of indigo ink were all she could make out. A harmless design?

Or something nefarious?

The interior of his car didn't allude to any ulterior motives he might have. Every inch was spotless, devoid of even an air freshener as decoration.

She was so lost in her observations she barely noticed when the squad car came to a stop before a pale blue farmhouse.

A house she knew all too well.

"This…t-this is the old Baker farm," she croaked, bolting upright. The property was directly behind her father's house, past the woods and a shallow stream. All in all, a ten-minute walk with time to spare if she ran the whole way.

The white barn near the west field was where she spent the most time these days. Achingly aware of the loss of the apple and carrots, she felt her hands clench at the air.

Then a chilling thought took hold.

Why on earth would he bring her all the way out here?

3

*T*he sound of the driver-side door opening startled Loren so badly she jumped.

"You okay?" Officer McGoven asked. He already stood before her, his expression blank.

"Y-Yes," she croaked, unhooking her seatbelt.

"Come inside. You can get cleaned up, and then I'll drive you to school." He headed up the pathway leading toward the house. Helpless, Loren found herself scrambling out of the squad car after him.

"Y-You live here?" she asked in a small voice.

In this house, resting in the center of the old Baker farm —*her* paradise. She spent so much time in the barn just a few paces away, that it never occurred to her someone might own the property. Not just anyone, but an officer of the law. At least, now she knew why her father had always forbidden her from this place.

A creaking sound jarred Loren back to awareness. Officer McGoven had climbed the front steps of the house and eyed her from the porch while holding open a battered screen door.

"Come on."

She hesitated, wrestling with the building panic within her. The fact that he lived *here* of all places was an even bigger reason to avoid him. The smart thing to do would be to run and take her chances getting to school on foot.

Nothing was worth angering her father again—not with her new shoes on the line.

She even took a step toward the woods before the logical part of her brain kicked in. Sure, she could leave, but then *what*? Spend the rest of her life avoiding the police officer who just so happened to live in her backyard?

After all, he still had her backpack.

Left with no choice, she mounted the steps leading to a large wraparound porch that encircled the house on three sides. Genuine awe diminished some of her fear. She had always admired the sturdy, old-fashioned home. On her visits, she made sure to catch a glimpse of it from the barn at least once. It was the polar opposite of her father's dreary brown ranch-style house.

Up close, the old estate was far more impressive despite the peeling white paint and vines creeping as high as the upper stories. Would the interior look as decrepit and wild? Before the unease could steal her nerve, she gripped the handle of the front door and peered inside.

The second she glimpsed the foyer of the house, her guard dropped further. She had envisioned some plain furniture. Maybe a television and a beer-stained recliner, like the one her father owned.

Not a wide, open floor plan decorated in alternating shades of brown and emerald green. Both hues evoked the earthy, secluded feelings of the forest, and Loren could almost taste the scent of pine. Intrigued, she ventured deeper inside and found Officer McGovern in an open kitchen, rummaging through cupboards.

Past him was a spacious den, with a bookshelf along the far wall, stocked with countless leather volumes. The walls were a soothing shade of gray, and the wood floors gleamed beneath a fresh coating of wax. Ironically, there wasn't a TV in sight, though one could probably entertain themselves by gazing out at the view, showcased by a large bay window.

It was breathtaking. Jealously, she imagined McGoven sitting here with a cup of tea, gazing out fondly over the west fields, and the stream…

And the barn.

Her cheeks seared at the sight of it, clearly visible from this very spot. No wonder he knew her name. He probably sat here every day, watching her trespass onto his property.

Which brought up a bigger question? How did she miss the police cruiser parked around back? Though, to be fair, the front of the house faced east, and she had always snuck up directly behind the barn.

Not that the excuse would exactly matter once she was on trial facing criminal charges.

"The bathroom is straight back, down the hall." She flinched as Officer McGoven's voice came from the doorway. His tone wasn't angry, like someone gloating over her crimes against him might be. Merely impatient. "You don't want to be late. I promised to get you to school before the bell rings."

"O-Okay."

Off the living room was a hallway leading to a small bathroom. Closing the door behind her, Loren faced the mirror, steeling herself against what she might find.

A wild-haired, she-devil? Or perhaps the freak Naomi accused her of being?

Instead, a ghost watched her with mournful hazel eyes. Only a vibrant smear of blood gave the pale creature any definition against the white walls. Her chin was bleeding. Ironically, the injury was the only eye-catching thing about her. Lifeless brown hair tumbled down her shoulders, streaked with mud. Her sweater hung on her frame, making her resemble a child playing dress-up in their father's clothes.

Sighing, Loren hobbled to the sink and splashed some cool water onto her face, scrubbing away most of the blood. The motion brought attention to her fingers—the nails of which were encrusted in ruby-colored crud. With a shudder, she shoved her hands beneath the faucet and watched as reddish water circled the drain. Finished, she wet a paper towel and went to work on erasing as much of the mud from her sweater as she could. The tights were a total loss, soaked through.

Ten minutes later, she emerged, looking no less scrappy than before.

At least, Officer McGoven seemed to have found whatever he'd been looking for. Two sandwiches lay spread out before him. *Tuna,* Loren sensed with an appreciative sniff.

Not only that, but two shiny apples sat on the counter, complete with a stick of cheddar cheese. Hope swelled in her chest. It was more than she'd eaten last night. Hell, more than she ate most nights.

As if sensing the direction her thoughts had taken, McGoven cocked his head her way. "I take it that was *your* lunch smeared all over the sidewalk?"

Loren didn't know what to say.

"Here." To her immense shock, McGoven swept the food into a brown paper bag and offered it to her. "Is this enough to replace it?"

She nodded, too grateful to refuse. "T-thanks." Even as the word left her mouth, a sense of dread rushed to replace it.

These days, people rarely did anything without expecting something in return. *What would he want?* She snuck a glimpse of that unreadable face through a fringe of her hair.

There were only a few things someone like her could give him.

Suddenly, he frowned. "Wait—"

Loren nearly dropped the food as he opened a drawer. When he pulled out a knife, her heart sank.

Fearlessly, he brandished the blade and brought it down right over the middle of the second tuna sandwich. Taking one half for himself, he tossed the knife in the sink and nodded toward the remaining slice. "One for the road."

Loren stared at it for all of two seconds, before snatching the food as if afraid he might take it from her. Without hesitation, she crammed the entire thing into her mouth. She chewed so quickly the taste barely registered in her mind, but it was *good*—she knew that much.

And, she knew that he was watching her.

Rather than question, he quietly left the house.

Loren rushed after him, clutching the brown paper bag to her chest like a king's ransom of gold. Once again, Officer McGoven opened the car door for her, but he didn't speak.

She could have been invisible if it weren't for the fact that he silently cranked up the heat the second she began to shiver in her damp sweater. It was a cold, dreary day, even for fall, and the threat of rain seemed inevitable.

Loren just hoped that the storm held until she made it home. Tracking mud into the house was a surefire way to rile her father—if he wasn't already aware of the drama before school.

Luckily, the streets and plain buildings of New Walsh passed in a blur. Far too soon, she found herself staring at a sign reading New Walsh Academy.

As far as Loren was concerned, it could have read *hell on earth.*

To be fair, school itself wasn't all bad. She got decent grades, and there were a few subjects she liked—but the Naomi Tanners of the world excelled at spoiling even a glimmer of happiness. Ever since the day Loren dared to set foot inside New Walsh Academy, the blond had been there nipping at her heels with increasing viciousness. Judging from the mess this morning, it was only a matter of time before Naomi got her expelled.

Today might not have been that day, though—a certain pink car wasn't in the parking lot.

"Here we are, right on time," Officer McGoven remarked as he parked near the path leading to the front of the main building.

"T-Thank you," she whispered, gathering her belongings.

"I don't want to see you in this position again, Ms. Connors. If you don't mind me saying it. You recognize me, don't you?"

He angled his face her way, allowing the daylight to illuminate every sculpted plane. Her breath caught, her belly on fire with an emotion she couldn't name. The look in his eyes diminished the awe somewhat—he was disappointed.

"Yes," she admitted.

"I don't want to have the same relationship with you that I do with your father. Do you understand?"

Loren hung her head in shame. The double-meaning lurking within his tone was perfectly clear—*I don't want to see you in this position again...like him.*

"I understand." On that note, she gathered her things and scrambled out of the car. Protocol dictated she turn tail and run, but lingering gratitude made her look back. "T-Thank you," she stammered. "Thanks."

With a curt nod, McGoven leaned over to close the passenger-side door—but not before two last parting words slipped out to greet her. "Take care."

Loren watched him drive all the way to the end of the street, where he made a left and became lost in the bustle of traffic. The second he disappeared, she turned on her heel, skirted around the school building, and headed straight for the woods.

4

A torrent of rain fell the moment she set foot beneath the trees, but the thrill of freedom displaced any fear she might feel. Nothing compared to this —the slick earth beneath her feet and the cooling rain on her skin. Every falling drop caressed her as if in welcome, urging her further from the hostile New Walsh Academy.

She didn't belong there, in sterile hallways and suffocating classrooms.

This was her true playground, the forest. It and the Baker farm were the only places she felt safe these days. The open spaces contained no bullies waiting to attack, and the twisted branches above had no mysteries to hide.

There was simply nature. Invitingly, forebodingly, terrifyingly *natural*. Rarely did the environment fall out of step with that beautiful, terrible rhythm, and Loren appreciated the monotony. Biology was one of her favorite subjects merely for its focus on this wilder part of the world and the creatures who inhabited it. One creature, in particular, drew her interest the most—*Canis lupus.* Their social dynamics seemed so at odds with the moniker some attached to people like her. Lone wolves who shunned most interactions. Real wolves were fascinating predators, killing purely out of need, with the same instinctive desire, she possessed to breathe.

They didn't relish violence the way humans could.

Though, what's your excuse? a part of her sniped, conjuring the image of her straddling Naomi Tanner.

Loren shook her head to clear it as she ran even faster. She hadn't meant to hurt Naomi. Had she? Her fingers twitched as if to betray that hope.

She hadn't wanted to *hurt* Naomi. No, she wanted to destroy her.

Bite, scratch, tear. Make her suffer.

And you wonder why you don't have any friends, a part of her hissed. *You're a freak. Someone sick enough to fantasize about biting schoolyard bullies.* Though, if *anyone* deserved the brunt of her sudden viciousness, Naomi wasn't at the top of the list.

Her father might be.

Don't think about that. Loren pushed every thought from her mind, as the rain came down harder, soaking through her sweater. Thunder rumbled ominously in the distance as if warning her to take cover. In her peripheral vision, her father's house appeared and vanished.

When she finally came to a stop, chest heaving, she stood before a white barn, where the pungent stench of animals persisted despite the rain. Warily, she clutched her now soggy brown paper bag to her chest and hesitated. It was stupid to come here, especially now that she knew who owned it.

But…

Much like the wolves she studied, she couldn't forsake her duty to her pack. Even if said "pack" members weren't exactly her species. They loved her all the same, and a little food every now and again was the least she could give in return.

She saved the apple especially for Bunny—the old nag loved fresh fruit—and Esther would appreciate anything, even if it wasn't her beloved carrots. They were her friends. Or the closest things in the world she could apply the term to.

Therefore, trespassing on a police officer's private property was entirely worth the risk.

That didn't mean she wouldn't be careful, though. Cautiously, she peeked around the edge of the barn, toward the farmhouse, which seemed no less intimidating from far away. The driveway wasn't visible from here, but something told her that Officer McGoven had to be out on patrol, or whatever it was police officers did during the day.

Besides, she had taken a shortcut through the woods; he couldn't have gotten there so fast by car. Not with traffic to contend with. When he did return, she'd surely see him long before he saw her.

Five minutes, she told herself, as she entered the barn. As always, the main door was unlocked. Why hadn't that ever bothered her before?

She always assumed that someone came by to care for the horses, though the place seemed abandoned most days. There was a hole in the barn's far wall that had yet to be repaired, and this time of year, the drafty air seeped inside. Loren's teeth chattered, but her lips formed a rare smile as a triangular head appeared above the door to greet her with more compassion than she'd ever felt from a human.

"Hey, honey," she murmured, stroking the mare's gray muzzle. "I've got a treat for you, Bunny girl."

Bunny tossed her massive head as Loren presented one of the apples.

Nearby, on the wall above a line of saddle racks hung a set of tools that must have been used to repair the worn leather. From the selection, Loren took a knife and sliced the fruit into quarters, smiling as the others caught a whiff of the scent and demanded their treats with impatient nickers.

"I'll save some for you," she promised Esther as she gave two slivers of apple to Bunny. "You too," she called to Xavier, the quiet mustang in the corner stall who hadn't warmed up to her yet.

As the storm raged on outside, Loren lost herself in the busywork of giving everyone their fair share.

The horses were the one saving grace she discovered while living in New Walsh. In the early days after moving in with her father, she spent most of her time wandering the massive property behind his house.

The presence of so much empty land set New Walsh apart from the busier town of Ridgerton. It was quieter, too, with plenty of open space that invited exploration. One day, she strayed too far north and found a small white barn, where, just outside in the neighboring field, grazed three beautiful horses.

It didn't matter that Bunny, the old palomino, had a swayback and was far too brittle to be of much use. Or that Esther, the gentle mare with a glorious chestnut mane, had a long, jagged scar marring her left flank—animal attack, Loren assumed.

Xavier, with his ink-black coat and proud posture, was the only one of the three who truly seemed valuable. Too valuable, maybe, to spend his days cooped up in a small barn with two nags. But he was skittish. Loren could barely pet him, though he seemed to have no trouble snatching bits of apple from her hands.

Once the horses were fed, Loren curled up in the corner of the barn and waited for the rain to pass, telling herself that she'd make it home in time to intercept any call from the school about her absence. The storm was too dangerous to risk venturing out in, anyway. Heavy droplets of rain pattered off the roof of the barn like the frantic beating of a drum.

Winter's coming, she thought wistfully. *I wonder when it will start to snow?*

Would the barn finally be locked then? The prospect sent a pang through her chest. Winter was the time of predators, and there were stories of wild animals circling the outskirts of New Walsh. Primarily wolves, and the occasional bear. Other farmers in the area reported missing or injured animals every now again, and the morbid stories dominated the news.

But she had never heard of anything happening around the old Baker property. Looking back, she had been drawn to this place, despite plenty of other farms in the area—always creeping back to watch the animals graze, until she felt bold enough to view them up close.

Stupidly, she asked her father about the strange property so close to his—a question which earned her bruises that lasted for weeks after.

But it had been okay, a part of her reasoned with a cold sense of detachment; school hadn't started yet, so there had been no one to hide the injuries from. It was funny how her life had switched course. From *wanting* to be hidden to *having* to hide.

Even now. She didn't know how long she sat, listening to the drone of the rain play against the old wood. It could have been hours before her body felt too heavy—when the shelter of the barn and the soft murmurs of the animals lulled her into a drowsy state.

Her eyelids became heavy, drooping despite her best attempts to stay alert. It had been days since she'd slept through the night, and exhaustion tempted her to do the most dangerous thing she could in that moment.

She fell asleep.

angerous.

She's…dangerous…dangerous…

"She's dangerous—" The deep voice startled Loren awake.

Alarmed, she wrenched her eyes open, blinking against a harsh light. A wave of instinctive fear inspired her first coherent thought.

Was it morning already?

Her father would be angry if she didn't deliver the newspapers on time. Though, if she were lucky, last night's tally of beer might have left him too hungover to get out of bed. Though, she couldn't quite remember just how many beers he'd had. Or what she made for dinner. Or…

Ever leaving the old Baker farm.

Oh no! She bolted upright, finding the source of the light— a nearby table lamp. That was the first clue she wasn't in the barn. She wasn't home either. Instead of her father's moldy, second-hand furniture, she rested on a pristine leather couch. Draped over her legs was a woolen blanket too luxuriously thick to belong in the Connor household.

That wasn't all, she realized amid growing dread. It was dark beyond a nearby window, way past nightfall. Her father would be furious—but his wrath took a back seat to the present danger.

A familiar voice resonated through her body, but it definitely didn't belong to Fred Connors. "I didn't sign up for this. If you don't come up with a solution, I will—no, I don't give a damn about protocol. *Listen to me!*"

Loren obeyed, bracing her hands protectively over her face. As she eyed the room fearfully beyond her fingers, she realized the speaker's anger wasn't directed at her. He wasn't even in sight, but in another room close by, where his voice echoed off the walls.

"I agreed to watch *Connors*," he continued. "Not his damn daughter! She was supposed to be human. Well, guess what? She attacked another girl today. I practically had to drag her away. No. Thank God she didn't change, but she had blood all over her damn hands. If she's human, I'm the Queen of fucking England."

He paused, and Loren swore she heard a faint mumble as if someone was shouting at him, though from far away. A phone, maybe?

"You know damn well what I mean," Officer McGoven replied, just as heatedly. "Don't put this on me. She's just a kid. Hell, she probably doesn't even know what she is, but I don't want to be responsible for her. That isn't my place. She needs guidance. She needs... Are you even listening to me?"

He paused again, and fragments of his tirade ran ceaselessly through Loren's brain. *Responsible. For her.*

Could he be referring to Naomi? Though, it didn't matter. She had more important things to worry about, and she shifted her weight, freeing herself from the blanket. Heart pounding, she searched for her backpack next. How in the hell had she slept for so long?

Even so, it wasn't long enough to combat months of living with her father. She winced as the full effects of sleep deprivation seemed to strike all at once. She felt dizzy. Her throat ached. Her head throbbed, and the bottom of her chin stung as she swiped the hair from her face and tried to focus.

Think!

"No, I'm not going to calm down," Officer McGoven shouted, derailing her fragile train of thought. His increasing agitation triggered a tendril of alarm that ran down her spine. His voice was too deep—more guttural than her father's at his most furious. "Get the damn pack to take her in, then. Isn't that what you do? Protect your own? Invite the outcasts into your loving, *welcoming* family? She needs more than sentiments and meaningless platitudes,

Sonia. She needs help! Oh fuck, come here and see for yourself, then! Well, *do* something."

Loren lurched to her feet, swaying to find her balance. Confused, she eyed her trembling legs as if they didn't belong to her. In this moment…they didn't seem to. It was like they moved on autopilot, driven by two words. *Do something.* In fact, every nerve in her body prickled as if waiting for another command. *His.*

But why?

"I didn't ask for this," he said a fraction softer, and some of the uncanny tension in her muscles eased up. "She's not my damn problem. She's not some burden to unload like baggage. You have a duty to her, the same as I do. Oh, of course, you must beg your precious Alpha first. Call me back with his decision, then. Fuck!"

Presumably, he hung up the phone, but heavy footsteps alluded to him pacing. With every passing second, his anger only seemed to increase, smoldering like wildfire. Loren suspected at least some of it was directed her way.

Though, she didn't plan to stick around long enough to find out. The front door was visible from here, but her knees buckled as she staggered toward it, suddenly too weak to support her own weight. It seemed to take ages to reach the front door, but the second she did, the back of her neck prickled with awareness.

"Wait."

Just like that, she froze as if rooted to the spot. Heavy footsteps advanced from behind her, preceded by a scent that puzzled her the second she breathed it in—pine?

"I'll drive you home," McGoven continued, sounding paces behind her now. "I need to speak to your father, anyway."

Loren's blood ran cold. Helpless, she turned to find him standing in the kitchen doorway. He had shed his jacket, revealing a black T-shirt with short sleeves that bared his forearms. She swallowed hard at the sight. He had more muscle than anyone she'd ever seen in person.

"You brought me here," she croaked. Though it might have been far worse if he carried her home and her father witnessed. Still, she couldn't fathom why he hadn't. "Why? I'll be late. I need to get back."

He raised an eyebrow as if surprised by her line of questioning. "You seemed exhausted. I hope you don't mind, but I thought you might prefer somewhere warmer than the barn." The explanation seemed rehearsed, disguising his real reason for bringing her here.

Though she could have been paranoid. Rather than gratitude, a helpless jumble of words spilled from her throat the second she opened her mouth. "I can't...I...why did you let me sleep? Why didn't you wake me up? God, he's going to—" She had enough sense to break off before finishing that sentence. "I have to go home."

A task easier said than done—she couldn't move, not even as terror welled like bile in her throat. Her own body wouldn't obey the frantic commands her mind issued.

"I have to go home," she croaked as if saying it out loud would somehow make her limbs move.

"I know." McGoven's expression didn't betray a hint of emotion. "You don't need to be afraid. I will drive you home."

"No!" Frantically, Loren shook her head. "Please. I need to go *now*."

A strange note colored her voice. Like she was asking permission, but in a sense, it felt like she was. Something inside her seemed hung on his every word—compelled by them.

She couldn't move unless he told her it was okay.

"It's storming out," he replied in an even tone. Gone was the volatile anger he displayed on the phone call. "You'll catch your death if you walk home, and I'm not going to allow that to happen. You can wait for me out in the car. Go."

Finally, she could move again, and she practically ran from the front door. The porch steps were already slick, but she descended them swiftly—but that was as far as her autonomy extended. She fully intended to run past the driveway and make a break for the woods, but she approached the squad car instead. A persistent mantra dominated her thoughts, impossible to ignore. *Wait for him in the car.* But why?

The further she ventured from the house, and the man inside it, the more confusing her obedience seemed.

What's wrong with me?

It wasn't like she wanted to listen. Maybe there was just something broken inside of her that *liked* being at someone else's whim?

No, she thought as her hand reached for the passenger-side door. Without Officer McGoven in sight, the thought seemed stronger than before, resonating in her mind.

No. She couldn't stay. Her father would kill her.

Wait for him. Wait for him in the car.

"*NO!*" Stumbling, Loren took another step—only this time toward the looming fields she could barely make out in the dark. *No,* she thought frantically as she took another step. And then, another. And another.

It was hard. Like wading through thick cement poured up to her ankles. Painful even, as if a part of her hated leaving. *He told us to wait*, it cried mournfully. *We need to wait for him in the car.*

Sheer willpower pushed her to ignore it. A few more steps, and she was paces from the trees separating the farm from her father's neighborhood.

Just a little more, she urged her aching limbs, as if distance were the cure to the strange compulsion. Maybe it was. The farther she got from that house, the freer each step felt until…

Snap!

Like a breaking leash, the strange hold over her shattered, and Loren took off for the woods like a bat out of hell. She couldn't stop running. The need to move felt instinctive, and she had learned a long time ago to trust her intuition above all else. It told her to leave. *Now.* Before he found out, because if he did—

A shout rang out like a rumble of thunder, and she realized it was too late.

"LOREN!"

She winced and stumbled over her own feet. It was as if an invisible hook sank into her chest, pulling her back. *Dragging* her back.

No, she couldn't go back. *She couldn't!* Fear was a buffer, smothering everything but the need to escape. *Run!* Desperate, she raced toward the stream and blindly waded through the shallow end. The chill stole the air from her lungs, cutting her down to the very bone. Her shoes were a mess, the duct tape long since torn off, but the discomfort didn't faze her.

Couldn't faze her. If she stopped for even a second, all hell would break loose. She could feel it in the air—dangerous tension.

Luckily, she made it to the sleepy neighborhood beyond Baker farm without incident. Even so, she was shaking by the time she reached her father's backyard. She could barely mount the porch steps and wrestle open the door.

She didn't even make it over the threshold before she was struck in the face by an unseen force. *Wham!*

As pain seared through her cheek, Loren went limp like a rag doll, guarding her face with her hands. Tense with anticipation, she braced for the next hit. The next kick. The angrily growled "Care to explain?"

Instead, only the cool kiss of rainwater greeted her as the door creaked lazily on its hinges. When she finally peeked through her fingers, the porch light revealed her attacker— the handle of a broom that had fallen by her feet. Otherwise, the kitchen was empty, utterly dark.

With a sigh of relief, she crept inside, hoping the noise didn't wake her father. There was no sign of him downstairs, at least. The television was off, as were all the lights. The sole illumination came from a flickering red indicator on the answering machine.

The deceptively innocent device presented a new wealth of danger. Who could it be? Naomi Tanner's furious parents, demanding retribution for their daughter's injuries? The school calling to report her absence?

Feeling sick, Loren pressed the play button before fear could steal her nerve.

"Girl," the message began, rough with static. "Don't wait up. I've got some business to take care of over in Weller."

Click. End of story.

She played the message two more times before it finally sank in. Her father was gone, and the relief nearly knocked her over. She was safe for now...but for how long?

Unwilling to test her luck, she hobbled up the stairs to her room. After stripping off her soaked, filthy clothing, she ran the shower until the stall filled with steam, and she lost herself beneath the rush of hot water.

As inevitable as the sun rising and setting, she knew that this brief reprieve wouldn't last.

Regardless, she enjoyed the peace for as long as she could.

6

"—*T*he hell do you want?" The shout snapped Loren from a painful, dreamless sleep. Alarmed, she tried to make sense of the shadows blanketing her room.

Her father wasn't in view, though she certainly recognized his voice. Her bedroom door was still closed. He was in the house, but further away. Downstairs? The slam of the front door cemented that suspicion.

He wasn't alone.

Whoever replied to him spoke so softly only a few words caught her ears. "Here…about Loren…"

Shit! At the sound of her name, she shrugged off her cheap comforter and braced her feet against the floor. She knew of only one man with a voice that deep. What did she intend to do about it, though? The only available course of action was to listen.

"What about her?" Her father's voice was a hostile hiss in comparison. It was obvious he had been drinking.

"Not here to fight." McGoven's words were even harder to distinguish. Loren could only clearly make out two more —*her* and *pack*.

"The hell I will," her father grumbled, sounding insulted at the mere idea of...whatever they were talking about. "She doesn't need those bastards. A lot of good they've done you. Big shot William-fucking-McGoven. Hell, they shun you, and you still do their dirty work like a lost pup. It must be lonely out here without a bitch to keep you company. Is that why you're sniffin' around my girl?"

Officer McGoven's reply came in a series of guttural notes. "*Don't test me.*"

"The girl doesn't need *them*," her father insisted.

Was he referring to long-lost family? She had already had enough of estranged relatives. Like, *Uncle Bart,* who still haunted her nightmares.

"You don't get to make that decision," Officer McGoven said, sounding louder than before. "Especially if she's—"

"She's not. If she's any daughter of mine, she *wouldn't* be. Though you know that better than anyone, don't you, *Bill?* You fucking pure-bloods and your rules."

Bill. The oddly harmless name stuck in Loren's mind. *Bill McGoven.* The man would unintentionally get her killed if he mentioned her skipping school or falling asleep in his barn.

"Rules don't determine our ways—biology does. Even a mongrel like you can sense what she is. You know what could happen to her if you keep her secluded," McGoven said, in a tone decisively more somber. "She'll become isolated. Demented. You wouldn't want that."

"You don't know what the hell I want, Bill. Now, get the hell out of my house! I'm of half a mind to call that precious Alpha of yours. You aren't supposed to speak to me directly. Just report on my every move like a good dog—"

"Goodnight, Mr. Connors."

The sound of retreating footsteps echoed amid the slam of the screen door. Loren scrambled to the window in time to catch sight of a dark figure striding from the house to an awaiting patrol car. Right when he reached the driver's-side door, he looked up, and she swore his gaze fixated directly on her.

She jumped back as more footsteps broke the silence, only these were louder, inside the house, mounting the stairs.

A second later, her bedroom door flew open to crash against the wall. Dingy, orange light from the hall lamp illuminated dark hair, matched by two narrowed eyes set in a face that didn't seem capable of holding a smile.

"Girl," her father snarled. The whites of his eyes were bloodshot—he was most definitely drunk. "Care to explain why that fucking bastard McGoven just came over here asking about you?"

Loren could barely squeak in her own defense. "I-I don't know."

"You don't know?" He lumbered forward, his hands in fists. Compared to McGoven's bulk, he appeared scrawny, swallowed by his stained T-shirt. Loren cowered anyway.

She used to wonder why he never took her in after her mother's death, despite being listed on her birth certificate. He never visited, never called. The first time she met him had been the very day social services dropped her off after a failed placement with a distant relative. Not long after that, Loren realized the grim truth—Fred Connors wanted nothing to do with her. In fact, they looked nothing alike. His hair was sandy blond, and their eyes were shaped differently. They may have had the same, wide, oval face, but so did her mother.

"You didn't talk to him?" Her father's tone was dangerous, daring her to slip up.

Careful, Loren thought. "He stopped me on the way to school," she began in a tentative whisper. When that didn't seem to spark a rage, she continued. "He spoke to me—"

"And what did you say?"

"N-nothing—I mean," she croaked. "I-I was polite, but I didn't say anything. I told him to leave me alone. I swear."

He appeared to mull her answer over in silence. Finally, he turned, bracing one of his fists against the door.

"The next time he tries to speak to you, you tell him to go to hell, understood? He's a fucking pervert. Probably heard down at the station how much money I get for you from that bitch's insurance. That's what he's after."

Loren winced, but he was already stumbling down the hall to his own bedroom. He slammed the door after him, but she didn't dare move a muscle.

Neither did she have the nerve to close her bedroom door, or even creep into the hallway to switch off the light he'd left on. She stayed frozen until morning, when the dull light of dawn entered her window in a silent reprieve.

*I*t was Saturday.

"Lazy day" her mother used to call it, a weekly holiday they would spend in pajamas, eating cereal, and watching cartoons.

Those days were long gone. Loren didn't even realize it was the weekend until she hastened downstairs for the bag her father kept the papers in, only to discover that it wasn't there.

Saturday was the only day of the week he delivered the newspapers himself. Mainly, Loren knew, because he used the time to collect on his gambling tab from a man who lived across town.

A good thing, too, she thought once she returned to her room and fished her battered shoes from the corner. They were beyond salvageable. Mud and rainwater had dissolved the remaining duct tape, and both soles held on by only a thread.

Who knew how she'd get to school on Monday. Or how on earth she was going to find the money for new shoes.

Don't slip up this time, she told herself. *Ask again. Get him in a good mood.*

With that goal in mind, she busied herself with the many chores her father demanded she complete. As always, the living room was a landmine of empty beer cans and scattered TV dinners. She cleared those first, only to discover a bigger mess waiting for her in the kitchen.

She tracked mud in last night. Either her father had been too drunk to notice, or he just didn't care. Regardless, she'd been spared at least one beating for the day.

It took an hour of scrubbing to get the floor remotely clean, and then another run with the mop to erase all traces of muck. Once the house was decent enough, she curled up on the couch and savored what little peace remained until her father returned.

While Saturdays weren't exactly "lazy" anymore, they were still one of the rare moments she had the house to herself. Usually, she'd spend it at the old Baker farm.

Bunny might get to stretch her legs today, she thought while glancing out the window to see a faintly cloudless sky. The old nag loved being in the pasture.

Xavier, too, she assumed with a smile. The stallion needed plenty of exercise to stay happy. She was so lost in the thought that she didn't hear the first knock on the door.

But the second rap sent her scrambling from the couch. Her initial fear was her father had locked himself out. He'd blame her if she kept him waiting too long.

Heart pounding, she raced to the door, but—as if held back by some force she couldn't comprehend—her hand froze over the knob. *Pine.* Her nostrils flared, catching the strange scent in the air.

A scent that didn't belong here. At that exact moment, a stern voice seeped through the wooden barrier, impossible to resist.

"Loren. Please open the door."

She jumped back, slamming her hip on the couch. Amid her smothered gasp, McGoven's voice rang out clearly.

"I just want to talk. You can let me in."

No, a part of her warned, even as her body disobeyed. Robotic steps carried her forward and, despite her panic, her fingers deftly undid the lock. The door opened from the outside, revealing the man dominating the doorway.

His voice sounded calm, but he looked angry. His eyes were narrowed, glowing in the pale daylight.

Loren swallowed hard as a potential explanation for his visit came to mind. Had Naomi decided to catch her unguarded on the weekend? She braced herself for the moment he'd slap her in handcuffs. Surprisingly, all he seemed inclined to do was watch her.

Silently.

Being ogled by strangers was par for the course as the new girl in town, but his scrutiny felt different. Probing. Penetrating. His gaze seemed to pierce her clothing, weighing every inch of her beneath. How did she measure up?

As a disappointment, apparently. The worn lines around his mouth deepened by the second, exaggerating his frown.

Fortunately for her, what he thought didn't matter. His presence alone could get her punished.

"You can't be here," she blurted, scanning the sidewalk behind him as if her father might appear at any moment. "Please. I—"

"May I come inside?"

The request threw her off. It wasn't *really* a request, though. His low tone proclaimed something else that spurred her limbs into motion. *Let me in. Now.*

"I can't," Loren insisted. As the words left her mouth, she jerked aside to let him pass anyway.

"Thank you," he said, and he almost sounded genuine.

She didn't want him here—and he knew it. He seemed as out of place in their cramped living room as a wolf in the middle of a sheep's pen. He was too close—even though a good ten feet of space separated them, and she had her back pressed against the wall.

"M-my father isn't home," she said in a small voice. "You shouldn't talk to me without—"

"Naomi Tanner decided not to press charges." Officer McGoven's baritone cut over her easily. "I don't think you want your father to know that. Do you?"

Loren could only shake her head, flinching as those gray eyes found her again. She felt minuscule beneath his scrutiny. Like a child shriveling beneath a police officer's perusal all over again.

They had all seemed the same back in those days, a bunch of featureless faces topped by a dark uniform. Only he wasn't wearing his now. Instead, a green polo revealed his muscular forearms, and a simple pair of jeans were tucked into his leather boots.

The boots held Loren's attention. They looked firm. Sturdy. If only she could manage to talk her father into buying her a pair like that. Though if Naomi had her thrown in jail, she might never wear shoes again.

"D-do you know why?" she asked, focusing on the topic at hand. "Why she didn't press the c-charges?"

McGoven shrugged. "She decided it may not have been in her best interest."

In other words, he convinced her not to. Was Naomi susceptible to his commanding voice like she was?

"She won't be bothering you again," he added as if to confirm that unspoken suspicion.

"T-thank you," she stammered, but a gnawing sense of paranoia ate at her gratitude. *What did he want in return?* Nobody did anything for free.

Sure enough, he met her probing stare with one of his own. "Loren, I need to ask you something."

"Y-yes?"

He seemed to hesitate, taking time to inspect the modest living room furniture—a stained couch and musty recliner. His gaze lingered, appearing to note everything down to the dust in the corners—but Loren still sensed the second his focus returned to her.

"What do you know about your father?"

She frowned. "Not much." Only that his name was Fred Connors, and after her mother died, his house was the only place she had left to go. "But he is my father, and I…love him."

Everyone else accepted that generic answer. It might have been true to some extent. After all, this home was better than the last one.

Rather than satisfied, McGoven looked… Uneasy. His probing stare intensified, demanding the truth she was too chicken to say.

He's a monster—not in the literal sense. She didn't know why it seemed essential to make that distinction. Sure, he might not have had claws or fangs or bulging yellow eyes, but real-life monsters were always the worst. Just ask the average serial killer, who seemed more frightening than the story of *Little Red Riding Hood* any day.

Give her a real monster, complete with fur and a spine-tingling growl, and Loren knew she could hold her own. Somehow. Her father, on the other hand? He was a far more formidable threat.

And if he knew she had a man in his house, he'd kill her. The thought consumed her, and she barely heard what Officer McGoven said next.

"What about your family?" he pressed. "What do you know about them? I heard your mother wasn't from around here—"

"My mother's dead," Loren replied before she realized what he probably meant. Other family. Grandmothers. Grandfathers. Cousins.

"My mom was all I had," she added. "I-I mean *besides* my dad."

Officer McGoven didn't seem to like that, and Loren swallowed at the emotion that contorted his expression too quickly to name. Anger?

"Have you ever heard of Black Mountain?" he asked.

"No." She wasn't too familiar with the area around New Walsh. Up until a few months ago, her entire existence had consisted of the small town of Ridgerton.

"You haven't. What about any mention of a territory up North? Friends of his?"

"He doesn't have friends," she replied. "Outside of his gambling buddies, anyway."

And if he did, he certainly hadn't introduced them to her.

"I'm sorry," she blurted as McGoven's eyes flashed. Anger was definitely the emotion she failed to name before. For whatever reason, he seemed determined to disguise it from her. He turned away, but his posture was too tense. Furious. "Fucking bastard," he snarled under his breath.

Her? Or her father? At the thought of him, her entire body went cold.

"My dad will be back soon," she lied. "He won't like it if you're here. He won't—"

"I'm leaving."

He was in the doorway before she could blink, but the fluidity of his movements sparked a grudging appreciation. Despite all that muscle, he moved with easy grace, like a dancer.

But he hesitated. "Oh, before I forget. You left your bag last night." Sure enough, he had it slung over one shoulder. She didn't know how she had missed it before.

Maybe because her eyes never left his face for longer than a few short seconds? Her fingers shook as she reached for the bag. From the weight, she could tell all the necessary materials were inside it.

"Thank you," she murmured, staring down at the floor. There was only one place he could have found it—his barn.

How could she have been so stupid? Forget Naomi; would *he* pursue charges?

No, something told her, even before she saw the decidedly un-angry gleam in his eye. He would just extend his visit and abuse her gratitude to ask more questions. "What happened yesterday?"

Her mood shifted from hopeful to ashamed. "I'm sorry. I shouldn't have skipped school. I just—"

"No, not that," he said over her. "Naomi. I called the school, and they sent me your file. You've never gotten detention, let alone into a fight. You have straight As. Honors courses. Not even a warning."

Her file. Could he do that? Apparently so. His uncanny authority must work even on school officials. But why the interest in her?

"She must have done something to provoke you, Loren. You drew blood." He didn't sound accusatory. Just curious. "What happened?"

"She…" Loren bit her tongue.

The truth wouldn't matter to him—it never did. People like Naomi, with their money and influence, would always win over people like her. If McGoven was looking for a reason to avoid pressing charges, he wouldn't find it here.

Though, to be fair, he didn't seem to care about this in his capacity as a police officer. His interest went beyond duty. It was like he was hunting for something. An answer he wanted her to give.

"What happened?" he demanded, his eyes flashing.

"Nothing! I mean, she said—"

"I don't care what she did. What did you *feel?*"

"Angry," Loren admitted. Her cheeks flamed. It was such a childish response.

"That wasn't it," McGoven pressed, unsatisfied. "What else? When you knew you'd drawn blood? What did you feel then?"

"I…" Her true emotions were too insane to verbalize. She felt anger in the core of her very being. A fury that still raged even now. It demanded more than an apology from Naomi to soothe it. It wanted retribution.

Blood.

"Did she hurt you?" McGoven was closer, his voice impossible to resist. That strange scent of pine she smelled whenever he was near, it wasn't the forest. It was him. His very being seemed infused with the essence of the earth.

But she didn't feel the same calm she felt while out in the woods. Her belly flipped, her toes curling. Whatever this feeling was, it made her pulse race. It felt...bad. Uncontrollable.

"Loren?" he prodded. "Is Naomi the one who hurt you?"

She shook her head, struggling to keep up with the conversation. Every word he uttered made her feel dizzy. "I'm fine—"

"Your left hip is bruised." He spoke with such conviction she blushed.

Then, she looked down, irrationally convinced she must have answered the door naked. But she wasn't. Her thick sweater should have disguised every ache on her body. Unless he searched her while she'd been unconscious...

"I-I don't know what you're talking about," she croaked, crossing her arms over her torso. The thought of him eyeing her body made her feel violated, but she couldn't shake the feeling that he would never do that.

There had to be another explanation. Like...he just knew.

At her denial, his eyes narrowed. With a sweep of his gaze, he homed in on her chest.

"There is a bruise on your left hip," he reiterated with unnerving confidence. "Two... Maybe three days old. Another fresh injury is on your chest. On your left forearm is an older mark. Your right shoulder, too. Left upper back. Left lower back. There are more, but they span weeks—"

Suddenly he surged forward, and there was nowhere to run but to press herself against the wall.

"Were these all caused by Naomi Tanner?" He raised his voice only a fraction, but she cowered as if he shouted. The muscles of his neck were corded, his face dangerously close to hers. "Answer me!"

"I-I don't..." Panic wiped her mind blank. Had her father been right about him after all? No...

Rather than fixate on her mouth, or a part of her a pervert might be interested in, he just...

Inhaled. Over and over, his nostrils flared with increasingly rapid intakes of air. Whatever he smelled made him swallow, and a sound rumbled in his throat a heartbeat later, too deep to form audible words. No, it was something that a part of Loren hesitantly attempted to name. A growl?

"How do you know?" she asked, barely able to form the words. "How?"

"You know I can smell them—" He snapped his teeth shut, and a muscle in his jaw twitched. He seemed to realize how it sounded—he could *smell* a bruise.

Loren knew she misheard him. "W-What?"

Suddenly, he was across the room, heading for the door. "Don't worry about it. I was wrong. Have a good day, Ms. Connors. I... I think it's a good idea if you stay away from my property from now on."

Loren nodded, still shaken. Somehow, the loss of her haven mattered more than his strange interrogation. Did he know about her previous trips?

His face gave nothing away. With one last raking glance, he left the house entirely, slamming the door in his wake.

Creeping to the window, she noticed that he entered a green pickup truck instead of the squad car.

In a matter of minutes, he was gone.

7

The rest of the day passed in a blur. In the absence of McGoven she felt oddly calm. With every passing second, his strange behavior became a distant memory. She could barely remember exactly what he'd said —but she didn't dare question it.

Instead, she threw herself into busywork, desperate for a distraction. As a result, she cleaned the house—twice—and watched a staticky program on the television. Afterward, she did her homework, and when five-o-clock neared, she started dinner.

The evening came and went, with no sign of her father. After another hour passed, Loren left his plate in the fridge and crept into bed.

I'll just wait, she told herself. She wouldn't fall asleep. As soon as he came home, she'd ask about the shoes.

What felt like mere seconds later, she wrenched her eyes open as a monstrous sound shattered the quiet. It was her bedroom door flying open and striking the wall. Before she could react, a brutal force seized her arm and yanked her into the hall. The stench of stale beer gave away the intruder's identity. Her father.

He was shouting incoherently, hauling her toward the staircase. Loren reached for the banister, but a shove to her back robbed her of balance. The air rushed past in a whoosh as she struck the topmost steps. Then another. Another.

Tuck. The instinctive voice had saved her too many times to count, so she threw her hands up to guard her face as her body tumbled like a ragdoll. It felt like an eternity before her descent came to an abrupt stop. Blinking, she found herself in the living room, tasting blood on her tongue and instinctively clutching at her left side. God, she hurt.

Ignore it, that inner voice told her. *You can cry later. All that matters is staying alive.*

Because she was in danger. Her father stood over her, still raging. His voice echoed off the walls, but she could only hear the blood rushing through her ears. From the way his lips moved, she could piece together the gist of his tirade —*care to explain...*

Something.

Her mind raced, parsing through which event could have enraged him.

Naomi? School?

"Did you hear me, girl?"

She saw his leg fly out, delivering a blow to her side. The rush of pain seemed to snap the sense back into her, and she could clearly understand what he snarled next. "Care to explain why you had that asshole McGoven in my house?"

McGoven. Paralyzing fear raced down her spine. How did he know? She cleaned the house twice. Every trace of Officer McGoven had been scraped, wiped, and vacuumed away.

"Well?" her father bellowed. His next kick caught her ribs. Long-honed practice was the only thing that held in the scream.

"Huh, you little bitch? Answer me!"

"He wouldn't leave," she croaked, gasping for air. "I'm sorry—"

"What did he say to you? What did *you* say to *him*?"

Loren shook her head. "N-Nothing—"

"He had to want something." Her father glanced her over with disgust, settling on the high collar of her nightgown. "He thought you were one of those pompous little bitches. What lies did he feed you, huh? That he could take you away to paradise? And what the fuck did you give him, you little slut?"

When he reached for her, Loren flinched, breaking that protective, blank shell. Like a shark sensing blood, he caught wind of her fear. It made him bolder. Louder. Angrier.

"Huh?" He snatched her sleeve, wrenching her unceremoniously to her feet. "What did you do, you little slut?"

"N-Nothing," Loren stammered. "He j-just asked about us," she added, voice tight with pain. "He asked if I had any other family—"

It was the wrong thing to say.

Wham! She barely saw him form a fist before it collided with the side of her face. Sparks danced before her eyes as the world swayed beneath her feet. The next slap caught the other side of her face, sending her into the wall.

"And I'm sure you told him everything, didn't you," her father snarled. "Didn't you?"

For the first time in years, Loren forgot all about being a turtle and making herself a small target.

She ran.

The kitchen was her only refuge, though deep down, she knew it was pointless to hide. She was boxing herself in and merely prolonging the inevitable. It didn't matter. The need to move was instinctive, too urgent to ignore. *Run!*

"Where the hell are you going?" He was paces behind, taking his time as if confident she wouldn't make it far.

Run, Loren thought frantically. With no other option, she raced for the back door.

This time was different. She could taste it—sense it, right down to the inevitable stench of death on her own skin. He had hit her in the face, without bothering to worry about bruises. He had kicked her without concerning himself with how loudly she might scream.

He was angry. Angrier than she had ever seen him before, and when she fumbled with the lock on the screen door, he caught her by the waist.

As if she weighed nothing, he threw her aside into the counter.

Thwack!

Wincing, she caught herself on the kitchen sink and scrambled upright. By the time she regained her balance, her father was closing in with the eerie, predatory grace of a wolf. It was as if the rage had a calming effect on him.

He was enjoying this. Even the look in his eyes was different. Sharper. Colder. Meaner.

Run!

Loren jerked on her feet, unsure of what to do. If she resisted, he'd only hit her again. Hit her harder. Kill her…

Stop! That calm, commanding voice returned, snapping her limbs into action. *Focus!*

Trembling, she wrenched open the nearest drawer. There, ready for the taking, was a knife—the same one her father ate his steak with. God, she couldn't really use it… Could she?

She *had* to.

"What the hell are you going to do with that, girl?" her father demanded as she gripped the brittle handle.

It felt so damn heavy. She could barely lift it, though the metal was that cheap, synthetic kind and not real steel. *Hold it,* the shadowy part of her hissed, and she didn't dare hesitate.

"Lo-ren," her father sing-songed. She rarely heard him say her name, let alone like this. Playfully. Hungrily…

"Huh, girl?" he demanded with a cold laugh. "What you gonna do with that?"

Use it? She had never intentionally hurt someone. Ever. *Liar,* a part of her hissed. *You hurt Naomi, and you enjoyed every damn bit of it…*

"Stop!" Loren didn't know if the plea was directed at herself, or the man still advancing at a lazy, casual pace. "P-please. Just leave me alone."

"You've been a bad girl, Lo-ren," he growled. "*Very* bad. Just what did you say to that damn McGoven to get him sniffing around you, huh? Just what did you give him, girl?"

He lashed out for the neckline of her nightgown and yanked. With a violent *rrrriiiipp,* the cotton tore down to her navel, revealing pale, bruised skin.

Shame flooded her cheeks as she scrambled to shield what she could with her free hand. "P-please stop—"

"You let him take you, you little slut?" her father shouted over her. "You let him have you? Mark you? I bet the bastard would love a little bitch like you. Just as easy a slut as your damn mother."

NO! Loren didn't know what happened. She saw him reach for her and her own grip tightened over the knife, lifting it…

But it was like something else took over, guiding the blade in a wide arch.

"Son of a bitch!" Howling with rage, her father stumbled back, clutching his arm to his chest. A sharp scent tinged the air—one she recognized with a shudder. Blood. "You cut me!"

There wasn't time for fear. Loren took her shot and lurched for the back door, wrenching it open. It was raining hard. The torrent churned the earth into a slippery soup that coated her bare feet as she jumped off the porch and raced for the woods.

"Loren!" His voice rang out behind her, punctuated by a harsh laugh. *Where ya going, Lo-ren? You can't run from me…*

But she tried. Panting for air, she navigated the darkened woods while her thin nightgown bunched up around her legs. The soles of her feet ached. She couldn't see anything but looming, endless black.

But she could hear him well enough. "Where ya running to, darlin'?" The drunken endearment seemed to come from every direction at once. Far away. Too close.

Inside her head.

"Darlin,' Darlin'... Where you going, Darlin'? Don't you know I'll always find you?"

Noises crashed through the underbrush just paces behind her.

"H-help!" Forsaking stealth, she screamed. "H-help...me. Help me...help!"

It was too late.

A flicker of movement from the corner of her eye was her only warning before she went sprawling, thrown by an impenetrable force. Boneless, she tumbled down a hill, landing in a heap near the bubbling path of the stream. Sometime during the fall, her nightgown tore completely, hanging open as she scrambled to her knees.

A desperate hope grappled with the building terror. Somehow, she made it all the way to the Baker farm. She was close enough to view the barn through the trees.

But would anyone hear her?

Sucking in a breath, she put her effort into making sure someone would. "Help me! Please—"

"Get back here, you little bitch." Her father's voice reached her in advance of his heavy footsteps. He took his time, seeming to leisurely pick his way through the underbrush.

You're dead, a part of Loren whispered. *Dead, dead, dead.*

But she still had the knife in her hand. Her knuckles whitened over the handle, not that it would help one damn bit.

"You think you can run from me?" Her father posed the question casually as he appeared at the top of the hill. "You think that I would just let you *leave*? So you can take all that fucking money for yourself?"

No, Loren thought sadly. She had always known how this story would end. One final chapter concluded with violence.

"You deserve this, don't you?" He came clearly within view, his arms at his sides, lips quirked into a cold smile. "Say it."

He waited for her to nod. Give up. Acquiesce. She always did, submitting to being a punching bag.

But this time... She just eyed the night sky, unconcerned by the raindrops speckling her face. If this night was to be her last, then she might as well go out with her dignity intact.

Be blank...empty. Don't let them see...

"I asked you a question, Loren." He crouched and snatched her chin, forcing her to meet his gaze. "You deserve this, don't you?"

LANA SKY

She said nothing, too exhausted to play along.

Fresh anger distorted his features to an alarming degree. His eyes seemed to glow, his jaw lengthened. Those yellowed teeth even seemed sharper…

She was hallucinating. She had to be.

"You deserved this." As he spoke, his tone deepened, becoming more guttural. "Say it, you little bitch!"

He raised his fist but reached for her throat instead. Using the grip to pin her down, he turned his attention to the skin bared by the torn halves of her nightgown.

Loren froze. He never touched her. Not like this.

"You didn't wait long to let that ass, McGoven, have you, did you?" He breathed harshly. "How long have you been fucking him, huh?"

Loren frantically shook her head, squeezing her eyes shut, trying to breathe. *No.*

"If I had known what a little slut you were, I would have used you to pay off my damn debts, rather than work my ass off—"

His hand trailed to the strap of her bra, tugging, and that was the last thing she remembered.

Gggggrrrrrrrrrrlllllllll.

The growl shattered through everything. Even the earth seemed to ripple with the force of it. It could have been a roll of thunder, but as the thought crossed her mind, some part of Loren snickered—*Ha-ha, you wish.*

"Fuck!" Whatever it was, the sound startled her father. He withdrew from her, scanning the forest frantically. "The asshole wouldn't dare." His voice quivered. He was afraid.

Of what?

"I'll deal with you on my own damn property. Come on—" He reached for her again, and a part of Loren knew that it was her only chance.

The knife was still in her hand, but she had no conscious control of her limbs. With an eerie sense of calm, she felt that impulsive force take hold of her again. Her arm moved, bringing the knife into something firm that grunted at the blow.

And then suddenly...the knife was gone, ripped right out of her hands.

When she stood, the only thing she was aware of was the falling rain on her skin.

Keep moving, Loren, that calm voice commanded. *Just keep moving. Just move. Don't stop.*

She didn't make it far.

After a few steps, she stumbled and went down face first. By reflex, her eyes flew open, and everything fell into focus. She saw the silvery rain that pelted her outstretched fingers...mingling with a darker, more vibrant color.

Red.

"No!" The wail ripped from her throat. Helpless, she curled up in a ball, knowing the truth in her gut even though she never turned her head to look. She couldn't look.

She didn't know how long she huddled there, screaming out wordless howls as the rain died down to a whisper. But she knew the exact moment when *he* came.

By then, the rain died down to barely a cool mist as if to herald his arrival. Even nature didn't dare to challenge him.

He approached her slowly and watched her for what felt like an eternity. His presence alone penetrated deeper than even physical touch. *I'm here,* he seemed to convey without saying a word. *It's alright.*

Weakly, Loren turned toward him. Though she couldn't make out any of his features, she had no doubt who the man above her was.

And as concerned as he seemed to be, one fact would tarnish any pity he might have felt toward her.

"He's dead," she croaked, watching those silver eyes flash in response. "I...I-I killed him."

8

*W*ait here.

He didn't say so out loud. He didn't have to. One look conveyed the order and more. *Wait for me.*

Though, it wasn't like she had any place left to go…

She lay there, freezing, as the horror of what she'd done set in.

Murderer! You killed him.

It didn't matter that he seemed intent on killing *her*. Though, she never confirmed it for herself. Maybe she'd only injured him? *He could still be alive…*

"Shit." The gruff curse came from nearby—McGoven. He didn't sound like a man confronted with a still-living victim. No, he sounded horrified.

Dejectedly, Loren stood and stumbled toward the stream, driven by an impulse to put as much space between herself and anyone else. She was a monster. The icy water felt like a slap against her bared toes, but as the water reached her calves, she sank to her knees and attempted to…what?

Gather her senses? She didn't have any damn sense *left*.

Nothing but the overwhelming horror of what she'd done. *I killed him.* Not only that, but she had shown up practically on an officer's doorstep, complete with the body, murder weapon, and all.

McGoven would drag her to the precinct before the blood on her hands even dried. She would spend the rest of her life behind bars—and how damn ironic was that?

Out of all the monsters who'd done her wrong, *she* would be the one punished in the end. There was only one way out…

Slowly, Loren eased herself forward, and the Autumn chill biting into her skin faded away. The scent of the rain-drenched forest, marred by the metallic odor of blood, drifted into oblivion. *Bye-bye* went the sounds of approaching footsteps.

She just sank beneath the ice-cold water of the stream and let it drown out everything else. The frigid temperature knocked her sideways, even as she allowed her body to go limp, submerging her head completely.

What the hell are you doing? a part of her cried as her lungs screamed for air. *Are you insane?*

Probably.

But she was so damn tired…

"What are you doing?" The shout accompanied a harsh grip that dragged her back from the water, pulling her higher up on the stream's bank until she landed on her back in the mud.

Breathless, all she could do was stare into endless silver.

Officer McGoven stood over her, though he looked far from an officer now. He must have been in bed. His hair hung loose instead of slicked back—as if he'd run the whole way there, through the wind and rain. Though, that wasn't all Loren realized as her eyes tiredly glanced him over. He was…

Naked.

Completely. He wasn't even wearing shoes.

Thick, sinewy muscle coiled under every single inch of golden skin. Sculpted limbs branched from the broad expanse of his chest, down…to where Loren attempted to keep her gaze from traveling.

It did anyway, catching sight of a dark trail of black hair leading from his navel down to… Mercifully, there wasn't enough light to see where. Faint moonlight pierced the cloud cover, glinting off the rest of him. Each strip of muscle stood out in definition. The man resembled a carved statue more than a living, breathing being. Every inch of him seemed rock solid.

Lethal. *Dangerous*, a part of Loren whispered. Though on second glance, he wasn't entirely perfect. Scars speckled nearly every inch of his body, adorning the brawn. They were thin, jagged lines, glimmering like streaks of silver. Ten. Twenty. More. Too many to count. Was he whipped? Either that or fed to tigers—the only animal Loren could think of capable of leaving such brutal marks. Even her own many scrapes and bruises paled in comparison.

"Loren."

She flinched at the sound of her name, feeling her heart pound in her chest as if his voice alone zapped some life back into it. Though what was the point of living? Every thrum of her pulse echoed as if to drive home how worthless her existence had become.

Loren, Loren, Loren.

Loren Connors, that girl who killed her father. Stabbed him in cold blood—though the newspapers would probably come up with some way to lay on the drama, by mentioning years of suspected abuse. Her tormented past.

"*Traumatized girl murders father in the woods.*"

"Loren."

She blinked to find him closer than before, crouched on one gloriously bare knee.

"Look at me." He spoke slowly as if in the space of a few minutes, she had reverted to a child. "What happened?"

Helpless, she shook her head. She couldn't say it.

"Loren—"

"No, no, no…" Her voice was so shrill. She sounded hysterical. Crazed. Some poor little girl in the middle of a nightmare that needed to be woken up. "No, no, no, no—"

"*Loren.*" He didn't have to raise his voice. She *felt* rather than heard her name come from his lips. The sound encased her, blocking out everything else but *him.* "Look at me."

She did, and the sight of those gray eyes filled with concern set everything over the edge. He would have to take her soon. Shove her in the back of that squad car and drive her into town, where strange looks and whispers would follow her for the rest of her life.

You know, Loren Connors—that crazy girl, who…

"Loren, breathe!"

She was hyperventilating. Her breaths wheezed. She felt dizzy…

Look at me!

The command erupted inside her skull, too authoritative to deny. When she raised her head, gray eyes held her captive more securely than any handcuffs.

"Loren… Shit!" His eyes cut down to her front. Judging from the cool breeze tickling her chest, her nightgown was completely in tatters.

"Damn it." The curses flowed from him, one right after the other, matching the anger that had him reaching for her breast. She didn't have the strength to panic. His warmth leeched into her skin—he was so damn hot. Like a furnace, throwing off heat.

Even his fingertips felt like hot pokers on her skin. She flinched at the contact—had she escaped one nightmare only to jump right into another? But no...he only grabbed for the torn edges of the gown and held them closed.

He noticed her reaction, and his grimace made her feel guilty for shying away.

"Did he...fuck!" He turned, glaring into the trees as if he couldn't even *look* at her and pose the question. When he spoke again, his voice was barely audible. "Did he *hurt* you?"

Loren shook her head, sensing that he wasn't referring to the bruises forming all over her body.

He remained silent for so long that Loren almost wondered if he had turned to stone right before her eyes. A living, breathing statue. Slowly, he faced her again, but his expression made her heart sink.

A grim frown warned that, whatever he'd decided, it wouldn't be good... Not for her.

She tried to move, stand, run away—*anything,* but his presence was like an invisible weight, holding her down. Keeping her in place. At least until he gave her *permission* to move.

"Loren, listen to me. This was an accident—"

"Please…" She didn't want him to paint a bright shade over the stark, grim truth. "I'm a monster."

"No," he said in a tone she felt down to her toes. "You aren't. But, if you let me…I can take it away. I can *take* the pain away."

She blinked.

Then she waited for the laugh. The cruel smile to tell her that it was all some sick joke. Neither came, and after a few seconds, panic set in.

He was serious.

"I can take it all." His tone all but promised there was a catch. "I can *help* you…but you have to trust me."

Trust?

Loren glanced down at her hands, painted red with her own father's blood. There was nothing left *to* trust. She was a monster. A freak…

"Just let me die," she whispered, cutting her gaze longingly to the lethal waters of the stream.

"I can *help* you!" The offer was a growl, whispered heatedly into her skin. "It won't be easy. You won't like it…but I can help you."

He can help, that calm, familiar voice whispered tiredly from the back of her mind. *We can trust him. Just let him…*

In the end, she didn't have much of a choice. When he lunged, pinning her with his full weight, the decision was made.

She couldn't even scream.

9

*S*he was drifting, floating aimlessly from one cloud of delirium to the next. She had no clue where she was, but she wasn't alone. At some point, bits of conversation reached her like static through a faulty radio connection.

Had to.

The only way.

I couldn't leave her.

"The pack wouldn't take her in. It was the only way."

All at once, the world stopped spinning, and Loren fell unceremoniously back to earth. She was on a bed with a mattress softer than any she could remember sleeping on before. The air smelled safe, rich like the forest. She couldn't see—it was too dark—but she could sense other people nearby.

Two people.

"Did you call them when you found her?" a gentle voice prodded. Someone female? "Did you *ask*?"

"No—" this voice was gruffer. *Definitely male.* Familiar, too. A name didn't come to mind instantly, just a breathtaking face set with silver eyes. "But the other day, you all didn't seem to give a damn about her anyway."

"Don't lump me in with them, Bill. I told you that it wasn't my choice."

"There is always a choice!" Anger penetrated his voice in guttural notes, and Loren shivered. Though, for the first time in her life, it wasn't out of fear.

Discomfort? She didn't like that he, whoever *he* was, was angry. It made *her* feel something that could have been anger as well. Her pulse raced, surging through her limbs as if electrified.

"She looks so young," the first speaker remarked. "Are you sure she's even old enough to—"

"Birth records claim she's eighteen," the man replied. Loren could tell from his inflection that he was uneasy. "But... She claimed that the bastard hadn't touched her tonight—I don't think he did. But she was covered in bruises. Her memories are like a fucking nightmare. I can't—"

"Oh, no. That poor girl."

Poor girl, Loren agreed amid a rush of sympathy. Whoever they were talking about, she seemed to deserve the pity.

"But you can't really keep her *here*," the woman added. "You said she doesn't even know the truth. What makes you think that she'll—"

"I'll handle it," the man replied. *Case closed.*

"Alright. But at least let me talk to Lukka again. Obviously, she's one of *us* if…if she's mated to you. He has no choice but to take responsibility. She needs a *pack*. She needs to be around her own kind. Even he will have to understand that."

Mated. The word seemed to convey several meanings at once. Bound, tied, linked. Connected.

Chained.

"Talk to the bastard," the man didn't seem to care either way. "Let him take her off my hands—*I don't want this.*"

"Then why get involved?" the woman asked. "Why mate her at all? I hate to play the devil's advocate, Bill."

"Who's playing? You are an advisor to Lukka, after all—"

"I'm not here to fight; I'm here to help," the woman insisted. "And, playing devil's advocate, one might think that you didn't have to get involved at all. She's lived as a human. Human laws could dictate her future now."

"So she can attack an inmate next? Rip out someone's throat while in shackles? I thought your precious Alpha valued discretion above all."

"It could have been better for her in the long run. Better than being plunged into a dynamic she doesn't understand."

A gruff laugh boomed like thunder. "Forget human laws. Why not try her by ours? Committing patricide should be enough to make her the next fucking Alpha. It worked for Lukka—"

"Bill, please!" The woman sounded pained. "You know I can't hear you speak ill of him. Besides, I'm not blaming you. You had no choice. I believe that. I just want to make sure you can defend this against the barrage of criticism we both know is coming. So… Can you?"

There was a long silence, and Loren imagined them both straining to compile a logical response. It took minutes before the man cleared his throat.

"Sonia, I couldn't leave her like that," he began haltingly. "She tried to *drown* herself in the fucking stream. You should have seen her. Smelled her. She was covered in blood, terrified. Only God knows how long he's been terrorizing her before this. She had no one. You know how it feels to be cut off. Alone. I warned that asshole Connors what could happen if he didn't take her to the damn pack—"

That *asshole Connors*. Some nameless girl wasn't the subject of this debate, but *her*. Which meant the man dominating this conversation could only be…

"What's going to happen to her, Bill?" The woman seemed to hesitate. "The police, will they—"

"I've handled it," McGoven snapped. "They think the bastard got what was coming to him. He had more gambling debts than we could keep track of. He even put his fucking house up for collateral. It was only a matter of time before one of his enemies came to collect. As for the girl, Loren will stay with me until... Until I decide what to do next."

"It's funny, Bill," the woman remarked after another brief silence. "You always swore that you wouldn't take another mate—"

"She isn't my mate," he countered coldly. "She is my problem until I figure out a better solution."

"I mean in general," the woman said. Her voice was softer. Wistful. "For so many years, you seemed set on your hermit ways, shunning everyone who tried to prove you wrong—"

"Who would want me?" he argued just as softly. "You might have a short memory, Sonia, but everyone else *doesn't*. Offering me pity isn't the same damn thing as accepting a murderer with open arms."

"You always swore that you were done with pack life," the woman continued as if he'd never spoken. "Only now, it's as if it just fell into your lap, regardless of whether you wanted it or not. Some might say you did this purposefully, though. With a mate, you could form your own pack. Challenge Lukka directly—"

"That isn't funny," the man growled. "I called you here because you're the only one in that place I trust. So do your duty as my friend and as an emissary. Call Lukka. Convince him to come. The sooner he can take her off my hands, the better—"

"Bill," the woman scolded, still utilizing that gentle tone. "No pun intended, but she's not just some puppy you can pawn off."

"Don't be cute. This isn't funny, and you know better than anyone that she'll be better off without me—"

"Look, I'm honored that you still trust me after everything we've been through," the woman insisted. "But I don't have the influence you seem to think I do. What could I possibly say?"

"You wanted to play devil's advocate? Well, here's the truth —I don't want her here longer than necessary. Despite what *they* might think, I don't want a fucking mate, and I'm asking Lukka to do the job he wanted so damn badly and fix this."

"I understand," the woman replied. "But that poor girl..."

Wasn't that the irony of it all? Loren thought drowsily. Every person who so-called "rescued" her, never wanted her in the first place.

*I*t was morning.

Her father would be angry if she didn't get up soon. After all, the papers wouldn't deliver themselves. Then there were her chores to contend with. Wallowing in bed wouldn't make those looming problems disappear, either.

Hurry up, Loren told herself. With a sigh, she rolled over and attempted to peel her eyes open. *You can still make it if you hurry.*

Once she finally caught sight of her surroundings, delivering papers was the last thing on her mind. She wasn't in her room. This wasn't even her house.

The walls weren't covered in peeling gray paint. Instead, dark wooden paneling encircled a room large enough to contain both her father's living room *and* kitchen.

The blue curtains shielding the window weren't stained. In fact, the window itself was massive, stretching almost the entire length of the wall, beyond the foot of the bed. A large, *spacious* bed, covered in a blue comforter, and a gray blanket draped over Loren specifically.

Because her nightgown was gone. So were her bra and underwear. She didn't even have on socks.

The foreign room, the bed, the nakedness—Loren figured they should have affected her, but the only coherent thought to flood her mind was the same word in a soothing mantra.

Safe. This place was safe. This room was safe. This house was safe. The feeling seemed ingrained in the very foundation, more obvious than if someone had erected a sign proclaiming, "Nothing can hurt you here."

When she tentatively placed her feet on the floor, she wasn't afraid. But something was off. The pain was still *there*—her entire body ached—but it was as if it were held at bay by an invisible wall.

She could sense it lurking just beyond that boundary, but it couldn't touch her. Nothing could. Just peace. It permeated the air like perfume, smothering any trace of fear before it could rise. And boy, she should have been afraid the moment she stood—wrapped within the blanket—and crept into a hallway that seemed way *too* familiar.

The stairs led directly into an open kitchen overlooking a modest living room. She could see a white barn from here, visible through a large bay window.

The smells of cooking food drew her notice, and she padded toward the kitchen, following the scent. Someone sat at the center island, watching her approach.

Despite the strange calm, Loren knew instantly that she didn't recognize this woman. She was beautiful, whoever she was, with curling dark hair and large blue eyes set in a delicate face that instantly conjured images of a porcelain doll.

"Hello," she said warmly, fingering the rim of a steaming cup of tea. "You must be Loren. I'm Sonia, and I think we really need to talk."

10

*H*e smelled her everywhere. Her scent permeated his bed, his house. Even the fields were impregnated with it.

She didn't smell like most women did, or even *wanted* to. Loren Connors reeked of a strange mixture of horse, fresh air, and the faintest hint of cleaning supplies, as if all those things had become a part of her. Ingrained.

After last night, he could add *blood* to that list. Rage ripped through him, mingled with regret. He should have never let her go back there. Any idiot could see how terrified she was of Connors. Hell, she reeked of fear.

His only comfort was that he didn't spend enough time around the bastard to truly know him. His job was to keep his distance, watch, and report. Before Loren's arrival, he avoided that damn house unless necessary—though he still wound up being called out at least once a month while on duty. Fred Connors was the sort of man who didn't need lycan instincts to cause trouble—his alcoholism and inclination toward violence were more than enough. Nothing about the man screamed suitable placement for a minor. Bill hadn't even known about the man's supposed daughter until the day she appeared.

Loren Connors had thrown a wrench into his life long before he chose to intervene. There was something about her, an intangible quality that people like Naomi Tanner and Fred Connors were drawn to. A part of him sensed it, too. *Easy bait*, her aura proclaimed. Weak, broken spirit, won't bite back. She was the mortal personification of a mouse, always hoping that a hawk wasn't watching.

Though, the proverbial hawk in this equation was *always* watching her.

He could recall the exact moment she first set foot on his land. He had been gathering firewood when her scent hit him with the strength of a punch to the chest. Struck dumb, he stood there *counting* the milieu of flavors composing that foreign, feminine aroma.

Animal musk, stream water, *Mr. Clean.*

It amazed him still that his first instinct hadn't been to hunt down whoever dared to trespass onto his property. Had it been her damn father, he wouldn't have hesitated, but her...

Instead, he waited, puzzled by how her presence melded into the environment like it belonged there. This was *her* land, that wild aroma told him. He was just living on it. Instant attraction had been only natural—or so he told himself. As much as it disgusted him to admit, he'd felt a pull then and there—the primal urge to claim a lone female wolf who dared to venture so close.

Until he saw her and realized his mistake. That frail waif of a girl was no lycan. She couldn't be.

The second time she came, he intentionally left those horses out, curious how she would react to them. How they would react to her. From a distance she could never fathom, he observed her approach. When she saw them…

It was *because* of those animals that he believed she was human. They let her go near them. Touch them—a courtesy they never tolerated from him, despite the years he owned the property. It was instinct. To them, he reeked of a predator's scent. The dark one had even tried kicking him once, but they never showed the same fear toward Loren Connors.

If she really were lupine, he couldn't explain the exception —not logically, anyway. At least her visits gave the animals some social interaction. Sure, they let him put food in the stable and bring them out to pasture, but that was it.

Once, he considered hiring human stable hands, but humans were instinctively nosy, and he relished his privacy. Fortunately, Loren kept to the barn, never venturing any further than that.

He was *convinced* she was human…

Witnessing her on top of the Tanner girl was enough to challenge that belief. So much for being a mouse. With barely any provocation, the prey sprouted claws on the spot. Growled. Got its first taste of battle-worn blood.

And *liked* it too—he recognized that hungry look in her eyes. Instinct had awoken, transforming her from hunted to hunter. It was a good thing that he stopped her—otherwise, who knew what she would have done?

Though, if he were honest with himself...he *shouldn't* have stopped her at all. It wasn't their way. Were they in the pack, protocol would dictate she assert herself and scratch out her place in the pecking order.

If only that asshole Connors had taken her to the pack when he had the chance. Their laws would have forbidden them from refusing her. Lukka, that arrogant prick, would have had to listen.

However, as long as there was any doubt, they could ignore her existence entirely.

In retrospect, Bill figured he should have taken her his damn self. His only comfort was purely selfish—Fred Connors couldn't possibly be her father. That low-level bastard couldn't sire a lycan.

But therein lay the drama. Which one of those pricks in the pack had fathered the girl and then abandoned her without a second thought?

Ironically, there wasn't a law for punishing that action. To be fair, there was no need. Children ensured a legacy, and most men acknowledged their bastards, if only to guarantee their bloodline lived on. It was primal instinct rather than honor. Loren's sire either didn't know of her existence, or he was as much of an anomaly as she was. Though, for now…

No other family mattered. She was *his.*

From now, until he released her, she could never go anywhere he didn't allow, or do anything he didn't give explicit permission for. A part of her would always be connected to him. Like in this very moment, when he sensed she was awake.

A possessive urge to protect her flooded his veins, strengthening by the second. *Mine.* It went beyond logic. Emotions. Morals.

Still, disgust mingled with the newfound bond. As much as he tried to rationalize it to Sonia, he didn't *want* this. Not since Emma—though this time it was different. So different, the contrasts blew his damn mind.

Emma had wanted him. They had shared their thoughts and emotions through their link, almost greedily. With Loren, the connection to her was completely sealed off—*for her own good,* he told himself. The only parts of her he allowed himself to access were her emotions. Her pain. Her fear. Those damn dark memories—he prevented her from feeling any of it. It was the least he could do.

Until Lukka…

Damn, he just hoped the bastard came soon.

He couldn't keep her here—even though her scent already seemed like a permanent part of the atmosphere…

11

"*H*ave a seat," Sonia told Loren, gesturing to an empty stool. "Would you like anything to eat?"

There seemed to be plenty. Loren sniffed, sensing eggs, bacon, and pancakes. All things she hadn't eaten in years. Cautiously, she crept over to the stool, holding the blanket to her body so tightly that her hands shook.

The food wasn't the only aroma flooding the house. That familiar scent of pine lingered in the air…on her *skin*. It was everywhere.

"Something wrong?" Sonia asked, noticing her uneasy expression.

"T-This is Officer McGoven's house," Loren croaked while attempting to mount the barstool without losing her grip over her covering. "How did I... How did I get here?"

Sonia's warm smile remained frozen in place. "I'm a friend of Bill's," she began, ignoring the question. "I want you to know that you are safe here. Don't worry about anything else. Did you sleep okay?"

She paused as if waiting for a reply.

Loren couldn't think of one.

"I'm here visiting for a few days," Sonia went on, still smiling. "So, how do you feel?"

Loren thought it over. "Strange," she whispered after a long minute.

Something wasn't...*right.*

Much like Sonia insisted, she felt safe—when she shouldn't have. She'd woken up in a stranger's bed, for one. A stranger who just so happened to be an officer of the law. Now, here she was, talking to an even stranger woman in said officer's kitchen over an offer of breakfast.

And why on earth was she naked? Why did scrapes and bruises seem to cover every inch of the skin that wasn't shielded beneath the protection of the blanket? Strangest of all, why didn't she seem worried about spending the night in a man's house, while her father...

Fear stabbed through her chest, shattering that invisible barrier. *Her father.*

"I'll make you some tea." Sonia shot to her feet. "And how about some eggs?"

Before Loren could reply, she retrieved a pan from the stove and scraped a heaping pile of food onto a plate. Minutes later, Loren found herself served with a full meal, complete with two strips of bacon.

"Eat up," Sonia urged, reclaiming a stool. "You must be starving."

Loren felt way too uneasy to be hungry—though, Sonia seemed to possess the same unspoken authority McGoven did. A fork was already in her hand, and she shoveled a helping of eggs into her mouth before she could help it.

She chewed woodenly, inspecting the large kitchen all the while. A few things stuck out to her. The fridge was devoid of any decoration or random clutter—even her father kept a magnet from one of his favorite beer companies on the front of theirs.

Moving on, the sink was spotless. The center island was clear, save for her plate and Sonia's tea. Even the countertops didn't hold anything of significance other than a potted plant and a coffee maker.

No empty beer bottles, crushed soda cans, or the remnants of a late-night poker party. It reminded Loren of one of those fancy show kitchens in a magazine. Perfect, but oddly uninviting. *Unlived* in.

"Your food's getting cold."

At the prompt, Loren choked down another mouthful of eggs, but as she swallowed, Sonia's cheerful expression faded.

"Loren, how much do you remember? About last night?" Anxiety colored her voice. She was worried.

"Last night?" Loren set her fork aside and mulled over the question. She remembered sleeping in her own bed...only to be awoken by—

Suddenly, she gripped the counter, trembling from head to toe.

"Are you alright?"

Loren shook her head, fighting to suck in air. *Remember.* Once the memories started, it was like watching a train wreck—she couldn't look away.

She had been dragged out of bed by her father. Thrown down the stairs.

Beaten.

Her father chased her into the kitchen, she grabbed a knife, and...

That was where her recollections ended like a movie cut short. The rest was blank. Empty.

Erased?

But he's dead, a part of her whispered. She knew that much.

"I think... I'm an orphan." Her voice sounded flat. Empty. The despair she would have imagined feeling was absent. It could have been a normal day.

No. The thought prickled at the back of her mind like an unreachable itch. *Think! This is wrong.*

"Loren…" Sonia suddenly reached across the table and grasped her hand. "I'm so sorry about your father. They think it was a robbery gone wrong, or at least that's what Bill told me."

A robbery. The only hole in that theory was that her father didn't have anything worth stealing, let alone killing him for. Though, she could just be in denial.

His death meant that she was truly alone. An orphan at eighteen.

"Bill thinks that it's better if you stay here," Sonia added. "At least, for now—"

"Why?" Loren blurted. She should have been in a shelter. Or, perhaps, the interrogation room of the police station. After all, she'd been in this position before…

"He was the one who found you. In the woods." Sonia eyed the wall behind Loren's head as she spoke—anywhere but her face. "He thinks that maybe the person who killed your father attacked you too. It might have been revenge over his gambling debts. You'll be safer here. He's cleared it with the station and the school as well. Everyone agrees this is the best situation."

Loren mulled over that in silence—but it didn't make sense. In fact, *none* of what Sonia had said made sense. The so-called mysterious murderer. Her being found wandering the woods in the middle of the night alone…

Before she could think too hard on it, the front door opened.

Pine. The scent rode a gust of cool air, more pungent than ever—preceding the exact moment a dark-haired figure entered the foyer. He paused, stomping mud and rainwater from his boots. He wore a thick navy windbreaker and jeans that alluded to the cold temperature outside. It must have been raining too, because his hair dripped as he slicked a hand through it. Only then did he finally glance in her direction…

And the world made sense again.

Sonia said something, her pink lips moving, but Loren couldn't hear her. She lurched to her feet, clutching the blanket. It was an impulse as unavoidable as a heartbeat. Instinctive—*Get up. He's here.*

And all along, something within her had craved him from the second she awoke. It had been waiting for him. His presence was an anchor against any doubt. She could feel the calm taking hold as his eyes flitted over her.

But then he turned away, addressing Sonia. "See if these will do."

For the first time, Loren noticed the duffle he carried over to the counter. As he set it down, Sonia withdrew its contents, mainly clothing. Not only that…

They were hers. *Her* ratty sweater still encrusted with mud. Her oversized T-shirt. Her one pair of jeans, and two long, shapeless sundresses. The only things missing were her white nightgown and her shoes.

"This is it?" Sonia sighed at the meager collection. "Are you sure?"

Officer McGoven followed her gaze and nodded. "Everything else was his."

"This will have to do for now, but you *have* to get her some new clothes. If you need the money, I can give you a few hundred—"

"I don't need your charity, Sonia." McGoven's eyes narrowed, and Loren felt an answering emotion ignite within her. Irritation. He was right. They didn't need charity. They just needed…

Him. She needed him to look at her.

"It's not charity," Sonia insisted, while folding the clothing strewn on the countertop. "After all, if Lukka does accept her, I'm sure you'll be compensated."

"Compensated." McGoven scoffed and began to pace, eyeing the floor. "That is if he doesn't conjure some old law out of thin air that declares this a crime."

Loren held her breath as he passed by her position, but he never looked up.

Please, a part of her whined. She twitched on her heels, possessed with the desire. *Look at me. Look at me.*

"Oh, Bill." Sonia sighed and placed a hand on his shoulder. "Don't be—"

"Look at me!" The voice sounded like Loren's—but louder than she would ever dare to speak. In unison, McGoven and Sonia turned to see her standing there in her thin blanket.

Sonia gasped, but Loren ignored her. Nothing mattered but those gray eyes. Finally, they met her gaze, and her heart raced, her tongue went dry, even her palms started to sweat.

This is it, a part of her murmured excitedly. *Look at me. Acknowledge me...*

"This will have to do, for now," he grumbled, returning his attention to the woman at the counter. "I'll take her out tomorrow. Though, I don't know what the hell I'm going to do about her school."

"Maybe just get her assignments?" Sonia pitched, but her eyes darted warily in Loren's direction. She hadn't missed the outburst. Both she and McGoven seemed to be deliberately ignoring it. "At least for the first week—"

"But do you think that'll—"

"Why...why can't I go to school?" *Bad girl, Loren,* she thought as both sets of eyes turned to her again. Only Sonia's lingered for longer than a second.

"It's not safe," McGoven replied, eyeing the window.

Not safe, that persistent voice in her head echoed. But no. That wasn't all.

"Why?" she asked.

His head seemed to swivel in slow motion. Like lasers, his eyes went to hers, penetrating with a single, searching stare.

She'd gotten her wish. She made *him* look at her.

But he didn't seem to like what he saw. Not one bit.

12

He took her in vertically, starting with her wild, tangled hair, before moving down to her battered face, her throat, and finally, the bits of her visible from beneath the blanket.

He drew the observation out to the last second. Stalling. *Please*, that voice in her pleaded. She waited for those gray eyes to lock with hers. Waited for him to say something— anything. But there was no spark of recognition. No expression, whatsoever, played over that handsome face.

And it hurt. It physically *hurt* to be denied…something. A look. Reassurance. Her heart panged, her stomach in knots.

Please…

He cleared his throat and turned to the window again, inspecting the gray sky with unusual interest.

"You've been through a lot, Loren," Sonia said to fill the awkward silence. "It might be better if you just rest for a few days."

Was that what he wanted? Loren couldn't take her eyes off him.

He was ignoring her. She could tell—but that silver gaze flitted her way every few seconds as if he couldn't help it. He took stock of her in pieces. Her trembling frame. Her *eye* especially, which throbbed whenever she blinked.

Abruptly, he turned back to Sonia. *Do something,* that gaze demanded, almost helplessly.

"Loren," Sonia's voice was suddenly strained. "Why don't you get dressed?"

She fished a garment at random from the pile on the counter. "This is lovely," she exclaimed with more enthusiasm than necessary, holding up the straps of a pink paisley sundress. "Why don't you wear it today? Here—" She returned the dress to the duffle and handed it to Loren before she had the chance to reply. "Do you need me to show you where the bathroom is?"

Loren shook her head only to belatedly realize that the offer had been a not-so-subtle cue to leave.

Now.

Stiffly, she retreated into the living room, still gripping the blanket, but she couldn't stop herself from glancing at *him* one last time.

He stood nearly the entire length of the kitchen away, his back to her, as if a spot on the wall was far more interesting than she was.

You're being ridiculous, she tried to scold herself as she turned into the hallway. *You're a half-naked freak standing in the middle of his house.*

But still…

Why won't he look at me? The thought chased her into the bathroom, where she shut the door and faced her reflection with a heavy sense of dread.

Her appearance could explain his reluctance. She looked awful. Her hair was a mess, her face swollen and battered. An ugly mark stretched along the length of her jaw, contrasting with the pallor of her skin.

Just as alarming was a twin bruise encircling her throat…

She turned away from the mirror in favor of inspecting the clothes. They weren't all the duffle contained. There was also a toothbrush, hairbrush, comb, and underwear—all hers. There was only one way Officer McGoven could have gotten them, but the thought of him prowling through her father's empty house made her shiver. At least she didn't have to wear the blanket any longer.

She washed up on autopilot, pulling the dress on after. It was long enough to disguise the worst of the bruising, though the thin straps left her arms bare. Ignoring the sight, she focused on her hair.

A part of her just wanted to coil the mess in a bun and be done with it—but that would mean no protective covering to hide behind. Though, McGoven seemed to have no problem probing beneath her protective measures. In the end, she settled for dragging a brush through the worst of the kinks and then braided it, like her mother used to, all those years ago.

Once finished, she felt weirdly exposed. A turtle without its shell. Before she could change her mind, she entered the hall, leaving the blanket—folded neatly—and duffle behind.

Sonia and Officer McGoven seemed to be in the middle of an intense conversation, huddled together near the center island.

"What are you going to do?" Sonia asked in a hushed whisper.

McGoven shrugged and braced his hands against the counter. "Have you called Lukka yet?"

"Y-Yes, but…"

"But what?"

"He says it will be at least a week before he can come to see her. Even then, he made no guarantees that he would accept her into the—"

"Fuck!" McGoven slammed a fist onto the counter, and Loren felt an answering twinge through her chest. It was as if she were a mirror, reflecting whatever he felt. Now? More than rage plagued him. Fear?

"What the hell is he so busy doing that he has to wait a whole week?"

"He's the Alpha Bill," Sonia said softly. "If he says he's busy, then he's busy. Besides…as cruel as it sounds, she's not one of his—at least not yet. He has no responsibility to her. Why should he hurry?"

"Because I don't *want* her, that's why." McGoven groaned in frustration, cradling his face in his hands. "What the hell am I supposed to do with her for an entire damn week? It's hard enough smoothing over that mess with her father. Sooner or later, the wrong people will start asking the right questions."

"Help her," Sonia suggested. "Protect her. Keep her safe. I know this is a lot to ask of you, but she doesn't have anyone else. Look at me, Bill."

He did, and something inside Loren lurched. It was the same envy she'd felt while Naomi pranced around in her fancy boots—but times a million. Poisonous jealousy. *No,* that voice within her cried. *He shouldn't look at her. Not her. Me!*

Her jaw ached with the restraint it took to remain silent. This was insane. She had no right to be upset.

Then, Sonia placed her hand on his shoulder, and her mind went blank. *NO!* The protest ripped through her skull. Her body—as if Sonia simply touching him went against the fabric of her entire being.

Her lips parted with the impulse to voice just one word. Scream it. *Mine*—

"Loren, are you okay?" Sonia had both hands against the counter now, her head cocked with concern.

No, she wasn't. Heart pounding, Loren darted past the kitchen for the front door. Outside, the cold air felt like a slap, but it didn't help to knock any sense into her. She couldn't erase the sight of them from her mind.

He can look at her, a part of her cruelly whispered. *He seems to have no problem touching her—it's you he can't stand.*

He said so himself. *What am I supposed to do with her for a whole week?*

Apparently, he was waiting for this *Lukka* to come for her. To take her where?

She had no idea. But wasn't that how the game of her life seemed to be played? People just came and shuffled her from one place to the other, and she never had any say.

Well, I do now.

Gritting her teeth, she descended the porch steps while the wind tore at her braid and her bare feet sank into fresh mud. The slight discomfort wasn't enough to make her turn back.

Where could she possibly go, anyway?

Run, that familiar instinct urged. *Just run away. No one will miss you…*

It wasn't like she had any ties to New Walsh. Her father was dead. That crappy ranch house at the end of the street was empty.

She had nothing left. Except…

Her feet carried her forward without any input from her brain. Almost on autopilot, she reached her destination—the barn.

She was freezing by the time she muscled open the door and pushed her way inside. Once enclosed by the familiar four walls, she felt safe. It was with an almost dream-like calm that she went over to the saddle rack and grabbed a set of tack at random, then headed for the back stall.

Bunny and Esther greeted her warmly, but Loren only had eyes for Xavier. Out of the three, he was the only one fit enough to ride and, as if knowing her intention, he didn't shy away for the first time in months as she opened his stall.

She had never ridden a horse before, though she seemed to instinctively know how to clip the reins onto his halter and lead him fearlessly to a nearby bench that made for the perfect makeshift mounting block.

A strange sense of urgency drove her on—*Hurry, hurry, hurry. Can't let him see.*

Though what did it matter?

Officer McGoven didn't seem to give a damn about her. The loss of his animal was the least he could suffer in exchange for having her out of his hair once and for all.

Determined, she hiked up her dress and braced one foot on the bench while swinging the other over Xavier's ebony back. Once she sat, fully mounted, that rebellious sense of determination faltered.

What now? She had no clue. On the other hand, Xavier seemed to know exactly what *he* wanted. When the horse bolted into motion, Loren just held on.

Experimentally, she tugged the reins to one side, and Xavier followed, storming through the gate and down the muddy path. She felt her eyes drawn to the house, watching anxiously for any sign of movement.

Would they notice her?

Even if they had, she was already out of view. Xavier flew across the earth, apparently eager to stretch his legs. When Loren squeezed her thighs, he seemed to have no trouble going faster. She had only a second's warning to grip his mane before he broke into a gallop over the hill.

She hung on and tried to breathe. For the moment, nothing else mattered but the icy chill of the wind bearing down her back. Who knew where she'd end up?

Anywhere was better than where she wasn't wanted.

13

*T*he ride seemed to last an eternity, but it could have only been a few minutes later that they neared the edge of the Baker farm boundary—and that was when the horse lost it.

Suddenly, he reared, kicking up mud and earth in a stinging spray. A frantic whinny rippled from his massive chest, sending a chill down Loren's spine.

Her first thought was that something had spooked him, and she patted his flank, murmuring soothing words. She tried twisting the reins in another direction, but once again, he shied back. And then again, when she tried another direction. It was as if an invisible wall prevented him from crossing the property boundary.

"Come on, boy," Loren urged. She shifted, intending to dismount and lead him on foot.

The second she moved, all hell broke loose.

Xavier reared again, bellowing a high-pitched cry that would haunt her nightmares. Loud, terrified—panicked. Dislodged completely, she fell from the animal's back. No, it felt more like an invisible hand caught her collar and yanked her down *hard*. She braced for the fall, but when she finally collided with a firm surface, there was no pain.

Just noise. *Thunder?* No, this sound went even *deeper*, rumbling beneath her skin. Words? Yes, but it was a long, dizzying minute before she could make out any clearly.

"What the hell is wrong with you? Are you *insane?*"

Probably, Loren realized as her nostrils flared, catching the scent of pine. She wasn't on the ground after all, but in someone's arms.

14

"*A*re you alright?" her rescuer demanded, his eyes a chilling silver. He crouched, manipulating her onto her knees before him. "Are you hurt? Are you injured? ANSWER ME!"

He was shaking her, Loren realized. *Physically* shaking her. Her head lolled back and forth as he wrenched on her shoulders.

"Can you speak? Loren!"

"I-I'm fine," she managed to choke out.

Abruptly, he let her go and stood, hissing in relief. Her response seemed to console him, but marginally. He was still angry, but above all else, he looked…worried?

"Do you have any idea how dangerous they can be? Fuck, you could have been—" He broke off abruptly and turned toward the west end of the field. In an ebony blur, Xavier bolted as if the devil himself were at his heels.

You could have been... A vivid imagination allowed Loren to fill in the blanks. She could have broken her neck or been crushed beneath a flurry of racing hooves. In fact, the only reason she hadn't been hurt at all, was because of him. McGoven. Though, how had he caught up to her in the first place?

Silent, she took in his wind-swept hair and heaving chest. Both pointed to one insane conclusion. Had he run after a galloping horse on foot?

"I'm sorry," she blurted. Fear for Xavier especially made her sick with guilt. "I'm sorry."

"Shut up." He didn't yell, but her mouth snapped shut instantly.

Then she winced. Her lower jaw was on fire. *Swollen,* she remembered, though the cause was hazy. A punch? Gingerly, she traced her bottom lip, only to freeze the second she contacted the tender flesh.

He was watching her. Worriedly, his gaze traced the planes of her face, and he was on his knees in a heartbeat. One of his hands reached for her, but visibly hesitated, before brushing her bruised cheek.

Every muscle in her body tensed at his touch. Not out of fear, but he was warm. So warm. A foreign emotion bubbled in the pit of her stomach. Greed maybe? His heat traveled hungrily through her skin, inciting an urge that had her aching to move closer. Become engulfed in that furnace-like warmth.

The look in his eyes stopped her, though—something told her that if she *did* touch him, he wouldn't hesitate to bat her hand away.

I don't want this! The memory of the declaration was almost as painful as what he said next, "Don't you *ever* do this again. Ever. In fact, don't ever leave this property without my permission. Do you understand?"

Her heart sank beneath the weight of the order. *Never again.* She nodded, but he was already on his feet, his focus beyond her.

"I need to find the horse. Come with me." He took off, and she followed robotically, cutting across the field.

Xavier had carried her farther than she'd realized, and it seemed to take an eternity to return to the heart of the property. McGoven remained silent during the entire trek, but his tense posture spoke for him. *I'm angry. Don't you ever do this again. You could have been killed!*

She was shivering by the time they reached the farmhouse —not only because she walked barefoot in a sundress. Dread was another reason her teeth chattered. She knew that look in his eye. One way or another, she would pay for this little stunt.

But is there any room left? she wondered, glancing at her fresh bruises. It didn't really matter. When they mounted the front porch, Loren tensed in anticipation of a blow.

But—even though he seemed just as angry—the only move McGoven made was to sidestep Sonia, who rushed to greet them.

"Is she okay?" the woman asked breathlessly. "Bill? Is she okay?"

He didn't answer. With single-minded focus, he stalked off in the direction Xavier had taken off in. Simmering fury battered off him in waves, cutting through the icy mist.

"Ugh, *Men*." Sonia clucked her tongue and rolled her eyes. "So damn dramatic. You okay? Bill nearly had a heart attack when we saw that you'd gone off on that horse." She bit her lower lip at the memory. "They can be a little wild, as I'm sure you've found out. To be frank, I'm surprised he hasn't sold them yet. Keeping them here has probably caused them more stress than anything. Not to mention the expense. I guess it's out of loyalty. The rogue who used to live here kept them for so long—" She broke off, shooting Loren a worried glance. "Oh dear, you still look a little shaken. Your hair is a mess. Let me—" She attempted to finger a lock of wayward hair, but Loren nearly tripped off the bottommost porch step in her haste to back away.

While Sonia might not hurt her, she couldn't say the same for everyone on the property. Fearfully, she eyed the direction Officer McGoven had marched off in, only to find that he'd vanished from view.

"I'm going to have to give him a little *talking to* about proper ways to express our anger," Sonia muttered ominously. "Come on inside. I've made some chamomile tea. Oh, you're feet! Let's clean you off first."

Loren waited while Sonia ran inside to fetch a towel. Once clean, she retreated to the couch, and Sonia reappeared armed with a steaming mug of tea. As Loren took a sip, she eyed the window, just in time to witness a dark shape streaking across the west field.

Xavier. But something else was hot on his heels. Or make that *someone,* who easily herded the animal straight into the barn. Still holding the stable door, the figure turned as if seeking *her* out through the distance.

"Oh! Loren!" Sonia was staring at her, wide-eyed. "You're bleeding."

Sure enough, she had unintentionally bitten her bottom lip. Warm beads of blood dribbled down her chin, but she barely felt the sting.

"Wait here," Sonia said, before racing down a hallway. "I'll grab the first aid kit!"

Loren remained on the couch, tucking her knees beneath her chin. That inevitable ache in her gut that always preceded one of her father's rages plagued her ceaselessly. That "shit's about to hit the fan" feeling.

When she heard the sound of approaching footsteps, she tensed, but it was only Sonia sitting beside her with a white case on her lap.

"This might hurt a little," the woman warned as she fished out a length of gauze. "But we don't want it to get infected—"

"I'll do it."

Both women turned to the doorway, where officer McGoven stood as if he'd been there all along. The only signs that gave him away were mud-caked boots and tousled hair. The scent of fresh air diluted his unique smell, and Loren couldn't help how her nostrils flared. He smelled wilder than ever.

Ours, the voice within her purred as if thrilled by his disheveled appearance. His clothing clung to every straining bit of muscle, damp with sweat.

"Are you sure, Bill?" Sonia clutched the med kit to her chest. "I can—"

"No." He stepped forward, his voice ringing with authority. "I'll do it."

Sonia shrugged and retreated to a corner while Officer McGoven continued to approach. As he came close enough to touch, Loren cleared her throat.

"W-Wait." She didn't know what made her speak up. Maybe guilt. "X-Xavier? Is he alright?"

"Is who alright?" Sonia asked. McGoven frowned, equally confused.

No wonder. Loren's cheeks flamed as she realized her mistake. Esther, Bunny, and Xavier were names *she* had given the horses. Unlike the portrayals of stables on television, Officer McGoven didn't have his animals' names on the doors to their stalls, so she named each one based on its personality.

Esther, for her big, soulful eyes. Bunny, for those droopy white ears, and Xavier, who seemed too regal to be called anything else. It had never really entered her mind that their *real* owner might have called them something else.

"The horse," she croaked, forcing herself to meet that piercing gaze. "Is h-he alright?"

Officer McGoven gave her the strangest look. "No."

Loren's heart sank. "Oh, God…I'm so sorry—"

"He's spooked," Officer McGoven explained matter-of-factly. "He's winded…but he'll live."

"Oh." Relief nearly barreled Loren over. Xavier was okay.

"See?" Sonia began tentatively. "You were worried for nothing. Bill, it's fine. I can fix her up. You don't have to—"

"I'll do it." He shifted to deliberately block Sonia's path.

With a sigh, Sonia turned to the kitchen. "I'll just make more tea."

Nervous energy filled the air as she left. She seemed like the type who needed to keep busy, feeding everyone, or soothing emotions during a crisis. The natural-born mom.

Officer McGoven, however, eyed the first-aid kit as if he had no clue what to do with it.

"Hold it for me," he ordered after a moment.

Loren scooted to the very end of the couch and wrestled the kit onto her lap. Seeming to change his mind, he took it from her, and she had nothing better to do with her hands than fidget with the hem of her dress.

It felt thinner than tissue paper as he sank to one knee before her. His scent flooded her lungs, intoxicating. Powerful. The first aid kit resembled a toy box in his large hands, flimsy and fragile.

"What were you thinking?" He posed the question so softly she barely heard him. "You could have been killed."

"I just thought…" That somehow, stealing his horse would be okay in the long run if it got her off his property. "I'm sorry. I thought… It would be better if I left."

His frown gave her the excuse to stop talking. He lowered his head, propping the kit on his knee. "Do you even know the first damn thing about riding a horse?" he asked.

"No."

He made a deep sound in the back of his throat. *Interesting.* "Do you realize that the horse you took is a full-grown stallion who could have *thrown* you the second he wanted to?"

She had known that much, at least. "Y-yes."

"*And*—" Officer McGoven continued. "Do you realize those horses will never leave *my* property unless I give—" Abruptly, he changed the topic. "Open your mouth. You're still bleeding."

He gave her no warning, and she tried not to flinch as one of those massive hands cradled her chin. If only he felt as dangerous as he looked. Despite the muscles coiling beneath his skin, his gentleness was a shock. He barely touched her at all, just softly eased her head back so that he could dab at her bottom lip with a bit of antiseptic liquid smeared over the cotton ball.

Their eyes met, and Loren expected anger. Hatred. Rage. What she found in his gaze only confused her. Fear? Genuine fear that didn't seem to ease until he wiped away most of the blood and set the first aid kit aside.

Rather than withdraw, he remained crouched. Then, much like Sonia had tried to, he tucked a loose piece of hair behind her ear.

She didn't recoil—she couldn't. It was like her body became magnetic, drawn to his touch. Her toes *curled,* and an unfamiliar emotion flooded her belly. Another time she might have flinched at the sensation, but she was paralyzed.

It felt…nice having him there. Right.

Ours, that voice murmured, louder and more insistent. *Ours. Mine. His.*

She felt as though she could endure his touch for eternity. Longer, even.

Though nothing in the world could have prepared her for the moment he leaned forward and pressed his mouth against her jaw.

15

*H*e didn't kiss her. Instead, his lips ghosted over what had to be the only unmarked sliver of skin she had left.

Panic stirred at the back of her mind, but something in his movements made her relax. He wasn't brutal or rough. Just…patient. He angled his face, but carefully, ensuring his skin contacted hers. As a result, his breath basted her skin, lessening some of the discomfort in the bruised areas. It was strange. His mouth nudged a tender bruise on her cheek next. Rather than pain, she felt…

Better.

It was as if his touch was magic—but he didn't stop there. His lips blazed a trail along her entire jaw. Her nose. Her swollen upper lip. When he finally stilled, his mouth hovered inches from hers.

His nearness made her dizzy, but though her heart pounded, she wasn't afraid. Not even as she felt his fingers untangle the remains of her braid to cup the back of her skull. Like lightning, a million thoughts jolted through her all at once—*stupid* thoughts.

The main one being that he couldn't mean to... He couldn't possibly *kiss* her. Her lip was busted, and he didn't even *know* her. Not to mention the fact that he had to at least be in his mid-twenties, several years older than her.

None of that, however, mattered more than the simple fact that he *couldn't* kiss her because...

"I'm making cookies!"

The excited proclamation came from the kitchen, and Loren recoiled against the couch while Officer McGoven stood, crossing his arms.

"What the hell did you just say?" he bellowed.

"Cookies," Sonia cheerfully reiterated, poking her head through the doorway. "I found some stuff in your cupboards."

"Sonia..." McGoven rolled his eyes, but, overall, his expression revealed none of the shock Loren felt. As if it were the most natural thing in the world to press his mouth against a stranger's face and walk away with no explanation.

She wasn't so unaffected. Boys her own age were an enigma, and men... In her experience, their touch only inspired terror, nothing more—until now. Her cheek tingled, but not like the slaps she was used to enduring. In fact, her face felt better overall. Numb instead of throbbing.

On second thought, McGoven's unshaken demeanor seemed to be an act he put on for her benefit. His eyes kept darting to the window—the woods. While he'd safely wrangled Xavier, something had him worried. Suddenly, he cocked his head as if picking up a noise.

Loren strained her ears but heard nothing. A heartbeat later, McGoven was storming across the room.

"You came alone?" Belatedly, Loren realized he was speaking to Sonia.

"Yes." The woman barely looked up from the contents of a bowl she was stirring. "Why?"

"Nothing—" His frown deepened, and he eyed the window more intently. Did he see something? Suddenly, he lunged for the doorway. "Stay here. I'm heading out."

He was at the front door before Loren could blink.

Sonia didn't seem worried. "Kay," she called back. "I'll save you some cookies."

McGoven only grunted in acknowledgment before leaving, letting the door slam behind him. Alone, Loren crept into the kitchen. Without his cold mystery as a contrast, Sonia flitted across the space with childlike energy that betrayed her youth. She couldn't be any older than her early twenties.

"I hope you like sweets?" she asked once she caught Loren staring. "I think they'll have to be sugar, though. He doesn't seem to have any chocolate chips. He always was a health nut. You know, he used to eat tuna by the can every day.

What a freak of nature—" Beaming, she looked at Loren only to realize that she wasn't in on the joke. "Oh… Well, let's just say where we come from, beef is the most common thing on the menu, cooked rare, if at all."

Her father must have been from the same place. Steak seemed to be all he ever ate—unless beer counted as a meal item. The thought unnerved her for some reason, tugging at a memory on the periphery of her consciousness. Why couldn't she remember?

"Where are you from?" she asked absently. Now that she thought about it, McGoven didn't seem like the other citizens of New Walsh. He wasn't stuck-up like Naomi Tanner, or hostile to outsiders like her father.

"Somewhere far from here," Sonia said warily. "Bill and I grew up together. In a place called Black Mountain. Ever hear of it?"

Loren shook her head.

"Really?" Sonia's eyes widened, but she disguised her surprise behind a tinkling laugh. "Well, it's beautiful, but not exactly a haven of culture. Tuna fish is about the most exotic thing on our menu. Though, luckily, we do love our cookies. Wanna give me a hand?"

"S-sure."

Beaming, Sonia tossed her a small glass bowl and three eggs. "I love to bake," she chirped, still stirring her mixture. "It gives me something to do with my hands. Though, I probably *should* go and check on Bill."

Loren followed her gaze out of the window above the sink. Visible against the backdrop of the forest was the hulking shape of Officer McGoven. He wasn't heading for his truck, or even the squad car—both of which were parked in the driveway alongside a blue car she assumed was Sonia's.

Instead, he marched toward the woods with a determination that made Loren suspect he wasn't going for a lighthearted stroll. No. She could...feel his unease. It flavored the air like smoke, warning of impending danger.

Did he sense something out there? she wondered, creeping closer to the window. The same something that had spooked Xavier?

She opened her mouth to ask, only to be presented with a bowl of tan-colored gunk. "Wanna add the eggs?" Sonia asked.

Woodenly, Loren added all three to the mixture. As Sonia stirred, she glanced at the window again. Already, McGoven had vanished.

"Don't worry about him. He'll be back. Bill is..." Sonia sighed, following her gaze. "Well, he can seem grumpy at times. Perhaps a bit cold. Don't take it personally. He's been through a lot, and let's just say he isn't used to carrying on a full conversation."

"What happened?"

Sonia eyed her sharply. Her tongue flitted across her lips, and Loren suspected she was weighing whether or not to tell her this piece of McGoven's past. But suddenly...a part of her needed to know—craved anything that could lessen his mystery.

"Please," she croaked.

"Well, he had a… *Wife*. A wife once, but she died. It was awful—" Pain constricted Sonia's features, and she leaned against the counter for stability. "Bill changed after that. He left home and took over this farm. It's been five years, and this is the first time I've seen him."

Five years. A wife. Those new bits of information seemed to devastate that newly woken inner voice in Loren's mind. *We didn't know…*

"I'm surprised to find that he's kept this place in good shape at least," Sonia said, forcing a smile. "Old Josiah, the man who used to own this place—well, he wasn't fond of visitors for a start. I only came here once in those days, but I think Bill has done his best to update the interior."

"Josiah?" Loren hadn't heard that name before.

"Josiah Baker. He was a…friend of Bill's father, more like an uncle to him than anything. After he died, Bill took over the farm and all its little eccentricities. Josiah was never happy at the compound, under our laws. The second he left, I think he bought those horses merely to prove a point. At his core, he saw himself as human. Nothing else. Um, I mean, as a cowboy at heart," Sonia added in a rush. Her cheeks were faintly pink, but she huddled over the sink, hiding her face. "Anyway, Bill's lived here ever since."

With another sigh, she inspected the empty driveway and shrugged. "Well, I suppose we should get these in the oven."

Without mentioning McGoven, Loren set about obeying any task Sonia sent her way until the cookies were cooling on the counter.

Every now and again, her gaze drifted to the window, as those remnants of his past played on her mind. He had a wife once. Someone he loved.

Someone she knew she could never compare to—not that it mattered. To McGoven, she was a burden.

Nothing more.

16

*H*e didn't return. At least not before nightfall. By then, Sonia hustled her off to bed with a yawn, promising to wake her in the morning.

Once again, Loren found herself in that strange room, on an unfamiliar mattress, helplessly eyeing the ceiling. The gray blanket from before was gone.

But she could still smell him. This was *his* room; it had to be—but that wasn't the realization that made her breath catch. No, it was the fact that he had shared this bed with her at least once. Her body just *knew*, even if she couldn't remember. Had it been the other night?

She tried to picture him there, that bulk lying beside her, not too close—but close enough to feel that warmth. Her traitorous body tensed, longing to feel it again. Without the presence of someone else, this room was too big. Too cold. The mattress creaked with every movement, and as crazy as it seemed, it didn't feel *natural* lying on his bed without him.

Hit your head a little hard, when you fell off that horse? she wondered, annoyed, turning on her side.

She couldn't sleep, though she wasn't sure how much time passed before the front door finally slammed open.

He was back. His presence filled the entire house, relieving some of the tension she hadn't been aware of until then. That inner voice murmured excitedly. *He's here. Ours.* Anticipation flooded her veins with a sudden need to see him. She had to. The urge felt as vital as breathing.

But he never came upstairs. Instead, those heavy footsteps retreated toward the living room, and Loren could guess his final destination with a pang of despair.

The couch.

She didn't know where Sonia was, but at the thought of him near her… Loren bit down on her already tender lip.

You don't know him, a part of her argued. *He's a police officer, and he doesn't even know you!*

None of the excuses could penetrate that stubborn inner voice insisting the opposite. He belonged *there*. The only reason he *wasn't* was because of *her*.

The thought followed her into a dreamless sleep, where a barrage of nightmares awaited. She was running. Running, racing, falling. No matter where she went, she couldn't find peace. Safety. Monsters lurked on every corner, and she just wasn't fast enough...

"Loren."

She jolted awake, heart in her throat, as the remnants of the dream washed over her like ice water. Gradually, the darkness faded, and she was shaking beneath the covers.

Safe, a part of her insisted firmly. Then a familiar scent flooded her lungs, calming her racing heartbeat.

"Get dressed."

She whirled to find someone watching her from the doorway. McGoven, fully dressed in his navy windbreaker and black slacks. His eyes were sharp, betraying none of the exhaustion she felt after waiting up for him.

Safe, that voice insisted again. As long as he was there, nothing in the world could touch her.

"Sonia made breakfast, but I'll—" He turned away, and the rest of his words were grumbled, barely audible. "I'll be out in the truck. Come join me when you're done."

Breakfast? Sure enough, it was morning already. Bright light spilled in through the curtains shielding the window, illuminating the plain surroundings. Already she could tell it would be another rainy, overcast day.

At least now she didn't have to face it *naked.* Per Sonia's suggestion, she had gone to bed wearing her oversized T-shirt. At least until "Bill" could find her something else.

Rather than new clothing, someone had placed her duffle at the foot of the bed. After a quick appraisal of the contents, she chose her muddy sweater and jeans and headed for the bathroom with her toothbrush in tow. The one upstairs was larger than the one below. In it, she dressed quickly, and stumbled downstairs minutes later.

"Morning," Sonia called tiredly from the kitchen. Compared with yesterday, she looked less chirpy and more…exhausted. Had she waited for McGoven all night, too? Without saying as much, she yawned and gestured toward a steaming plate of bacon and eggs sitting on the center island.

"I made breakfast. Eat, and take your time. I'll make sure he waits."

Aware of McGoven's warning, Loren snatched a piece of toast from the spread and gobbled it greedily. Then, she rushed out the front door before Sonia could call her back. Her heart pounded as she raced down the porch steps and bounded the length of the driveway.

That green pickup idled near the road leading from the farm. When she finally clambered inside, Officer McGoven inspected her, an eyebrow raised.

"You could have eaten breakfast," he said. "I would have waited."

Loren shook her head. "I'm okay."

She was starving. Despite eating some of Sonia's cookies last night and a dinner of spaghetti, she could have easily devoured that plate of eggs and then some. Part of it was just greed. She wasn't used to having so much food on demand. Though, the thought of him waiting on her was *worse* than hunger.

Officer McGoven shrugged and drove into town without any comment. Gazing from the window, Loren tried to smother her curiosity. Soon, the anxiety turned into downright panic the closer they came to the heart of New Walsh.

This was it. He was taking her to the police station. There, she would be questioned about her father's so-called murder, and everything would start to unravel. There was no way around it. Things didn't add up with the whole "murder/robbery" story—who knew what the police officers thought?

She was on edge, nearly rising from the seat the moment the car came to a stop—to bolt or just run inside the station herself? She had no idea. Fearfully, she faced the window, only to discover the elegant façade of New Walsh Academy, not the station.

It was that twilight hour right before the doors opened. The calm before the storm. Loren had no idea what he could possibly expect to do here so early. She didn't even have her backpack.

But, obviously, explaining wasn't his strong suit.

"Come on," Officer McGoven commanded as he exited the truck first.

Loren moved to follow him only to realize, the moment her bare foot hit the pavement, that she was completely barefoot. When she didn't appear beside him, he turned to see why, eyes darting directly to her filthy feet.

"You forgot your damn shoes," he began in a hiss.

Loren shook her head. "No, I…"

There weren't any "shoes" left to wear. Her *Kicks* had all but disintegrated and weren't even among the things he retrieved from her house. He flinched, and she could imagine him running over the contents of her bedroom in his mind—*Were those pathetic sneakers the only ones she had?*

"Never mind." He turned abruptly, waving her off. "Wait here."

Sick with worry, Loren watched him enter the school. Though he wasn't in uniform, he looked no less intimidating in slacks and a windbreaker—an odd outfit considering how cold it was. Loren was freezing in her thick sweater.

She huddled on the front seat, feeling like a kenneled puppy.

He was inside a long time. Already, the trickle of students heading into the school was starting to pick up. It felt strange to not be a part of the morning rush. Even stranger to be sitting in a police officer's truck.

When he finally exited the school building, she sat bolt upright, tense with anticipation. His expression alone revealed nothing. He wasn't smiling or frowning. With no explanation whatsoever, he wrenched open the door on her end and dumped a pile of books onto her lap.

"Sign it," he demanded, nodding to a document resting on top of the pile.

Loren took the pen he offered and complied, scanning the document as she did so. It seemed to mention something about termination—withdrawing from academic activity.

Before she could read more, Officer McGoven snatched the page and shoved it into his pocket. Then he returned to the driver's seat, started the engine, and peeled out of the quickly filling parking lot.

"From now on, you'll do your assignments on your own," he explained while turning onto the main street. "Someone will drop off the work and turn it in for you. This way, you won't fall behind. At least until..."

He seemed to deliberately keep himself from saying more, but Loren had a grim idea of what words filled in the blanks.

Until Lukka comes for you.

Dazed, she eyed the textbooks on her lap. They were for all the subjects she was taking, along with a few notebooks from her locker.

She didn't dare ask any questions, not that Officer McGoven seemed inclined to tell her anything else. Silently, he drove through the heart of town, finally parking along the busiest street. Here, various stores sold everything from clothing to ice cream.

"What size are you?" he asked gruffly.

Loren blinked, but her hesitation only earned her an impatient scoff.

"Your *shoe* size. What shoe size are you?"

Confused, she inspected her bare feet. She had always just grabbed a pair that fit, without ever worrying about that little number on the bottom.

When she shook her head, Officer McGoven palmed one of her knees without warning. Shock paralyzed her as he lifted her leg, cupping her bare foot in the center of his palm. He seemed to weigh it, inspecting the shape. Satisfied with whatever he'd observed, he released her and left the truck, slamming the door behind him.

Loren waited, wondering what on earth he could possibly need with her shoe size. When he finally emerged from a nearby store, she saw the box first. Big and beautiful, it consumed her attention as McGoven approached and shoved it unceremoniously onto her lap.

"Try them on."

Without even explaining what "them" was, he headed toward the driver's seat.

Loren had an idea, though... Her fingers shook in anticipation as she wrestled the lid off and set it aside.

A mixture of shock and awe left her dizzy. She couldn't even speak. "Them" was a pair of boots. Sturdy hiking boots, to be exact. Naomi Tanner wouldn't be caught dead wearing a similar style, but Loren thought they were the most beautiful things she'd ever laid eyes upon.

"Try them on," McGoven insisted, his voice slightly less gruff. "They should be snug but not too tight."

Heart in her throat, she removed each boot gingerly. Someone had shoved a pair of novelty socks in each one, both decorated with ribbons and trees for Christmas. She pulled them on first, then the boots lacing them tightly. Marveling at the feel, she gave her foot an experimental kick.

"How do they feel?"

"P-Perfect," she stammered. "Thank you…but I can't—I can't possibly pay for these."

He gave her an exasperated look and started the truck as if he needed the distraction to compile a response. In the end, he grated four words through his teeth, "Don't worry about it."

They didn't speak all the way back to the farmhouse. The second he parked, Officer McGoven grabbed her stuff and mounted the porch where Sonia stood in the doorway to greet him.

Loren took her time, relishing the feel of her new boots.

"Nice," Sonia said appreciatively as she mounted the porch steps—but Loren could read the unease written over her face.

"What's wrong?" McGoven demanded.

Sighing, Sonia led the way inside and marched directly into the kitchen, where she fished a cookie from the plate on the counter.

"Lukka's called me back," she announced before taking a bite.

Loren sensed the words meant more than the obvious. McGoven's furious snarl proved it.

"What?" he shouted. "What the *hell* do you mean?"

"I'm sorry." Sonia's blue eyes darted everywhere around the kitchen but his face. "He called me back," she said once she swallowed. "He says that 'I'm needed' though he won't say for what. It doesn't matter. I can't refuse a direct order. I have to leave. Tonight."

17

"*Y*ou can't leave." Angrily, McGoven formed a fist, and Loren half-expected him to smash it into the wall. He flattened his palm against the countertop instead with an almost helpless groan. "Sonia, I *need* you here—"

"I know," Sonia said softly. "But, it's not like I can refuse him. He'll see it as a challenge—especially if it's to stay with *you*. Besides, if we piss him off now, he might never come and see her. We can't take that risk."

Loren froze as they both turned in her direction.

Sonia looked miserable, but the man beside her... He looked crazed. Desperate. His eyes were molten silver, his throat cording with tension.

"What the hell am I supposed to do without you?" He sounded like a child pleading not to be abandoned.

"The same thing you've *been* doing," Sonia said gently. "This could turn out to be a good thing, for all of us. While I'm there, I can speak to Lukka directly. Now that I've met Loren, I can vouch for her. You... You were right, Bill." Her tone conveyed a double meaning.

"Yeah," McGoven hissed. "I'm sure he'll love to hear you say that. He'll roll out the fucking red carpet!"

"I'm sorry." Suddenly, Sonia stood on tiptoe and pressed her lips to his cheek.

Loren dug her nails into her palms. The intimate expression startled her—not because of the warmth in it, but because she wanted...

She wanted to march over there and drag Sonia away, by her *hair*. Shout, kick, scream—better yet, order her to never touch him again like that.

She didn't know why, but she couldn't ignore the building anger. It clawed through her chest like a living creature. It *hurt*.

Just as quickly, Sonia withdrew from him, and the unwarranted anger diminished slightly. "I'm leaving tonight," she said. "You'll be okay. I know you will. But I'll call—"

"Don't bother," Officer McGoven said ominously. "You have a point. There, you can convince the asshole to see her in person. If he hasn't sent his spies already."

Sonia raised an eyebrow. "What are you talking about?"

McGoven tossed Loren a cautious glance. Then he squared his jaw and said, "You saw how that horse bolted the other day? I thought it was because of the territory markers, but when I checked the perimeter, I caught a scent."

"What?" Sonia's eyes widened. "Another rogue?"

"No. They were too careful—much like a scout. I didn't recognize their scent, but I know your Lukka has been building his ranks, letting in plenty of outsiders to swell his numbers. All that talk about loyalty. You thought I didn't know?"

Sonia's cheeks flamed. "Bill, it isn't my place to—"

"I'm not asking for your political opinion, Sonia. I'm asking this—why the hell would your precious Alpha send a scout on the heels of a trusted advisor?"

A hard gleam sharpened Sonia's gaze. In an instant, the girlish charm vanished, and she looked on par with McGoven as far as maturity went. Just as shrewd and just as angry. "Maybe Lukka didn't give me exact permission to come," she said cagily. "I may have left on my own."

"You?" McGoven crossed his arms. "Go against your precious Alpha? What is this world coming to?"

"Don't mock me," Sonia snapped. "You called me, so I came. If he forbade me outright, I wouldn't be here."

"Or he let you come here as a distraction. Then he sent a guard dog after you to scout my property and report back," McGoven said darkly. "What the hell is he playing at?"

"You know what he's like."

"Oh, yes." McGoven's eyes flashed the color of steel. "I know exactly what he's like. That's what I'm worried about."

Sonia choked out an exasperated sigh. "*You* are the one who left us, remember? Lukka has done his best to keep order. You want so badly for him to fail, but he hasn't. We're doing fine under him, and I won't deny that because of your… history. I'm sorry if that upsets you."

"That's not what I meant," McGoven said softly. "I just want to know you're safe."

"*We* are."

"And… Is Kyle still his second?"

Loren stiffened. Irritation prickled her skin suddenly, white-hot. It didn't stem from her—just him. His face may be blank, but the guttural way he uttered that name left nothing to the imagination as to how McGoven felt about this man. Kyle.

Pure, unadulterated hatred.

"H-Huh?" Panic flitted across Sonia's features before she smothered it behind a cheerful smile. "Enough pack gossip. Don't worry. Please. It will only be a few days until Lukka comes himself. You'll be fine. Both of you. As for what you sensed… I'm sure it was just a scout, making sure I arrived safely."

"Even so, his scout most likely picked up her scent. Then, all of a sudden, your Alpha calls you back. Why?"

Sonia stammered. "Um...."

Loren didn't miss the way they both glanced at *her*. The tight-lipped expression could only be described as...wary. Whatever the source of their unspoken tension was, it had to do solely with her.

"I'll sort this mess out," Sonia insisted. "I promise."

This time, she didn't sound as optimistic.

18

OUTSIDE NEW WALSH

"*H*e smelled me," the dark-haired youth murmured excitedly, bouncing on the passenger's seat. "I *know* he did, though I think he was more worried about that horse, but I saw her—"

"You did?" Kyle cocked his head, his interest piqued. "Well, what did she look like?"

The boy, barely nineteen, shrugged. "I couldn't get a good look. She's pretty, though. Tall and skinny. Lukka might want her, after all—"

"Get your head out of your cock, kid," Kyle scolded. "What about her *eyes*? What did her damn eyes look like?"

That detail might reveal who her real father was, at least.

The kid paused. Judging from how long it took him to process the damn question, Kyle's suspicions were confirmed—he was a fucking idiot.

Figures. When it came to reconnaissance, he always got saddled with the bottom of the barrel. At least, this latest fool—his name was Micha, or something like that—could shift at will, and he was fast. You *had* to be to outrun Bill McGoven on his own damn property.

"Green. I think," Micha announced. "Though, I wasn't really looking at her *eyes,* if you know what I mean—"

"I don't," Kyle snapped. "Now shut the fuck up. I need to think."

He palmed the steering wheel, eyeing the deserted road they were parked alongside. McGoven's property was over an hour away, but he could still sense the bastard. He just hoped McGoven had noticed him in return. Wouldn't that make for an interesting reunion?

"Why hasn't Lukka taken her in?" the boy asked, fidgeting in the passenger seat. While skilled physically, he was apparently too stupid to heed a direct order. "He takes in outsiders all the time. He took me in—"

"Because we aren't a damn halfway house," Kyle replied. "And you and the others *earn* your keep."

Besides, the scrawny rogues were nothing more than cannon fodder—though Kyle didn't mention that. He also didn't mention that the girl in question was as good as dead. Lukka had made that clear. The Alpha may hide behind the fact that no law stipulated he *had* to take the girl in, but that was just a cop-out. Whatever helped him sleep at night.

The truth was the girl was mated to Bill McGoven. For that alone, she had signed her own death warrant. This was personal. It didn't matter that the asshole claimed he'd had no other choice or whatever bullshit that bitch Sonia had spewed to justify the action.

He was in *exile*—forbidden from ever partaking in pack life. Lo' and behold, taking a mate was a *major* fucking part of pack life. *Kyle* hadn't even taken one yet, and he was well past the age when his wolf called out for a mate of his own.

But hey, he could wait. By jumping the gun without permission, McGoven had gone too far. If losing the girl was what it took to make him realize the gravity of the situation, then so be it. The last time Kyle had checked, rogues in exile couldn't fucking take any woman they wanted.

And obviously, his little female wasn't just *any* old woman. Why else would he keep her so close? Days after their joining, and he barely let her off his property.

The fucker was hiding something, which was why Kyle was here in the first place, hours from pack territory in the middle of bum-fucking nowhere. Lukka was too much of a pussy to do his own dirty work.

Kyle was used to it. Even before he took over, Lukka preferred using his brains over brute force. Not like the great and powerful Bill McGoven—the same man everyone assumed would be the future Alpha once upon a time. As it turned out, *Lukka* claimed that mantle, and only the Alpha could decide who was worth saving or not.

This poor little mated female *wasn't,* and Kyle would see to it personally. Though…it wasn't like he could just stroll onto that farm and drive a stake through her chest himself.

Not with McGoven and the Carlisle woman there. Micha might have been fast, but Kyle doubted the pup could hold his own against a full-grown wolf like McGoven. Even that little bitch, Sonia, could put up a good fight if she wanted to.

Besides, they had to play nice. For political reasons, of course. After all, it wouldn't look good on Lukka's part to be responsible for the murder of a young girl just because he happened to hate the bastard who claimed her.

Yep, they had to play by specific rules, make it look like an accident. Kyle already had a few devious ideas in mind, but it wasn't like he could put any into practice without narrowing down the playing field by at least *one* hostile wolf.

Right on cue, his cell phone buzzed at his hip.

"Go," he told the runt beside him. "Scout for a mile. Make sure the coast is clear."

"Okay!" Micha bounded from the truck without a backward glance, and Kyle brought the phone to his ear.

"Yes," he grumbled the second he sensed the runt beyond earshot.

"The Carlisle girl's out." Lukka's voice crackled from the other end of a bad connection. "She'll leave tonight. Tomorrow, you move in."

"Excellent," Kyle said around a cold smile. "I'm bored babysitting."

"But you know the drill," Lukka snapped. "Be clean about it. I don't want this in any way traced back to me."

Yeah, yeah. Mentally, Kyle rolled his eyes. That was Lukka. Sure, he could *order* a murder easy enough, but when it came to the grisly details, he blanched. Though, how hard could killing one girl be? Hell, even McGoven seemed to want her off his hands. In a sick way, they were doing the bastard a favor.

"Don't make her suffer," the Alpha added.

As if he really gave a shit.

If McGoven had *really* wanted her, Kyle figured he would have been ordered to string the girl up by her toes and make the asshole watch him kill her. It wouldn't have been the first time Lukka had him get "creative" to prove a point to a rival.

Still.

"It'll be neat and clean, Lukka," Kyle promised. "Your little problem will be wiped away, and McGoven will once again be solely at your beck and call."

It was a win-win for everyone, really.

Except for the girl, of course. She got the short stick in the end. But in a twisted game of power and revenge, someone had to be the pawn.

19

*L*oren bolted awake, a scream poised in her throat. *It was dark. So dark. She couldn't see anything— couldn't see him—but she knew he wasn't there. She had been searching and searching, but he was never there…*

"You're alright." The stern voice encased her in an eerie sense of calm. Instantly, her fear vanished.

Safe…

"It's alright. You're dreaming," that same someone told her, their voice gentle and deep. Something brushed the top of her head. It took a second to identify it, but her heart fluttered once she did—warm fingers stroking through her hair. "You're alright."

Shivering, Loren glanced up. Her first thought was that it was the moon she saw, glowing through the oppressive dark. Make that *two*, both filling her with peace, while that familiar voice vibrated down her spine.

"It's alright," he repeated. "I'm here."

The words conveyed more than comfort. They were a promise. A vow.

I'm here.

Loren felt her eyes drift shut, her body heavy. A second later, she was asleep, so deeply it was as if she'd never woken up at all.

*L*oren was shivering. Once she opened her eyes, she realized why—she was curled into a ball, on top of the covers.

Icy daylight streamed in through the gap in the curtains, falling over her like a spotlight. When she finally found the strength to move, she fully expected to find someone right beside her.

Instead, there was nothing on the blue comforter but her own puddle of drool.

Puzzled, she stumbled into the bathroom to brush her teeth. Then, she got dressed, this time in the other sundress. The dull, brown cotton hung down to her toes, giving her *some* protection from the cold.

But not enough to erase the building dread that she was alone. The bottom floor of the house seemed just as deserted. For the first time in two days, there was no aroma of cooking breakfast. No cheerful Sonia to greet her with a plate and a smile.

The only things waiting for her on the center island were exactly two pieces of toast and a note. *Be back soon. Stay here, Bill.*

Bill. Loren shivered as her fingers traced the firm, steady handwriting. A glance out the window revealed the driveway was empty, save for the green pickup. He took the patrol car today, though she wondered where he could have gone so early, when the sun had barely risen.

Puzzled, she downed the toast in a few bites and padded into the living room, feeling as out of place as a mouse smack dab in the middle of the cat's den.

What should she do? The only likely option seemed to be to start on the massive pile of schoolwork the school assigned her.

Some of it was stuff they had already covered, though the new material didn't seem that hard. Loren finished it all in no time—way too soon to fill the hours of empty space that stretched on and on...

By the time lunch rolled around, she made herself a peanut butter sandwich, feeling guilty with every single bite. He didn't seem to be keeping her prisoner—at least not the whips, chains, and forced starvation version. Of course, he meant for her to feed herself while he was gone... Right?

Not that it mattered. By late afternoon, he hadn't returned.

Loren sat in the kitchen, drumming her fingers against the center island. Waiting. When she heard a sudden knock on the door, she raced for the foyer. It was only then that a part of her realized he wouldn't have to knock to get inside his own house.

As she hesitated, whoever stood on the other end opened the door without an invitation.

"Well, well, well." The husky purr accompanied the familiar green eyes that took her in with one calculating sweep. Definitely *not* Bill McGoven. "I was wondering what kind of loser would take both Advanced Microbiology *and* Calculus."

"N-Naomi?" Loren blinked as if just doing so would transform the hostile blond into someone else.

No such luck.

"The one and only," the blond snapped, pushing her way inside. "You gonna invite me in, or do I have to freeze my ass off?"

"T-This isn't my house," Loren stammered. Judging from the pile of paperwork she held, she figured that *Naomi* was the person the school assigned to deliver her work.

"I know," Naomi said, glancing around the spacious entryway with a sniff. "*Yours* is all covered in that caution tape shit. What the fuck did you *do?*"

Loren flinched. It had to be all over the news by now that her father was dead.

"You must have done something pretty bad for a *police officer* to take you in," Naomi added suspiciously, fingering a lock of blond hair.

Apparently, the fact that Officer McGoven lived on the Baker farm wasn't much of a secret.

"So, where do you want to be tutored?" the blond demanded, crossing her arms over the front of a sleek, designer sweater. She looked as bitchy and perfect as always —minus the large, square bandage stuck to the left side of her cheek.

How did she explain that to her minions? Loren wondered. *Plastic surgery?*

"I don't need a tutor," was all she could think to say.

Naomi shrugged. "Tough shit. It comes with the territory. They want to make sure that you 'understand the material' before attempting it on your own." She even utilized air quotes.

Loren bit her lip against a groan. First, she woke up naked in a stranger's bed to learn her father was dead. Now the girl she'd attacked was here to teach her calculus?

What next?

"I guess this will do," Naomi sighed, traipsing into the living room uninvited.

To Loren's immense shock, she took a seat on the couch and proceeded to open a workbook.

No threats. No veiled efforts to insinuate that she might press charges. No references to the scratches hidden by that bandage. It was as if she truly didn't care about the incident at all.

Or, that inner voice whispered. *Someone made her forget.*

"Time's ticking," she snapped when Loren didn't move. "I have a hair appointment in an hour."

"Why are you here?"

From what little Loren knew of the homeschooling system at New Walsh Academy, students *volunteered* to deliver the work. Call it skepticism, but she doubted that Naomi would do so out of the goodness of her heart.

"You're in advanced courses," the girl said as if it were obvious. "Surprise, surprise, *I'm* the only one qualified to tutor you—"

Loren raised an eyebrow. She vaguely remembered something about Naomi taking AP courses, but she had always just assumed that the blond had bought her way in or something.

"There are other students," she countered.

"I'm the only one with a *car*," Naomi added, flashing a cocky smile. "Now, can we get this over with?"

Loren claimed an armchair, unsure of what to expect. Submitting to this "tutoring," seemed more like a convict being tortured slowly before execution.

But, to her immense surprise, being tutored by Naomi Tanner wasn't *all* bad.

The girl was rude, snippy, and impatient, but she managed to make the math make sense at least, describing the complicated equations in a way that even the teacher, Mr. Hollings, couldn't.

But she wasn't nice about it.

Within an hour, they finished the last assignment. Not a second later, Naomi gathered up the work, plus what Loren had already done beforehand.

"Same time tomorrow," she said with a heavy sigh as if their session had been the most excruciating way to pass the time possible.

"Okay."

Loren watched her head for the door without so much as a parting jibe at her expense. Before she could open it, someone else did. A dark figure appeared in the doorway, draped in shadow.

He's here, a part of Loren murmured excitedly. Those silver eyes sought her out as she lurched to her feet, and her heart swelled. *Yes,* that inner voice murmured happily. *Ours.*

Abruptly, he turned to Naomi. "Ms. Tanner. This is a surprise."

"H-Hey, Officer McGoven," the blond stammered, swaying slightly on her feet as if his presence had shifted the universe. "I was just leaving."

Officer McGoven nodded, easing aside so that she could stumble past. "Tell your father hello for me." He was polite —at least until the door shut behind her.

When he turned to Loren, his gaze was questioning. "Why was Naomi Tanner in my house?"

"*She's* who the school sent over with my schoolwork," Loren said softly, barely believing it herself.

"Really?" That eyebrow shot all the way up. "I can call and have it changed if you want."

"No." Loren shook her head. Doing so would only give Naomi some sick sense of satisfaction. "I can handle her."

If anything, that reply made him *more* skeptical. The intensity in his stare seemed to skewer her, right through skin and bone down to the pit of her soul. "That's what I'm worried about."

With that, he headed for the kitchen.

Loren followed him, noticing how the muscles of his back strained the fabric of his blue windbreaker. The sight did something to her. Made her belly flip and parts of her body heat. Her cheeks. Her throat. Between her legs…

The last sensation alarmed her. Her face flamed, but she couldn't tear her gaze away. He was in uniform today, explaining away the all-day absence. A sudden concern sent a chill through her entire body, cooling the reaction he'd inspired.

Was he assigned to her father's case? She should have asked, but all she could focus on was how he still smelled inexplicably like fresh pine. Nature. The wild. She breathed deep, letting the scent travel through her stomach, right down to her toes. Gradually, that heat returned, growing hotter.

"Did you eat?"

She blushed as his gaze focused on her and shook her head. "No."

"Here." He turned to the fridge and withdrew a carton of what looked like tuna salad and a loaf of bread. Silently, he compiled two sandwiches, eventually handing one to her.

Sonia's words came back to her. *A health nut.* If tuna could give a man that much muscle, she wondered why everyone didn't hoard the stuff.

"Something funny?" McGoven asked. His voice was soft, not accusatory.

Loren realized her lip was quirked. "N-No," she said, taking the sandwich.

She ate it perched on the end of a stool, while he leaned against a nearby counter. Together they just…

Watched each other, like two wild animals sizing up one another for the first time.

Comically, Loren couldn't help but picture two stray dogs— a husky facing down a ratty little Shih Tzu. Who would sniff who first? Of course, *he* was the one to finally break the tension, tossing her a question after he swallowed his last bite of bread.

"You let Naomi in. You could have told her to go to hell. Why?"

Loren lifted her shoulder in a shrug. She didn't dare admit the truth. *Because I thought she was you.*

Instead, she improvised. "Because she's not worth it."

She had bigger fish to fry—starting with the confusing jumble her life had become.

Officer McGoven seemed to mull her answer over in silence. *Interesting,* she pictured him musing as he scratched the dark stubble along his chin.

"What's between you two, anyway?"

"I don't know," Loren admitted truthfully. She shifted on her stool, propping her elbow against the island's surface. "She just never liked me, I guess."

Though, how pathetic did that sound when said out loud? Frowning, she tried to explain it, that crazy, unwarranted hostility. "Naomi... She... Well, she..."

"What?" Officer McGoven demanded. His tone alone warned he wouldn't let her off so easy. *Don't put a happy face on it. Don't dress it up.*

The truth.

"She's a bitch," Loren blurted, surprising herself. "From the day I came here, she's had it out for me. I don't know why, but I can handle her."

The corner of his mouth twitched into an amused grin.

And the world stopped spinning. It blew her mind how something so simple could utterly transform him. Instantly, those eyes were less intimidating—more dove-gray than silver. His lips glistened, a welcoming pink.

Her own lips parted and closed. She felt dizzy. Hot. Then… confused. Shouldn't he be scolding her?

"Where I come from, you're expected to fight back when boxed into a corner," he said cryptically. Was that his way of signaling that he approved of what she did? If so, why had he been so angry that day? Furious.

"Black Mountain," she blurted, focusing on the most harmless piece of his statement. "Sonia said that's where you're from?"

The words barely left her mouth before she realized she miscalculated. This subject was a landmine. He sucked in a breath, his shoulders tensing. "Sonia…" He seemed to groan. Then he shook his head and met her gaze directly. "Something like that. Did she tell you anything else?"

Loren cringed, hating the thought of getting Sonia in trouble. She wanted to deny it—but she couldn't. "Yes," she gasped as if the confession were being ripped from her. "She told me you had a wife."

"A wife." His lips fell into a hard line. "Something like that."

Her heart twitched, hating the confirmation. He loved someone once. And yet, she wanted to know more. Needed to. "What was she like?"

Someone beautiful, she suspected. Full-figured and blond, with enough charm to reach a man as guarded as he was.

"She was… Emma." His voice turned hoarse, and Loren felt a pang in her chest. Pain?

"Your mother," he said, turning the tables. "What was she like?"

It was her turn to flinch, struck by the agony of memories. Words were never her forte, and even now, they failed to convey just who her mother was. "She was nice," she said haltingly. "Funny. I loved her."

"I'm sure she was," McGoven said. His words didn't ring hollow like the empty condolences she was used to enduring. It was as if he knew exactly how she felt and was acknowledging that in the most genuine of ways.

She tentatively met his gaze again, and she wasn't sure how much time passed before he cleared his throat.

"I'll be busy all day tomorrow," he said, tactfully changing the subject. "You can take the bed again tonight. I'll take the couch."

The bed, Loren thought with a shiver. A bed he just confirmed was *his*.

"I could take the c-couch—" The look he sent her way rendered her silent. *The hell you will,* his narrowed gaze conveyed.

"It's fine," he said tightly. "You need the sleep."

Apparently, chivalry *wasn't* all dead in the McGoven house.

"Don't wait up. I have something to take care of tonight," he added.

And they were right back to square one.

Loren fidgeted, trying to think of some way to undo the damage she'd done. Suddenly, a buzzing ringtone sliced the tension.

Never taking his eyes off her, Officer McGoven reached into his pocket for his cell phone.

"Hello," he grunted, pressing the device to his ear. He listened for a moment, and then all at once, his entire face changed, his brows furrowing. "Sonia? Slow down—"

A knock on the door gave Loren the distraction she needed to distance herself from what was obviously a private conversation. With her luck, Naomi had forgotten something.

"Sonia! Slow down!" She heard Officer McGoven bellow from behind her. "What are you saying?"

As Loren approached the door, the knocking slowed to a lazy rapping.

Tap, tap, tap.

Definitely Naomi—unless there was more than one person out there, who believed the world was full of peons whose duty it was to wait solely on them.

Sighing, she pulled the door open. "Did you forget something?" She began—only it wasn't *Naomi* standing there, drenched in the aftermath of another rainstorm.

This visitor was a man.

That was all Loren was sure of before a hand clamped down over her wrist, wrenching her toward the stairs. In that split second, a massive shape rushed to block her from view, swallowing the space of the doorway.

"What the fuck are you doing here?" Officer McGoven's voice was guttural, ripping from his chest like the roar of an engine. Or a growl.

With him blocking the door, Loren couldn't see how the visitor reacted to the hostility, but when they spoke, their voice didn't hold any hint of fear.

"Is that any way to greet an emissary?" His tone was equally low and slightly mocking, but overall business-like. Stern. "I come here on behalf of Lukka. For *her*. As you requested."

20

"*N*o!" McGoven surged, forcing the newcomer onto the porch. "*You* aren't taking her anywhere. Get the fuck off my land, or I swear to God, I'll send you to your Alpha in pieces."

Loren trembled. Obviously, this man was not Lukka—but he and McGoven weren't strangers. A subtle tension radiated between them. Hate? Something far deeper than mere aggression. She felt it in her bones, and that inner voice growled. *Enemy!*

"If Lukka wants her, then *he* can come for her," Officer McGoven continued. Strangely, there was no real anger in his voice. His point was perfectly clear.

The other man's reply came muffled. "He's a busy man. It might take him a whole month to find the time to travel all the way out here just to see one little pup—"

"That's his *duty*," Officer McGoven snarled. "He should have been here the second I called—"

"His duty is to protect his *own*," the stranger replied, just as harshly. "She isn't one of his—at least not yet. He doesn't owe a damn thing to her or to *you*."

The words seemed to land like a well-placed jab. McGoven flinched back—enough for Loren to finally view the figure standing before him in a puddle of cool moonlight.

He was tall, with bright red hair cropped tightly to his scalp and brown eyes that reminded her of a hawk's. They glowed the same way, visible even through the dark. Predatory.

"But, of course," he continued emotionlessly, "Lukka would never allow a stray to wander loose without pack ties. That's where I come in."

"Oh, really?" McGoven didn't even try to hide his skepticism. "And let me guess; you're here to welcome her with open fucking arms into your loving family?"

"Something like that." The stranger's eyes glowed with a mischievous light. "If Lukka can't come for her, then I'll just have to take *her* to *him*."

"Hell no." McGoven took a step, wordlessly forcing the stranger further from the doorway. "If Lukka wants her, he has to come and get her his damn self—"

"But that could take months," the other man countered. "How easy do you think this will be by then? How attached to you will she be in a few weeks? A whole month? Do you really want to play around with that kind of bond?"

A bond? The term confused Loren, but McGoven's shoulders slumped, and he looked back. His tormented expression said it all—*no*. Whatever this "bond" was, he didn't seem to want it at all.

"Why can't he come for her?" he demanded, turning back to the newcomer. "An asshole like you can't fill in for him for a few damn hours?"

The man's mouth curled into an icy smile. "Lukka doesn't work via substitutes. He is the Alpha; his word is the law. Do you think people can just 'go without' the law for a couple of hours?"

"Fuck," McGoven growled. He sounded torn, as if he were being wrenched in two completely different directions. "But why *you*? Why couldn't anyone else—"

"Who else could Lukka trust with something *so important* as transporting a stray female? Sonia Carlisle? She has other duties which don't concern acting as a liaison between her Alpha and a rogue. No. From now on, you deal only with me. I am his Beta, after all."

Beta. Loren didn't recognize the word, but the man's tone implied that it was something important. Too important for Officer McGoven to argue against.

But he didn't have to accept it, either. "Fuck." His gruff tone revealed more frustration than if he'd smashed his fist into the wall. Or the newcomer's face. "I'm guessing they won't let me take her myself? I'd prefer that to this."

"You're in exile. You stray within even a mile of pack territory, and you know the consequences."

Loren didn't like the way this conversation was headed. All of it—as everything had these past few days—seemed to center around taking her away. This strange man wanted to, but Officer McGoven…

"Fuck," he repeated.

All at once, the entryway seemed smaller as he backed inside, body hovering between the doorway and her position on the steps.

"There isn't any other way?"

"Of course, there isn't." The strange man cautiously took a step over the threshold—but the act seemed more monumental than that. A visual representation of how the tides of this silent battle were turning. With a shrug, he tapped his wrist, though Loren saw that he wasn't wearing a watch. "Time is ticking."

McGoven sighed. Then he turned to face her. His eyes went to her chest, avoiding her gaze. "Get your stuff."

Those three simple words sliced through her like knives.

"W-What?" *No*, a part of her pathetically whined. "No," she whispered out loud, surprising herself. This was *wrong*—her entire body trembled against it.

"Loren." His tone left no room for argument. "Go upstairs and get your stuff. Now."

He turned back to the stranger who watched them both with an unreadable expression, and Loren stumbled up the first few steps. *No.* The thought screamed through every nerve and muscle. She couldn't leave him. Her stomach lurched at the prospect, her throat dry.

Finally, she hesitated on the top step. "I-I don't—"

"GET YOUR STUFF!"

She tore into the hall, driven purely by his anger. Like an invisible hand, it pushed on her spine, forcing her into the bedroom to grab her duffle and shove her clothes inside of it. When she returned downstairs, Officer McGoven was in the kitchen—as far away from her as physically possible.

It was the stranger who stood to greet her at the bottom, his lips contorted into a mirthless smile. Whatever silent argument had waged between them, McGoven had soundly lost.

"I'm Kyle," he said. "You must be Loren—"

He reached out to help her down the bottom step, but she jerked back without thinking. *No!* The desperation wasn't solely hers. She could sense it, and her gaze was drawn to the kitchen where McGoven stood in the doorway, his jaw clenched.

Low, his voice resonated through the very walls to reach them. "You don't have to touch her." It wasn't a suggestion.

Wisely, Kyle stood back, holding his hand limply in the air. "You're right," he said, shoving the offending hand into his pocket. "That's *Lukka's* job."

His tone was intentionally cutting—insinuating something...

But what?

Officer McGoven's tight frown gave nothing away, but he shifted, keeping his focus on the man's visible hand.

"We should go," Kyle suggested, inclining his head toward the partially open front door.

Through the crack in the doorjamb, Loren could tell it was raining with a vengeance, reducing everything beyond the porch to a shapeless blur.

"If we leave now, we might be able to make it into the territory before midnight," Kyle added.

Six hours from now, according to the clock built into the coffee maker.

"Whatever," McGoven hissed. "Go now."

Kyle took a step and paused. Chuckling, he nodded to Loren. "I think you might have to tell *her* twice."

Loren flinched as a pair of gray eyes swiveled her way. His lips parted, and she braced for the sound of his voice. "Loren—"

"No!" The word tore from her throat. "No," she repeated, rocking on the balls of her feet. A rush of adrenaline fueled the disobedience. He was wrong—she couldn't go. Every muscle in her body told her to stay here. With him.

"*Please*. I d-don't want to go."

The man, Kyle, gave her an odd look—but he wasn't her focus. Just McGoven.

His upper lip pulled back from his teeth as if it pained him to deny her. And it did. She could feel it. "Go with him. It'll be okay. You'll be safe." His tone was gentler, though unflinchingly firm. *Shoo.*

"No," Loren whispered. Being abandoned by her mother, and rejected by her father had hurt, but this…

The pain tore at her. Tore *through* her.

She didn't even know him, but the thought of leaving made her entire body shake.

"Loren, *go!*"

She couldn't refuse. Robotically, she went to drag her new shoes from where they rested by the door and put them on.

Kyle watched her. "This won't last for very long," he said. "Once Lukka accepts her." It wasn't reassurance. It was a threat.

One McGoven reacted to visibly—he flinched. "He better." He raised his voice to carry across the entire room. "And if he *doesn't?*"

Kyle shrugged. "Then someone else will. You've done your good deed for the week. Don't worry, I won't bring her back."

Loren didn't miss the finality in his tone. *She won't be coming back...ever.*

"You won't make it back by midnight if you don't leave now," McGoven warned.

After the previous hostility, his tone was eerily casual. Even Kyle seemed shocked by the change, though he shrugged again. "Fine. Come on," he called to her.

Utterly numb, she took a step after him.

"Wait." A rush of air was her only warning before something heavy fell over her shoulders. Confused, she looked down to find a familiar blue windbreaker draped over her dress. It was so long that the hem reached her knees.

"It's freezing out," a gruff voice told her by way of explanation.

"She won't be able to wear that on Lukka's territory," Kyle warned, eyeing the jacket as though it were a snake. "You know the law."

"Sure I do." McGoven stood back, but Loren didn't miss how he adjusted her jacket until the very last second, ensuring it fell closed over her front. "She can take it off at the gate."

An angry flush crept over Kyle's angular jaw, but he didn't argue. Despite whatever power this Lukka person wielded, for now, McGoven had the upper hand.

Once she left the safety of the farm, what then?

"We need to go," Kyle insisted, jerking his head sharply toward the door.

Officer McGoven returned to the kitchen without a word—but Loren could read his body language. His shoulders were hunched as if her mere presence was an annoyance. *Go,* he told her without having to say it. *Get out. I don't want you here.*

No, no, no, that inner voice cried. *This is wrong. Wrong!*

"Come on." Kyle's voice was a knife, cutting through the panic in her mind.

It wasn't exactly like she could argue. After his command, her throat seemed clenched shut around any words that might go against what McGoven told her. *Go.*

Stiffly, she moved forward, huddled beneath the windbreaker. Near the threshold of the doorway, she paused, half-expecting...

Nothing. No command to stay. No goodbye, either.

The only sound at all was the muffled pitter-patter of rain as she stumbled into the darkness after Kyle.

21

*K*yle led her to a truck left idling in the driveway behind McGoven's.

He hadn't come alone. Someone sat in the passenger's seat, a dark-haired boy who lurched from the cabin to greet her, his green eyes flashing.

"This is her?" he asked excitedly. He was tall but slender and lean with an energy that made Loren envision an overworked puppy. "Wow. Up close, she looks even bett—"

Kyle nudged him firmly in his side. "Get in the truck," he snapped. His gaze was firmly fixed on Loren, almost as if daring her to run back to the house like every muscle in her body commanded her to do.

Slowly, she entered the truck instead, climbing in between the two front seats to sit on the back bench. Without a word, Kyle took the wheel, and the boy bounded into the passenger's seat.

"He just let her go?" he chirped, his attention on the house. "He really just let her go? With *you*? He really didn't want her? Wow, he must be—"

"Micha, shut up," Kyle commanded.

The youth clammed up instantly, still bouncing on his seat.

Loren swallowed as the truck lurched into motion, kicking up mud in a violent spray. Helpless, her gaze drifted through the rear windshield, noting the dark figure standing impassively in the kitchen window.

No, a part of her whined. The dread became a physical ache in her chest as the truck hurtled around a corner. Suddenly her pulse surged. She couldn't breathe. *I can't leave...*

"Hi!"

She blinked, staring directly into a pair of massive green eyes.

"I'm Micha," the chirpy voice belonged to the younger figure who twisted around to face her from over the headrest of his seat. "You're Loren."

"Y-Yes," she stammered, wondering just how he knew her name. Though, maybe she should have been wondering about a lot of things?

Like why Officer McGoven let her go with two strangers? Or why he seemed so determined to send her away in the first place? Why take her in, if all he wanted was to pawn her off on someone else?

Lukka.

"So—" The playful tone drew her attention back to Micha. "Why didn't McGoven want you?"

"Micha!" Kyle's tone deepened, not that Micha had the sense to look ashamed. His stare was persistent, demanding an answer.

Why didn't he want me?

"I...he found me wandering in the woods. He took me in, though; it was just for a little while." *Lies.* When said out loud, the explanation didn't make sense. What kind of person took in a teenage girl whose father had just been murdered? Not to mention...why hadn't he brought her to the police station—at least for questioning?

An interview?

To claim her father's body?

He hadn't even asked her about funeral arrangements. Overnight, McGoven had taken control of her life with little effort. Already, she was being shipped off to only God knew where, on his say-so, and...

You're just okay with that? a part of her wondered. Strangely enough, she *was.*

She didn't know why. Whenever she tried to question it, the same old thought would play through her mind like a bad song stuck on rewind—"Officer McGoven said..."

His words seemed ingrained in her mind, her very soul.

I don't want this.

Lukka can have her.

Loren go!

"You'll love Black Mountain," Micha gushed, once again intruding into her thoughts. "It's big. There's lots of space to run around, though I haven't lived there long—" He lifted his thin shoulder in a shrug. "When Lukka found me, I was little more than a stray myself. The Alpha of my old pack was a total—"

"Alpha?" The word dislodged some long-forgotten memory. McGoven had said it—though as if it were something comical. A mockery. "What's an Alpha?"

Micha gaped at her. Then, he looked at Kyle, who only curtly shook his head—*no.*

"Oh!" Those big green eyes got even wider. "You mean she really doesn't—" He seemed to stop himself from saying any more. Instead, he fidgeted in his seat, his dark curls bouncing against his scalp. "Oh, wow!"

Her apparent ignorance only seemed to increase Micha's interest in her. He didn't speak, but he never turned around, observing her intently as though she were some curiosity on display. "Wow," he'd murmur every now and again.

Loren felt uneasy. She wanted to demand they tell her something, but an instinctive part of her knew that Kyle would just shrug her off. He was impatient, glaring at the road, gripping the wheel tightly.

But, when Micha had mentioned the word Alpha, even he had shuddered.

Through the fog and rain, Loren couldn't make out much of where they were headed. All she knew was that Kyle skirted through the back of New Walsh, toward the country roads and just kept driving north.

Black Mountain, Micha said. The place where McGoven and Sonia had grown up.

"Is it cold there?" she found herself asking, barely audible over the staticky radio currently broadcasting show tunes. "This Black Mountain?"

"Oh yeah!" Micha turned back around, this time sticking his head between the two front seats. "I think so. I never really noticed before."

Loren raised an eyebrow at that. What kind of person lived on a mountain and didn't notice the obvious difference in the weather?

Obviously, Micha was not the brightest tool in the toolbox. But he seemed nice—which put him a cut above everyone Loren knew. He also apparently loved to talk. So, she decided to take the risk and draw out as much information from him as she possibly could.

"What's there?" she asked. Sonia hadn't given her much of a description of the place. "A town? A city?"

The questions earned her another impish grin and an incredulous look. "The territory," he said, as if that explained everything.

"Is there a school?" Loren wondered, thinking of the massive pile of work sitting on the end of Officer McGoven's couch. She only had a few months left, but already, after a few missed days, graduation seemed light-years away.

Micha nodded. "Of course! And a post office, and a town hall and all that boring stuff. But there's so much land. Lukka has more territory in this area than anyone else in the region. Well, maybe except for the Eislander pack—"

"Lukka?" Loren seized on the mention of the name and ran with it. "Who is he? The mayor?"

Obviously, he wielded some amount of clout. She recalled how Sonia had defended him to Bill—even when it seemed like she didn't exactly want to.

"Who is Lukka?" Micha's dark eyebrows shot right up into his dense tangle of hair. "He's the Alpha."

There was that word again. Micha didn't seem to notice her reaction.

"He controls Black Mountain—the entire pack," he went on. "He's probably the youngest Alpha in a century to dominate so much territory. He succeeded his father, who is a legend. Lukas Grehmaine. I'm sure you've heard of him, right? My mom told me stories when I was a pup about how he rebelled against his Alpha and forged his own territory. I heard rumors growing up, too, in a territory miles from here. About Lukas and his prodigy, Bill—"

"Bill?" Loren practically lunged out of her seat. "A prodigy?"

"Yeah," Micha said, frowning. "It's crazy how things worked out. That's why we had to come here. If you leave the pack, you leave our ways—all of them. He isn't allowed to hunt, or even marry. Especially not take a mate—"

"That's enough." Kyle reached and deliberately flicked the radio dial until the sounds of wavering country music filled the cabin.

With an apologetic frown, Micha shifted in his seat, and Loren couldn't silence a hiss of disappointment. At least for now, she wouldn't get anything else out of him.

What she had learned just confused her further. Prodigy. Pack. Mate? She didn't understand. Putting it from her mind, for now, she settled for staring from the window, trying to remember every detail of the landscape whizzing by.

The next few hours passed in utter silence. Micha had drifted off, resting his head against the window. Kyle just drove without so much as an attempt at conversation.

A part of Loren wanted to risk his ire just to ask *something*. More about Lukka, maybe?

She inhaled deeply to gather the nerve, but then her thoughts derailed entirely. *Pine*. That pure scent carried with it the wild aroma of the forest, faint musk, and the fresh flavor of the wind that whipped through the trees…

Wham!

She must have drifted off—somehow—because the next thing she knew, her body was being flung forward through the gap in the seats.

Quick thinking from Micha was the only thing that saved her from a bloody nose—his thin arm shot out, slowing down the momentum.

"What the hell?" he murmured sleepily. "What's going on?"

Loren was in awe of how quickly he'd reacted while half-asleep, and even more impressed once she realized why they'd stopped. The truck was stuck in a ditch. Hissing, Kyle jammed his foot on the gas, only to send mud churning from the wheels.

"Fuck. Something ran me off the road—"

"What?" Instantly, Micha's whole demeanor changed. He sat up straighter, and his eyes took on a sharper gleam. "Kyle, do you know where we *are*?"

"You think I'm a fucking idiot?"

Obviously, the thick forests and rolling hills that lined the road weren't this mysterious Black Mountain.

Not even close. As Kyle's gaze darted to the windows, even Loren could tell that he was uneasy. Micha was downright panicked.

"This is *Eislander* territory," he croaked. His nostrils flared as if the air inside the truck held a repulsive scent.

"The outskirts," Kyle admitted, wrenching the key from the ignition. "The usual road was blocked, so I thought we could take a shortcut."

From his defensive demeanor, Eislander territory didn't seem like an ideal place to be stranded in.

"Call Lukka!" Micha's voice was an octave higher. "He'll have to send Greg or Tom to come and—"

"No reception. The truck's transmission is shot," Kyle snapped, wrenching open his door. With fluid ease, he jumped down to land ankle-deep in the mud. "It's not far. One of us will have to head to the Michaelsons'. They could help."

"I'll do it." Micha was out in a flash. Literally. Loren barely saw him lope around the truck; he moved so fast.

"Take this." Kyle tossed him the cell phone and pointed to a thicket of trees. "Head north. Call Lukka the moment you get to the closest cell tower."

"Okay!" With that, Micha took off.

"As for you, girl. Get out of the truck." Kyle's voice reached her, as authoritative as a whip.

Loren scrambled out—but she had to admit that it wasn't because of that same instant pull she felt whenever Officer McGoven gave her a direct order. This time, her thoughts controlled the compulsion. If they were in danger, she needed to get her bearings. It helped that she instinctively felt better the moment her boots hit the muddied earth, and the fresh scent of wind filled her nose.

It had stopped raining, though the wind had taken on an icy edge this far north.

"I need to scout around," Kyle told her. He scanned the surrounding forests, as if at any moment an enemy might spring from the shadows. "You stay here—"

"By myself?" Loren couldn't help the apprehension in her voice. "I could come with you."

"No," Kyle snapped. "*You're* going to stay by the damn truck. I won't be long."

Before she could protest, he headed in the direction opposite Micha. And she was shocked to find that he was just as fast. Obviously, wherever they were from, the men knew how to keep fit.

In addition to abandoning people on the side of the road.

She tried to tell herself that he would come back. It was the middle of the night—even if this Eislander place wasn't friendly, who would notice three people stranded on the road this late?

They would, something told her, without elaborating on just who "they" were. Or what. *This is wrong,* that same instinct warned. *Be ready.*

On impulse, she climbed into the truck and pulled open the glove compartment. Her father always kept a knife in his, *just in case,* though he never explained in case of what.

Kyle didn't have anything like that in his. All she found was a small flashlight hanging from a keychain. The pale light barely cut through the shadows—not that Loren exactly needed it.

The moonlight piercing the thinning clouds was more than enough to see by, illuminating the road. Even the slight flicker of the branches swaying in the wind held an unusual clarity.

She couldn't hear anything. But something… Something deep down told her that the apparent calm meant nothing. The silence. The quiet—they were merely on the surface.

Something else stirred underneath, way too careful to make any noise. Hiding. Lurking, watching her through the trees —and it was hungry. Maybe not in the literal sense, but…

She wasn't quite that surprised when two men appeared in the middle of the road. They were too tall—not Micha or Kyle. They didn't seem like the type to offer roadside assistance, either.

Careful, that instinctive voice warned. *Easy. Watch…*

They stood there for a long while, just taking her in. Loren was almost willing to write them off as only two bystanders who'd happened by for a nighttime stroll. Until they moved forward, eerily in sync. Until she saw their *eyes*, glowing through the shadows.

Until they chuckled, as if they knew damn well she was there.

And that she was alone.

"Hey, little girl," one called, his voice a husky rasp that seeped into the truck. "You lost?"

"All alone out here, cutie?" the other one wondered though Loren could tell that he didn't seem very concerned. "Don't worry, we *like* to make friends."

Her first thought was to lock the doors and barricade herself in—but something held her back. That inner voice. *No. You'll just make yourself an easy target. Run!* Without questioning the impulse, she bolted from the driver's side and took off in the direction Micha had.

Kyle had told him to run north—there had to be something close by.

"Aw, baby!" one of the men called out. "Don't run away!"

Another joined in, "We don't have to do this the hard way!"

Run, run, run! Loren allowed the frantic thoughts to drown out the sounds of anything else.

She could see headlights, spilling through the trees—but the two men were in between her and the road. She could sense them behind her, picking their way lazily through the gnarled branches.

Laughing.

22

*L*oren forced herself to keep moving, sucking in painful breaths with every step. But while Micha and Kyle had speed on their side, she didn't.

Her foot caught on the edge of a root a few paces in, and she tripped, tumbling down into the mud near the base of a small field. Tall grasses cast wavering shadows, shrouding the two other figures already in the center. Waiting for her.

She had walked right into a trap. The fact was all but proven as mocking laughter reached her ears. Heart heavy, she turned as the other men approached from the direction of the road.

"We brought some friends, honey," one of them crooned. "We'll be real nice. Don't be afraid."

Run! Loren lurched to her feet, wincing as pain shot through her ankle. Ignoring it, she stumbled in a random direction. Almost instantly, someone was there to block her path.

"Easy, baby," the man purred as she stumbled back, the heel of her boot catching over the grass. "Don't hurt yourself, now. We don't bite—"

"Hard," another man finished for him, chuckling. "For you, I think we'll make an exception, though. That pretty milk-white skin looks so soft."

There were rumbles of agreement. A few even whispered suggestions as to just how her "milky" skin would feel—sick, twisted things, that would haunt her nightmares.

If she lived long enough to sleep another night.

Heart racing, she turned on her heel—only to have someone block her path again. And the next direction she tried.

And the next...

They were too fast, treating her like a living volleyball in some sick four-person game. Smirking, they surrounded her from all sides, closing in with the eerie grace of a pack of hunting wolves.

"So pretty," one of them murmured. "Such a shame."

"I don't think this little baby's *all* innocent, though," pitched in the man nearest to her, his bright eyes haunting in the darkness. "I can smell a man on her. Her mate, maybe?"

There was a chorus of "oh nos" and several mocking chuckles.

"I guess he'll just have to share," another figure suggested.

All at once, they moved closer, forcing her into the center of a makeshift ring.

No. That shadowy, calm voice was back—but different. Louder. Intense. There was an edge to it that Loren knew hers never had. *Don't let them get close.*

Go!

She chose two of the men at random and darted in between them. She barely made it a yard, before someone yanked her back—hard—by a fistful of hair.

"Aww, boys!" They chuckled, shoving her to the center of their circle. "This one's shy."

"Don't worry, honey," a man with blond hair crooned with false sweetness. "It won't hurt for very long. I promise, you might even like it…"

He reached for her, and Loren's entire body vibrated with adrenaline.

Fight!

She didn't think—only reacted. Her hand swung out, catching the bastard on his jaw. Instantly, she knew she'd drawn blood.

She could smell it, coppery and fresh. Inside her, something rumbled, like hunger—but different. A need.

"Bitch!"

Another man swung at her, striking her mouth. Stars exploded across her vision—but rather than fall back in the face of the pain, Loren lunged into the blow, opening and closing her mouth on the thickness of a finger.

Howling, the man tried to pull back, but she only bit down harder, feeling flesh and muscle give beneath her teeth.

"Shit!"

An oppressive flavor exploded on her tongue—*blood,* that inner voice smugly supplied. She could see the dark liquid dripping from his fingers. There wasn't time to be horrified. She had already pivoted—before her mind comprehended the motion—evading the remaining two men.

Had they been like her father and numbed by alcohol, she might have had a shot. As it was, the first of the two caught her easily, hooking his arm around her waist like a crowbar.

"The little bitch wants to play," he grumbled, the words vibrating down her spine. A cruel hand ruffled through her hair, snagging at her scalp, and forcing her chin into the air. "Let's teach her a little lesson about proper manners on the playground—"

Just what those "lessons" were? They never elaborated.

The next thing she knew, she was being shoved face down into the moist earth, with someone's unforgiving hand clenched around the back of her neck.

No! That shadowy part of her howled, filling her body with rage. *Fight! You need to fight!*

She kicked her legs. Lashed out with her hands, snagging skin and clothes beneath her nails. When struggling didn't loosen the restraining grip, she screamed. Piercing, long and sharp, the sound rang out through the clearing, droning on until a firm knee rammed into the small of her back.

She went silent with a moan, gritting her teeth and digging her hands into the mud, as a lazy hand wrenched up the skirt of her dress.

She wouldn't scream again, she told herself—she wouldn't give them the satisfaction. She clenched her jaw so tightly she thought she heard the bones crack. Her heart raced with panic.

She wouldn't scream...

The resolve lasted until she felt a clumsy hand rub her inner thigh. Then, she broke, mouth opening for a cry that instantly became swallowed up by the sound of something else.

Loud, it rumbled out over the weeds like thunder—but it wasn't. No. It was a *growl*—that was her only thought before something heavy slammed into her from behind, knocking the breath from her chest.

Wham!

She winced at the sound of crunching bone—only to realize that it hadn't come from her body. From above her came a harsh shout, cut short.

Oh, God. That growl came again. Deeper this time—triumphant. With her face against the ground, Loren couldn't breathe—couldn't see. Her lungs screamed for air. Until, all at once, the pressure holding her down eased, and she could finally lift her head.

"Oh, shit! It's a rogue!"

The shout was the last coherent statement she heard. The men scattered, darting in various directions, fleeing a presence that Loren could sense was directly behind her.

Before she could turn, the entire world shifted. A shadow seemed to fly across the earth, as dark and huge as if a cloud had drifted over the moon overhead.

Only it wasn't a formless shape. Unbelievably massive, it darted toward the closest of the running men—long, lean, and undeniable in what it really was. The man she'd bitten couldn't outrun it, and with a howl of pain, he went down, swallowed by shadow.

For the space of a second, Loren allowed herself to stare. Allowed herself to become awed by the ebony limbs, rippling with sinewy muscle as the creature turned from the fallen man to stare her dead in the eye.

Blood dripped from its mouth, sharp claws ripping at the earth as it tensed to lunge.

Finally, Loren ran. She couldn't see. Darkness encased her—that massive shadow rushing toward her, so huge it blotted out the light of the moon.

Loren, wait!

The plea, whispered around the edges of her mind, startled her so badly that she stumbled and fell. An ominous ripping sound came from her dress as she landed hard on one knee.

Don't look, a frantic part of her urged. *Don't look, don't look! It'll kill you too!*

That shadowy part of her was stronger. *Turn around,* it urged. *Face it. Face him.* Body shaking, she braced her hands over the cool earth and looked back.

The beast loomed only a few yards away from her. Not a man, though something just as large, crouched on four lean legs. It was a wolf, one three times the size of any she'd seen at the zoo.

A thick pelt of black fur covered it from head to toe— except for a crisscrossed jumble of silvery lines that marred the flesh of its chest. A deep rumble seemed to hum in the back of its throat. Another growl—but this time lower.

Reassuring.

And its eyes... They were familiar. A glowing silver, they stared unflinchingly from a triangular head, holding her captive as it took a slow pace in her direction.

Loren tensed, falling back with a gasp as the creature shifted. Its entire body seemed to ripple, like a disturbed reflection over water. That muscled body wavered, shrunk, and compacted into a leaner shape hunched over the earth. As Loren watched, that coating of dark hair receded, revealing tanned skin bulging with coiled muscle underneath.

The only thing the beast shared with the man that appeared in its place was a pair of piercing, silver eyes.

Officer McGoven didn't speak.

Not even as he stood, unabashedly naked.

23

He held her gaze for so long Loren felt numb when he finally turned away. Tussled and wild, his hair hung down his shoulders as he inclined his head without a word. *Come on.*

Shakily, Loren crept after him, wincing every time her ankle hit the ground. She felt nothing. No fear. No relief. It was as if an invisible hand held the emotions at bay, even as she spotted the still shape of a dead man lying only a few feet away.

McGoven didn't acknowledge the grisly sight. He merely slowed his pace so she could catch up. It was only when she winced, biting down hard on her bottom lip, that he turned to face her at all. Dangerously dark, his eyes went to her ankle, narrowing the moment she swayed on her feet.

A flash of silver was her only warning before he lunged. The next instant, she found herself swung into his arms, cheek coming to rest against the hardness of his chest.

She felt too stunned for shock. He was warm and cool at the same time. A light sheen of sweat, mixed with rainwater, clung to his skin. He smelled too. Like earth, mud, and everything dangerous and wild in between. Long and lean, his legs carried her through the trees as if he knew the way by heart.

This felt familiar, being carried in his arms, held against bare skin. The blood on his chin, however, wasn't.

He didn't speak. Not even a word of comfort to reassure her that what she'd just seen him do wasn't humanly possible.

What could she say? *Oh, by the way, you're not a beast, are you?*

There was no way around it. No explanation fit other than the obvious…

He was the wolf. Where the beast had been seconds prior, Officer McGoven had appeared. He even moved like one, weaving through the wilderness with an easy grace. It didn't help any that the logical part of her couldn't rectify why he wasn't wearing clothes.

I just saw someone murdered right in front of me, she thought —almost calmly while her heart hammered in her chest. *Two people,* she mentally corrected. *Ripped apart by the man carrying me in his arms.*

She figured she *should* have been terrified. But the only thought to cross her mind, as Officer McGoven darted in between the trees, was that he had to be freezing.

She was—even winded and breathless beneath his windbreaker, or what was left of it. A hole pierced the sleeve; it must have torn when one of the men grabbed her. Irrational guilt made her heart sink. Though, the state of his jacket seemed to be the furthest thing from McGoven's mind at the moment.

In no time at all, they reached the dark stretch of empty road—further up from where Kyle had hit the ditch. Parked in the center of the highway was a different truck. A darker, familiar one reeking of pine. Once McGoven settled her on the passenger's seat, he moved to close the door.

"Stay here," he commanded. Then he reached over her to wrench open the glove compartment. Unlike Kyle's, *his* held something a little more useful than a cheap flashlight—a gun, glinting lethally in the moonlight.

"Stay inside," he reiterated gruffly. "Lock the doors. If anyone comes close who isn't me, use it."

He shoved the weapon onto her lap and turned, loping easily up the road. He was back before Loren had the chance to feel uneasy. What seemed like seconds later, he appeared by the driver's side, wrenching open the door the moment she unlocked it.

More blood dripped down his leg but, rather than pain, a satisfied gleam glinted in his eyes. Something told Loren that the other two men hadn't made it very far.

Without saying as much, McGoven pulled on a pair of sweatpants snatched from the back bench and climbed into the driver's seat barefoot. It was only when he jammed his foot on the gas and drove straight down the winding road that some of the tension coiled in his muscles finally eased.

Some of it.

"Where is Kyle?" The question seemed deliberately spoken as if it had taken every bit of energy he had in him just to keep from shouting. Yelling. Breaking glass.

Loren shook her head. "I don't know. H-he and Micha left to—"

"*They left you alone?*"

She recoiled against her seat, eyeing him fearfully. When he spoke again, his tone was a fraction softer. "Did they?"

She nodded, and he swore, smashing a fist into the steering wheel. His jaw was clenched so tightly that a muscle in his cheek jerked. It was only when he attempted to ask another question that she understood the source of his anger. "Did those bastards in the clearing...did they—"

She shook her head, and he sighed. He didn't say anything after that, not that he had to. His body language spoke for him loud and clear.

She had never seen anyone so furious. Not her father. Not even McGoven himself when she took off on his horse. Loren was afraid that he might rip the steering wheel from the socket if he happened to turn it hard enough.

"How...how did you find me?" Her throat ached. She wasn't sure what made her speak at all. It probably wasn't a good idea. Her stomach lurched as he swiveled his head toward her, eyes like molten silver.

"I followed you," he said.

Oh. He made it sound so natural. *I followed you. I breathed. I blinked.* The next second, his gaze was back on the road, and overwhelmed, Loren slumped into her seat.

"I wanted to make sure," he added, through clenched teeth. "But I never thought that asshole would be stupid enough to cut through *Eislander* territory. What the hell was he thinking?"

Loren didn't have an answer right away. With shaking fingers, she gingerly lifted the gun from her lap and returned it to the glove compartment. Only then could she recall what Kyle himself had said.

"He said that a road was blocked—"

"Bullshit!" McGoven's voice bordered on a growl. "There is a protocol you follow. You don't trespass without permission. Not here. He should *know* better. And to leave you alone? To let them touch you—" He inhaled raggedly and became rigid. A heartbeat later, he had all the windows down to let in the freezing night air. "Four men. I could sense their intentions. All of them. Those sick bastards."

Loren swallowed hard, suddenly cold. He could tell that via smell? Though, this wasn't the first time. He once claimed to know the number of bruises on her body from their scent alone.

She wanted to ask him, make him talk. Something warned her not to. For the first time, that plaintive inner voice was muted around him. *He's angry,* it whispered. *Wait.*

Angry was an understatement. He glowered, his teeth bared. The muscles in his legs bulged as he slammed on the gas until the gauge on the dashboard ticked closer and closer toward the maximum. It wasn't until they were on the highway, far from the dark woods, that he finally slowed to a speed closer to the legal limit.

It was nearly eleven, she realized, glancing at the dash—almost five hours after she left with Kyle. That dangerous stretch of Eislander territory must have been close to Black Mountain, which explained why Micha seemed to have no problem running off on foot.

Was it just on two? a part of her wondered. Apparently, the men around here seemed to shift into four-legged animals at will. She inspected McGoven from the corner of her eye, watching the muscles of his shoulders ripple as he drove. Or, maybe they just did that constantly? Roiling with tension.

Some subconscious part of her knew that she should have been afraid. It flinched in fear as she pictured that same body, hunched in the middle of the field, dripping blood. But locked inside the cabin of the truck with him, breathing in that wild scent of pine...

She just couldn't find the energy. Though, she might as well conserve her strength for when he left her for good. They had to be close to Black Mountain by now—she was sure of it. Tense with anticipation, she stared from the window, straining to catch a glimpse of her new home.

An hour later, and she started to note familiar landmarks she'd already glimpsed on the ride with Kyle. Rather than north, McGoven was heading straight toward New Walsh.

With every mile gained, the air became thinner, flooded with pine. Her body lost that crippling anxiety, and her head began to loll with every motion of the vehicle.

Sleep overwhelmed her before she knew it, and a firm hand on her shoulder startled her awake what felt like seconds later.

"Loren—"

Drowsily, she blinked and found Officer McGoven watching her, with one foot out of the truck. "We're home," he said.

Home.

Obviously, he was referring to his property alone, but still. In that moment, *home* seemed like the proper designation for the big house before her, bathed in the pale light of dawn. She inhaled, greedily sucking in the familiar scent of wind, mud, and horses. *Safe.*

"Can you walk?"

McGoven was watching her. He kept his distance, but his eyes were on her ankle. Something told her that if she lost her balance, he'd catch her before she could even hit the ground.

Experimentally, she took a step. "I think it's okay," she said. The pain was sharp, but not unbearable. She'd felt worse. "I can walk on it."

Officer McGoven headed straight for the house without acknowledgment. He didn't look as angry as he had in the truck, but Loren wasn't fooled. The rage simmered within him, ready to boil over at the slightest provocation.

Like, when he turned and saw her weakly limping up the porch steps. His lips curled back from his teeth, and Loren half-expected him to shout. Yell. Smash his curled fists into something.

All he did was nod curtly toward her feet.

"The boots." His voice rang with authority. "Take them off."

Without questioning it, Loren sat on the worn wood of the porch and complied. Her feet ached after being confined for so long, but watching her toes, still in their Christmas-themed socks, flex against the floor, she wondered why he made the request at all.

Even more so when he jerked his head curtly to her body. "The jacket, take it off."

His voice sent a tremor through her body. It was deeper, impossible to resist. Robotically, she dragged the thin material from her shoulders. When she held the jacket out to him, he motioned for her to drop it. Now. He was stiff, his weight balanced on his toes, his eyes blazing as they raked over her battered, dirt-streaked frame.

Was he angry about the damage done to his windbreaker? No. He didn't even look at the clothing. Just her. A few specific things drew his attention—namely, the dried blood she could feel encrusted over her chin, and the long rip in her dress exposing her thigh.

He swayed when he saw that, and his eyes almost appeared to turn...black—but what upset him most of all, was whatever he sensed when he leaned forward and inhaled the air above her body.

"That dress. Take it off—"

"W-What?" Loren stiffened, crossing her arms over her chest. The brown cotton was filthy and matted with mud around the hem, but it still covered her for the most part. Not to mention, her other clothes were in Kyle's truck.

None of those concerns seemed to matter to Officer McGoven.

His gaze was as stormy as the rain clouds swelling overhead. His nostrils flared, and whatever he smelled had him crouching on the balls of his feet, practically lunging away.

"Loren, *please*," he choked out the words, fighting to keep his voice steady. For her benefit. He really wanted to bellow. Growl. She could feel the same urge nipping at her thoughts, foreign and overwhelming. "Take. It. *Off.*"

His anger scared her, but there was a desperate, pleading edge to his tone that had her reaching for the hem of her dress. Modesty didn't matter in the face of his pain. In jerky,

unsteady motions, she wrestled the garment over her head and tossed it aside.

Cheeks flaming, she huddled down, drawing her knees up to her chin, and tried to ignore the fact that she was outside, in the freezing cold, wearing only her bra and underwear. The nakedness exposed her to more than just the frigid temperature. He could see her. All of her.

There was nothing left to hide the scars. Nothing to shield the bruises on her arms and legs. Her father wasn't the only monster to mark her, and the evidence was painfully fresh. A streaky trail of mud painted her inner thigh, along with tiny scratches left by groping fingers...

He seemed to notice them at the same time she did. The guttural sound that tore from his throat had Loren cringing back so violently she almost fell off the porch.

"Fuck." With that, he wrenched open the screen door so hard it slammed against the wall. "Get in."

Loren limped inside, flinching as she passed him. For a rare instant, his eyes weren't on her, but scanning the horizon of trees along the property. After only a moment, he slammed the front door shut behind them both, leaving her clothes out on the porch.

"The bathroom." He led the way, unconcerned as she struggled to keep up.

Once there, he herded her inside the narrow room and turned on the shower at full blast. Loren stood by awkwardly as he snatched a towel from a shelf by the door, and fished a bottle of body wash from underneath the sink. He handed her both items and inclined his head toward the rushing water.

She hesitated. Did he really expect her to shower with him standing there?

As if reading her mind, something that could have been guilt contorted his expression, displacing the rage. Silently, he moved to stand just outside the door with his back to her —but that was all the privacy he seemed willing to give. His body language said it all—*I'm not leaving you.*

Strangely enough, a part of her wanted him there. His presence helped her face the mud and blood that washed off her without screaming. Without seizing up in fear at the memory of an unfamiliar hand inching up her leg. Imbued with the scent of pine, she washed up in minutes and blindly reached out for the towel.

"No." Officer McGoven still stood near the door, but the man seemed to have eyes in the back of his head. "Again," was all he said.

Loren lathered up in even more body wash. The second she started to rinse, another bellowed command came from the doorway. "Again."

She shampooed her hair twice.

"Again."

Another rinse. Another. It felt like ages before she felt clean enough—and at least three more passes of lather before

Officer McGoven seemed satisfied. A part of her almost instinctively knew when she could finally shut the shower off and shimmy nervously into her towel.

The second she was fully covered, a dark T-shirt appeared before her, thrown by an unseen hand. After making sure his back was to her, she dropped the towel and wrenched the garment over her head.

A glance in the mirror revealed a logo for the New Walsh police department stamped across the front of the gray cotton. It smelled like him—overwhelmingly. As if this was the very shirt he'd worn while tailing Kyle's truck, dripping with furious sweat. The mental image stole her breath.

Unfortunately, the ensemble didn't improve her appearance any. She looked a mess. Her hair hung limply over her shoulders. She wasn't wearing a bra, and the shirt's thin material clung to her in all the wrong places.

And he noticed. A glance out the corner of her eye revealed him watching her unashamedly.

Strangely… She didn't feel the same crippling impulse to hide she felt around everyone else. The sight of him inspired jealousy instead. Even streaked with dirt, and with blood seeping through the leg of his sweatpants, *he* still managed to look brave. Invincible. Strong enough to face a group of four men head-on without flinching.

"I'm sorry." Guilt instantly transformed him, making him look less fierce, and those eyes a little less silver. Nervously, he ran a hand through his hair, ruffling it into a messy tangle. "I shouldn't have yelled, but I couldn't bear to smell *them* on you."

The heat in his tone shocked her—or maybe it was the subtle possession lying beneath it? *I couldn't bear to smell them on you.* Was that why he kept his distance and made her shower until her fingers ached?

Hell yes, that dark gleam in his eye claimed. Not only that, but...she could tell from the way his fingers twitched at his sides that he wasn't satisfied with just wiping the stranger's scents away. No, he wanted to replace them. Needed to.

With his touch. His scent. The impulse was so strong Loren's knees buckled, and she gripped the counter. If she didn't, she might go to him. Demand he do...something. Anything.

That uncomfortable, prickling heat was back, building beneath her skin. Her chest. Between her legs. *Only him,* a part of her whispered, pleased. *Only he can touch me.*

Overwhelmed, Loren sat on the lid of the toilet, wrapping her arms around her chest. Where the hell had that come from? Obviously, she had hit her head during the attack. She even felt along her swollen bottom lip, hoping the pain might snap some sense into her.

"I'll kill him—" Officer McGoven stood by the sink, glaring at the mirror. He wet a rag and tackled his legs and arms haphazardly before washing his hands beneath the faucet. Afterward, he remained there, in between her and the door.

Massive, his body blocked her in, but for whatever reason, she wasn't alarmed.

"Kyle, that son of a bitch, will pay for this," he growled as the last droplets of water dripped from him. "He should have *never* left you alone. Not there."

But he *let her go in the first place*, a tiny voice inside her argued. If he hadn't followed her…

"Did you kill them?" Again, Loren didn't know what made her speak at all. She couldn't even look at him and stared down at her knees instead.

He didn't answer, but the look in his eye—once she found the strength to peek at him—said without words what he wouldn't.

"Loren, there is something you need to understand." He reached for her, and Loren jerked back.

Not out of fear, she told herself—for some reason, she couldn't bring herself to truly fear him—but…

The heat in his gaze startled her. No one ever looked at her like that. Ever. It was so much more than just anger or fear. No. Protectiveness? An emotion that drove him to kill.

"Loren…" Awkwardly, he held his hand in the air, inches from her face. "I would never hurt you. You know that, don't you?"

Something made her nod before her mind had even processed the words. He wasn't like her father or the men from the woods.

She knew that.

"They hurt you to get to me," he said. "They knew what you are... What you mean to me. If I didn't... They would have never stopped. Do you understand that?"

Tentatively, he reached for her again, coiling his fingers around her wrist. The air left her lungs. His touch traveled through every inch of her body, hot and electric. Through bone. Flesh. Muscle. Her mind whirled with the sensation, and she almost missed the moment he tugged, easily pulling her to her feet.

And into his chest.

24

*K*yle leaned against the wall of an alley an hour outside of Eislander territory, next to a crummy pay phone, and waited.

It was showtime. He had already mastered his "sad face" and had his sob story together. *They forced us off the road. The girl ran. There were too many of them. When I found her, she...*

He just hoped no one expected any more from him than that. Already, he'd spent too much damn effort making sure that this plan went off without a hitch. It hadn't been easy. The thought of staging something so close to Eislander territory, still made a shiver run down his spine. It was risky, but more than worth the danger in the end.

The girl was dead, and nothing could be traced back to him. *At least now McGoven no longer has the mating bond to worry about,* he thought around a chuckle.

It had probably been broken even before the girl had died. After all, the cheap bastards he'd hired to do the deed had only asked for one thing in addition to the money he'd paid them.

Any other day, he might have felt guilty. The poor female's last moments couldn't have been fun.

But who the hell cared? Lukka got his subtle revenge, and McGoven was back to being the brooding mate-less outlaw.

Win-win.

All Kyle had left to do was pat himself on the back for a job well done. *Piece of cake.*

Only when midnight rolled around without any word, his shoulders started to tense. By the time dawn approached, still without a peep, he had become downright panicked. His palms began to sweat. His already rapid heartbeat kicked it up a notch. He knew he was in deep shit even before the phone finally *did* ring.

"You fucked up."

The voice didn't belong to one of the seedy bastards he'd hired to kill Loren Connors. The power in it could only be conveyed by an Alpha.

"You hear me, Kyle?" Lukka snarled. "You. Fucked. Up."

"What the hell happened?" Kyle countered, feeling somewhat defensive even though he already knew *something* had gone wrong. The bastards never called to receive their second half of the payment, and there could only be one explanation.

Lukka growled. "I had my men scout the perimeter—"

For show, of course. Once Micha showed up, claiming attack by the Eislanders, Lukka would have had to put on his big boy Alpha panties and at least *pretend* to take the threat seriously.

"—only, they caught a whiff of McGoven in the area."

"What?" An uncharacteristic tendril of fear pierced through Kyle before he could help it.

No wonder the bastard let them go so easily. He'd expected a bigger fight, and assumed McGoven had been desperate to have the girl off his hands—but no. The damn rogue had followed them, and Kyle had been too confident to notice.

It was a ballsy move. Kyle might have been impressed— until he remembered that McGoven was a snake. If only he showed the same vigilance reserved for Loren Connors toward all his mates.

Emma might still be alive, in that case.

"I had the security footage pulled around that damn town where he lives," Lukka went on.

Mentally, Kyle had to chuckle at that. While the man might not have had the guts to pull off his own dirty work, he didn't seem to mind using the power that came with being the Alpha of one of the most powerful packs in the area.

Go figure.

"He was with the girl. She's still *alive*," the Alpha added, stating the obvious. "And he'll know that you tried to kill her."

"Why do you figure that?" Kyle asked, though more to stall than anything else.

Fuck. McGoven may have turned his back on pack life, but some instincts couldn't be forgotten—ignored. The mating bond went way deeper than any other connection. It outlasted mother, father, brother, friend, sister. Kyle could only compare it to what he'd felt for his twin—an instinctive pull, as though she were his other half. A piece of his soul.

Such a deep, lupine tie couldn't be forged on a whim. Seeing his mate in danger would have sent McGoven into a rage that Kyle shuddered to imagine. A fierce, primal need to protect at all costs.

He just wondered vaguely if there was anything left of the mercenary bastards that could be traced back to him. Though, his failure would mean more than a few dead contacts in the long run. McGoven would never release the girl now. And the longer the man remained bonded to a mate, the more dangerous he would become.

To be fair, revenge might have explained McGoven's tenacity, at least partly. The animosity between him and Kyle went beyond hatred.

It was personal; Kyle could admit that. Why pretend? If poor Bill McGoven lost his mate for a second time, then—

and only *then*—would he feel a fraction of the pain Kyle felt every fucking day. Until that moment, there could be no truce. No forgiveness. Not even an "order from the Alpha" could make him play nice.

"Did you hear me? McGoven will be out for blood," Lukka went on, sounding all "I hope you're happy"-like.

Kyle laughed. "No, he won't."

He covered his tracks too well. The men he'd hired weren't from Lukka's pack or the Eislander territory. They were shady, greedy little rogues who should have been honored to die as pawns.

Having McGoven fuck things up definitely put a snag in his plan, but he could be flexible. After all, the best revenge always came with a plan B.

"I'll handle it," he said.

"Before or after McGoven comes for your throat?"

"He won't get the chance," Kyle countered, confident of the fact.

As far as anyone knew, they had gotten stranded on Eislander territory. If anything, McGoven would just assume that *they* were the ones who attacked her.

In fact…

"You just sit tight, Lukka." Kyle grinned as a new plan unfurled in his mind. Sure, it involved a little murder and some finagling on his part—but he had always been creative.

"Be a good Alpha and offer your condolences. You can even throw McGoven a pity party if you want and lower his guard. Just leave the rest to me."

25

*H*is heat engulfed her, and despite everything she'd been through, Loren relented to the embrace. Eagerly. *Too* eagerly.

She couldn't get enough of him—of his heat, his scent. She needed him closer. Her body went limp as her chin settled against the hard line of his shoulder. Nose buried against his flesh, she inhaled, and the rush of his scent in her lungs was… Incomparable. Her belly flipped. The pressure between her legs was a constant ache—but it didn't feel wrong. Nothing to be ashamed of. Her reaction just meant…

He is mine.

Surprisingly, he allowed the embrace, but with restraint. He was careful, like one wrong move, and she might break. With utmost care, he ran his fingers through her hair, parting the wet tresses along her scalp while avoiding the area still throbbing from being pulled.

This is wrong, a part of her whispered. He was a stranger—and they were both half-naked. But she was so cold, and to be fair, he only seemed willing to *hold* her, nothing more. His warm breath ghosted the side of her cheek, alluding to the fact that his mouth was a respectful distance from hers.

Still, she didn't stiffen when his hands slid from their neutral positioning on her ribcage down to her waist. Before fear could even enter her mind, she felt his fingertips brush over his intended destination—the bruise left behind after one of the men had crouched on her back.

The memory made her shiver. If he hadn't…

She didn't even want to think about what might have happened—but he was. His nostrils flared, and she recalled something from what felt like an eternity ago.

"My bruises." She struggled to form a coherent question. "Can you really… Smell them?"

"Yes," he said heatedly. "Every one, just as easily as fresh blood. There is a slight difference, but our senses can pick up even the smallest injury."

"You saved my life," she choked out. Acknowledging that felt too important not to voice out loud. She needed to say more. "If you weren't there… Thank you."

He didn't answer. Instead, he cocked his head to bring his jaw against the crook of her shoulder. Loren exhaled sharply, her spine rigid with anticipation. She could sense his lips, a hairsbreadth from her flesh—but no closer. A ragged inhalation betrayed his intention—to breathe in her scent.

"I should have never let you go with that bastard."

Not, *I should have never let you go at all,* a part of her remarked—but it was close enough.

With a shaky breath, Loren copied him, losing herself in the heavy scent of pine.

She had forgotten what this felt like. Physical contact. Even a hug. Her body hummed, as if his nearness revitalized parts of her that had grown rusted with disuse. She hadn't experienced a similar embrace since her mother had been alive. Though McGoven was certainly taller than she had been. And wider, and stronger...

The muscles in his forearms alone were thicker than her own, but he utilized that strength with a gentleness that made her head spin. Even as he maneuvered her against the wall.

He moved too quickly to resist. Within seconds, both of his hands palmed the wall on either side of her, forming a cage of flesh and bone. Another soft intake of air was her only warning as he lowered his head, this time inhaling along the flesh at her throat.

In tendrils of whisper-soft warmth, she felt two fingers trail the length of her shoulder—so gentle, she barely even felt it. But she certainly felt him press the side of his face against her swollen, aching cheek.

He was still breathing, but shallowly, in and out. With every exhalation, his cheek collided with hers. Gently at first, then more firmly. Loren tensed for pain. Instead, a warm tingle washed over her entire being.

Her eyes widened with recognition. It was the same sensation she felt after she'd fallen off Xavier. This time, he concentrated the contact along the worst of the bruising while angling the rest of his body away from hers with what seemed to be a deliberate effort.

By the time he pulled back to observe her with that piercing stare, she couldn't feel anything at all.

"Better?" he asked.

She could only nod.

"Good—" Even the sound of his voice made her dizzy. Breathless, she slumped back against the wall. "I think you should go to bed."

She shook her head. "But…what—"

"I'll explain everything," he said over her. "Once you wake up. But now…" He trailed a finger down the side of her jaw, brushing back a damp tendril of hair. "You need sleep."

The words seemed to set something off inside of her. An intense exhaustion she hadn't even been aware of until then.

Go to sleep.

A part of her wasn't sure whether she made it to the stairs before her mind drifted into black.

*L*oren choked on the verge of a scream.

There were shadows everywhere—hunting her... chasing her through the trees.

She couldn't see—it was so damn cold—but they were gaining. She could tell that much. Their snarls rode the air, and the harsh snap of biting teeth nipped at her ankles. Any minute, they would catch her, and she was too exhausted to fight anymore—

"I'm here." The gruff voice shattered the nightmare, ripping her from the icy darkness of the forest, and leaving her curled up and warm on a bed.

Trembling, she inhaled the scent of pine and knew instantly that she was in McGoven's bed. Only she wasn't alone. Her companion's presence was unmistakable. They were big, with a muscular arm thrown lazily over her waist, holding her tight. However, when she attempted to look back, the comforting grip became a restraint.

"You're alright." That voice was a soothing rumble that echoed like the thunder sounding beyond the window, where a mid-afternoon rain came down in heavy sheets. "I'm here. You were only dreaming."

Drowsily, she allowed her eyes to drift shut, surrendering once again to the darkness. And all the while, that deep tone egged her on, as dexterous fingers stroked through her hair. "You were only dreaming…"

*L*oren woke up to the sound of a car door slamming shut.

Dazed, she rolled over, almost surprised to find that there was no one beside her. The red sheets had been draped neatly over her, tucked in along the edges of the mattress. There wasn't even the indent of another body.

With a sigh, she crept to the edge of the bed, shook out her hair, and…

Realized that all she wore was a man's oversized T-shirt—and very little else. Not to mention, her body ached all over, and the back of her head felt as if someone had taken a baseball bat to it. She traced her bottom lip with a trembling finger, shocked when the tip came away red with blood.

What in the world happened?

It was only when she tried to stand up, gasping as her ankle throbbed, that she remembered everything that happened in the woods.

Kyle, Micha…and Officer McGoven.

While not in this room, he was still in the house. She could sense *him* in the same way she felt her own heartbeat playing through her chest. *He's down below*, something told her. *Waiting.*

Her body trembled as she padded into the hallway and down the stairs. The instant she made contact with the first floor, a pair of gray eyes sought her out from the direction of the kitchen.

He stood at the center island, dressed in another pair of sweats…and very little else. In a rare display, his chest was bare, and every scar glimmered like silver in the waning daylight. As he pivoted on his heels, she snuck a glimpse of his naked back, and her breath caught. The man was a maze of flesh and silvery scars. And ink. For the first time, the tattoo on his neck was clearly visible—a simplistic design consisting of four lines, stretching down between his shoulder blades. Their deliberate placement brought to mind more violent imagery—claw marks.

Surprisingly, that wasn't the most shocking observation to catch Loren's eye. The fact that he watched her while holding a half-eaten tuna sandwich to his mouth was. In contrast to the man who took on four men to save her, it was a comical scene. Until his eyes met hers, as stern as ever.

"Naomi came by," he said, before taking a bite. "I had her leave your work. I thought you'd appreciate a reprieve from her for a day at least."

That explained the slamming car door. Sure enough, glancing out of the window, Loren caught sight of a pink car speeding down the road. It had to be late, if school had already let out—meaning she had slept all day.

"Thanks."

She stood awkwardly on the bottom step for at least another full minute, before she finally found the courage to enter the kitchen. He finished his sandwich while she approached. Then he stood aside to reveal a second, untouched sandwich on a paper plate.

"Have a seat—" He inclined his head toward an empty stool and placed the food in front of it.

Loren complied and began to eat. As soon as she took a bite, he placed a hand on the counter inches from hers.

"What are you thinking?"

The question threw her off, and she choked on a bite of tuna. He had to get her a cup of water, and she gulped it down, desperate to compile a coherent reply. What *was* she thinking? Her eyes trailed over that stern jaw, following the line of it up and across his face.

"You were the wolf." The words came out stronger than she would have thought. Steady.

But she had caught him off guard. Almost too quickly to track, he raised an eyebrow before his expression smoothed into a blank mask. He watched her for so long, she could sense the darkness thickening outside until it was fully nightfall.

Finally, he nodded. "I was."

He said it without any emotion, almost as if daring her *not* to believe him. And the funny thing was…

She did.

"How?"

How. Not, *You're crazy.*

This is insane.

I'm calling the police.

She didn't run from the room. Even stranger, was that the admission wasn't surprising in the least. All along, she'd sensed that he was different—from the moment she first stepped foot in this very house, in fact.

"It's in my blood," Officer McGoven said after a while, leaning against the opposite counter. "We call it lupine instinct." The careful phrasing implied something. Something…dark.

"Like a disease?" She didn't know what made her use that word. *A disease that makes you sprout hair and grow fangs?* Nervously, she crammed another chunk of sandwich into her mouth.

Officer McGoven didn't seem to take offense. "More like hereditary," he said. "An inherited trait. The beast you saw is a part of me, and I am a part of it. Think of us as two halves of the same coin."

Oh, Loren thought somewhat breathlessly. He must have rehearsed this speech, putting it into terms she'd understand. Though, most people inherited just their eye color from their parents. Apparently, *he* had inherited the ability to change into a beast at will.

"It's not how it sounds," McGoven added. He crossed his arms and frowned as if trying to come up with the right words. The awkwardness betrayed just how little he was used to holding an actual conversation. "It's *instinct*," he settled on finally. "I'm not a monster, or a mindless animal. Even in my other form, I am still me."

Loren trailed her gaze over his chest, across the scars, up to that thatch of dark, curling hair. Hair, the exact shade of a certain snarling wolf.

"So, you're a werewolf?" Her voice came out small, as she tried to recall what little she knew from horror movies.

Did he bray at the moon? Howl? Get fleas?

He flinched. "We prefer the term *lupine*. Lycan. Wolf-man —anything but *that*. And—" He paused deliberately, preparing her for another bombshell. "You are as well."

"I'm what?" Loren blurted stupidly before she realized what he really meant—one of *them*—lupine. She shook her head. "I'm not."

The only things she had inherited from her parents seemed to be an awful streak of bad luck, an inability to communicate with others, and a panache for making life difficult for those around her. Besides, one would think that if she *did* possess the ability to change into a wolf, she would have discovered it by now.

"You *are*." He met her gaze and held it, silently begging her to listen. "You must have inherited it from your father. That is how lupine blood is passed down. I'm guessing your mother was a human, but—"

"No," Loren said. "My father wasn't a werewolf."

Fred Connors had been a violent alcoholic, but he never sprouted claws.

"Fred Connors was not your father, Loren," McGoven said cautiously. "He couldn't be. Not if—"

"I'm not a wolf. I'm not—" She wracked her brain for the right word. Brave? Strong? Lethal? "Like *you*," she settled on helplessly.

"You are lupine, Loren. You *are*. I can sense it on you. Even now. You know I followed you out to that clearing, but you don't understand how. By your scent. I could feel every step you took—"

"S-stop." She dropped her sandwich onto the plate and scooted from the counter. Her heart was pounding, head throbbing, and, for once, the reaction had nothing to do with fear.

"Thank you," she stammered. "You've been so nice to me, b-but I'm not—I can't do this. I'm sorry."

He's crazy, a part of her thought as she scrambled for the front door. He had done more for her than anyone else—but he was obviously off his rocker. He had to be. Especially if he thought she was anything other than a messed-up teenager with nowhere left to go.

He didn't storm after her or stop her from leaving. The front door was unlocked, and the frosty night air hit her like a whip as she stumbled out onto the porch. After descending the steps, she hit the ground running and didn't stop, hair flying out behind her—though a part of her wailed in annoyance when she reached the one place that wasn't far from him.

The second she entered the barn, Bunny and Esther's heads appeared over the doors of their stalls in greeting. Xavier kept his distance, though, hidden firmly in the shadows.

Clumsily, Loren pulled open the door to the nearest stall and slipped inside, pressing herself against the farthest corner.

It didn't take him long to find her. Like a shadow, he appeared near the door, massive enough to block the entire exit. If she hadn't sensed him already, the horses' reactions would have alerted her—all three stomped their hooves, breathing heavily.

"Loren." His voice reached her easily above the clamor. "It's freezing out. Come back inside."

Loren felt like a child, fighting the urge to stick her fingers in her ears and chant, "Na na na na, I can't hear you."

"Loren. We need to talk—" He must have taken a step, because Bunny balked, and Esther shrieked, the whites of her massive eyes flickering.

Instantly, he retreated to the doorway, but he didn't leave. "Come here." He dropped the politeness. It was an order, one that had her flinching in his direction before she could help it.

Why is that? a part of her wondered helplessly. No one else had ever affected her with so much as a few simple words. Even when she obeyed her father, it had always been out of fear, but with him...

It was as if a part of her *needed* to obey, even as she dug her heels into the straw-strewn floor and gritted her teeth.

"Loren," he insisted, his tone deeper. "Get out of the barn."

Resisting him was like trying to hold her breath. After so long, her muscles ached, and every inch of her screamed with the need to give in. *Go!*

Gasping, she took a stumbling step toward the mouth of the stall, and then another... She could clearly see him now. He stood just beyond the doorway, eyes blazing against the darkened sky.

"Come here."

The words yanked her forward another few steps. *I have to*, a part of her insisted. *I have to listen to him.*

But why? All he did was confuse her even more. She was a turtle, content in its shell—and he was the eagle, trying to peck her out of it, all the while claiming that she really wasn't what she'd spent her whole life believing she was.

Regardless of her unease, her body continued toward him— but when he reached for her arm, something inside Loren snapped.

No! She lunged, taking off in the opposite direction, and his grasping hand caught only air. Any triumph she felt didn't last long. She could sense him on her heels, but he wasn't clumsy like the men from the clearing.

Her entire being shuddered with his presence. His scent cloyed in her throat, and she knew that, no matter how fast she ran, she'd never be able to escape him. Though, there was a tiny piece of her that really didn't *want* to…

Panting, she made it to the west field and took off randomly for the trees. *A little more,* she urged as her limbs started to burn. *Just a little more.*

She didn't even see him coming.

Wham!

She went down sprawling, trapped beneath a heavy force that pinned her to the ground.

No, she thought, fighting back the dark memory that threatened to overwhelm her—*darkness, groping hands, harsh pants. She would never get away!*

"No, no, no, no—"

"You're alive!"

The chirpy tone threw her off so badly that she blinked, forgetting all about the icy fear that crept up to swallow her whole. Instead, she twisted over the wet earth, coming face to face with two piercing eyes.

Instead of gray...

They were green.

26

"*Y*ou're alive!" The figure lunged, throwing their arms around her as if they were long-lost friends and not virtual strangers. Still, a name came to mind.

"M-Micha?"

He didn't seem to hear her. "You're alive. I thought... Thank God you're okay!"

When he finally withdrew, Loren noticed that—besides his lack of a shirt—a nasty bruise snaked along his jaw. His clothes, what little he wore anyway, were ripped and stained with mud. She wouldn't have been shocked if he claimed to have run the whole way here.

"No one would tell me what happened," he rambled. "Kyle's M.I.A. All they kept saying was 'an attack, an attack,' and I thought—"

He broke off mid-sentence as a shadow fell from above. He didn't even have the time to cry out before he was thrown backward.

Crunch! Loren winced in sympathy as Micha landed hard on the ground, a good ten feet away.

The next second, Officer McGoven stood over her, yanking her to her feet. "Are you okay?"

Without waiting for a reply, he was across the field, standing toe to toe with Micha. The moment the boy found his balance, McGoven shoved him to his knees. "You're one of Lukka's," he growled amid an audible sniff. "You were with Kyle—"

"Wait!" Breathless, Loren stumbled forward. Her ankle throbbed like hell, but it held up as she staggered toward him. "He wasn't doing anything—"

"Stay back!" McGoven's upper lip pulled back from his teeth as he inclined his head her way. He looked…feral. Coldly, he raked his gaze over her muddy knees, where his shirt had bunched up around her legs. Then, he turned back to Micha—only there was a lethal sharpness to his movements that made her heart lurch. He aimed to do more than shove him.

"Wait!" Clumsily, Loren moved forward. She hesitated, fingers outstretched, before bracing a hand against the skin of his bared shoulder. He felt hot, like the surface of an oven. His heart was racing, pounding beneath her palm. Anger battered off him in waves, along with something else. Something that a part of her marveled at...

Fear?

"He didn't hurt me," she said in a low voice. "I swear."

He shrugged her off but reluctantly lowered his fist. "You have five minutes," he growled to Micha. "So, you better start talking. What the hell are you doing here?"

Instead of launching into another whirlwind explanation, Micha bowed his head and raised one knee. The position would have been comical—he almost looked like a man proposing—but the thick tension in the air displaced any desire to laugh. Loren wanted to pull her hair out instead.

"I failed you," he said mournfully. "You entrusted your mate to us, and I—"

"You left her," McGoven interjected. "Alone in enemy territory, to the mercy of *thugs*."

"W-what?" Wide-eyed, Micha gaped at Loren. "Are you okay?"

"Don't you *dare* talk to her," McGoven bellowed. "Don't you even *look* at her. You left her alone in enemy territory. Do you know what they were going to do to her? I could *smell* their intentions. They planned to violate her in every way you can imagine. They wanted her to suffer. Should I go into detail?"

Micha flinched, but so did Loren. The inside of her thigh ached as if remembering that harsh, groping touch. She didn't think she could bear to have him elaborate.

Thankfully, in the end, McGoven released a harsh breath and cocked his head. "Why the hell are you here?"

Micha warily met his stare. Then he placed his left hand over his heart and sucked in a steadying breath. "I came to pledge myself to you. You can kill me. Have mercy. It's up to you. I accept your judgment—" He lowered his head, as if awaiting the bite of an executioner's blade. "For failing to protect your mate, I deserve whatever punishment you see fit. Even death."

"What?" McGoven looked confused. A black eyebrow twitched, threatening to disappear beneath a wayward strand of hair. The odd display seemed to diminish some of his anger—for now.

"That's an old law," he said finally. "I doubt that even *Lukka* would force you to obey it. Integrity wasn't his forte, from what I remember." His voice held so much derision Loren was surprised he didn't spit on the ground afterward.

Micha shrugged. "Sometimes, old ways are the best. My father was a member of the Oleron pack. It was how things were done there."

McGoven nodded. "There, maybe. Not here. Get up. I don't want anything from you. I'm sure your buddy Kyle had no shred of remorse, and neither should you."

"But—" Micha glanced in Loren's direction. "Kyle's not always right," he said, fumbling over the words. "And if you want to kill me, it's within your right. I won't even fight back—"

"Enough." McGoven scoffed, lowering his hands to his sides. "I'm sure you were just following orders—" Rather than sympathetic, he sounded mocking. "Though, *where* is your friend Kyle? Did he come to 'submit himself for my judgment,' as well?"

He seemed to eagerly scan the horizon.

The corner of Micha's mouth twitched. "Kyle isn't... Let's just say that I decided to face you alone after my own questions led me nowhere."

He gingerly fingered the bruise on his jaw. "Even Lukka doesn't know I left—but I just couldn't do *nothing*. You entrusted your mate to us, and we failed."

Mate, Loren shivered as he said the word, and so did Officer McGoven. She couldn't name the emotion in his expression. Whatever it was, made something inside her twist into knots.

"Get up," McGoven said to Micha. "Get back to your pack. You don't owe me a damn thing, and I don't want to see you around here again."

Micha seemed to hesitate. "But—"

"Go." Without another word, McGoven turned toward the house, and Loren followed him without him having to say a word. It just seemed natural—when he moved, so did she.

He didn't acknowledge her, but when he deliberately headed toward the path instead of cutting through the uneven field, she had a feeling that it had something to do with the way that she limped. Her ankle throbbed, and she practically hopped by the time they reached the front porch—but when she turned to stare over the darkening fields, a lone figure remained there, watching them from a distance.

27

*L*oren staggered to the couch the moment they entered the house. She could sense McGoven watching her, but all he did was crouch and prop her foot on his knee.

"It's not broken," he declared, though a purplish bruise discolored the skin. "But it's probably best if you don't walk on it for a while."

He reached for the med kit Sonia had left almost three days ago and withdrew a length of bandage. Carefully, he wrapped the foot from heel to toe. When he finished, she expected him to release her. Instead, he stared at her filthy toes, still cupping her heel in his palm.

She observed him in return, allowing her gaze to travel from that messy tangle of dark hair, down his chest, to the legs hidden beneath the bulky sweatpants.

And the blood pooling beneath him on the floor.

"You're bleeding!"

Freeing her foot, she sank down beside him and reached for the hem of his pant leg before he could stop her. His hand fell over her arm anyway, but not as a restraint. His fingers settled against her skin with a softness that made her pulse race. Focusing beyond him felt like wading through quicksand. The smell of his blood helped put her priorities in order, though. Gingerly, she pulled back the damp material to reveal a gash in his calf several inches long.

"You were hurt." She vaguely remembered him bleeding last night, but up close, the wound looked nasty. Way more debilitating than her ankle, but he hadn't even limped.

"You'll need to take care of this," she blurted, reaching automatically for the med kit and a bottle of antiseptic. "You don't want it to get infected. Or leave a scar."

"You know your stuff," he said. To tease?

Her cheeks flamed as she remained silent. Years of tending to her own injuries had taught her a thing or two. With a honed practice, she soaked a cotton ball in alcohol and cleaned the wound.

It had to hurt, but he didn't even flinch. His lips were quirked, seemingly with amusement. Her belly flipped with a sudden thought—he *had* been teasing her.

"It seems you didn't need my help after all," he said, presumably referring to his prior attempt at first aid.

"You may need s-stitches," she stammered while bandaging the width of his calf. "But I don't think that..."

His hand caught her wrist, and she broke off as a foreign emotion shot through her belly. Shock? Fear? Or *something else* that made her bare toes curl against the floor as he dragged the pad of his thumb carefully over the fragile bones?

At first, she wondered why, until she saw the way he stared, eyes dark with confusion, at a jagged section of skin that encircled each one. Scars, though far less pretty than the ones he sported. Hers were thinner, raised like bracelets formed of flesh.

His gaze found hers, silently questioning, but Loren just drew her hand away. The cause of those scars was one of the many secrets she'd shoved to the back of her mind—too dangerous to ever recall. Instead, she leaned back against the couch and sighed.

"Who is Lukka?" Her voice came out tired and strained.

Rather than deflect, McGoven copied her, sitting close enough that his shoulder brushed hers.

"He's the leader of a track of territory to the northeast of here." Loren sensed he deliberately avoided using another word—*Alpha*. "It's a place called Black Mountain, where a small community of sorts lives in relative isolation. Not a town like New Walsh. We have another name for it."

"You mean a pack," Loren said, utilizing that strange word Micha had.

Like wolves.

He nodded, gazing through the window as a flicker of lightning sparked over the horizon. "One of the largest in this region. At least five hundred strong the last I checked. Maybe more now. It doesn't sound like much compared to any town you're used to, but as far as our kind is concerned, it's massive." The words came hesitantly as if he expected her to argue. When she said nothing, he soldiered on. "Lukka controls hundreds of miles of territory. That's almost unheard of. Those born on Black Mountain can trace their bloodlines back generations. Centuries. The elders on his council have a wealth of knowledge between them. As far as packs go, his is the best around, especially for a young wolf. At least on paper."

The genuine admiration in his voice softened some of the sting of his reluctance to let her stay. He truly seemed to believe she would be better off at this place. One word, however, stuck out to her. "Controls?"

That definitely didn't sound like the political makeup of new Walsh.

McGoven nodded. "It might sound blunt, but that is how we live—under one set of laws, enforced by one person, the Alpha. Lukka has only been in power for a few years, but already things have…changed under his leadership."

He didn't elaborate on how. Sonia alluded to some of the changes, though. Lukka alone could decide if Loren would be welcome there or not—and that seemed to annoy them both.

"We have different ways of doing things," McGoven admitted. "But we don't turn our backs on our own. Never. The second I sensed the change in you, Lukka should have come to assess you himself that very night. Nothing could be more important than that. No fucking red tape."

It was like he'd read her mind. The intensity in his voice diminished more of her doubt. Crazy or not, he seemed to care about her. More than a stranger should, in her experience.

"If you think I'm…" She couldn't bring herself to say it, so she tried a different route. "Was my mother from there? My father?"

McGoven frowned. "Your mother could have been. Humans are sometimes allowed to live on the outskirts, but Fred Connors was one of Lukka's."

She didn't miss how he avoided calling him her father—though that wasn't the strangest revelation he let slip.

"You mean he was like you?" she asked.

"No." McGoven flinched as if the comparison were an insult. "Not like me at all. He was a made wolf—someone bitten by a full-blooded lycan. The Alpha accepted him into the pack out of duty years ago, but the bastard broke the rules and was exiled."

That sounded like him. No wonder he seemed to loathe New Walsh.

"It's the worst punishment among our kind," McGoven explained, his tone grim. "We are social creatures, more so than humans. Pack bonds are stronger than any other connection you can think of. We need it. We need to be surrounded by our own kind. Being excommunicated is a fate worse than death. In fact, most would *prefer* death over it."

"Why aren't you there?" Loren asked.

He grimaced and ran a hand through his tangled hair. "My job was to watch Connors. I knew that he took in a daughter, but I never thought that you would be—"

"Why?" she asked weakly. "How can you tell?"

He cocked his head in her direction. "What color are my eyes?"

"G-gray," she answered automatically. Though, now they glinted more like silver.

"That's how. It's as obvious to me as the color of your hair or eyes." He returned to his vigil at the window, and a flash of lightning reflected off his gaze. Rain had picked up again, running in rivulets down the glass. "I can look at you and see the instinct there. It's faint—but it's there."

Loren questioned that. When she looked in the mirror, all she saw was emptiness. Just what did this "lupine instinct" look like?

"How?" she gathered up the nerve to prod.

"Fred Connors was *made*," he continued as if she'd never spoken. "There is no way you could have inherited the blood from him. I'm sorry, but it is biologically impossible that he could be your father, Loren. He had to be someone else."

He sounded so sure, and strangely enough—if he *were* telling the truth—Loren didn't feel too much emotion at that. Was it strange to think that the man she'd been calling "dad" for the past ten months wasn't really her father? Yeah.

But when she thought of just how those ten months had been spent.

She felt relieved. *I didn't come from that*, a part of her sighed. *His nasty hatred isn't a part of my genes.* But then, what was?

"Was my mother a—"

McGoven shook his head before she even finished. "She was human, Loren. I'm positive about that. A full-blooded female would never give birth outside of her territory. Sometimes the Alpha offered protection to those without the blood. Victims of 'accidents' who weren't turned. That could be how she fell across Connors. I'll call Sonia and have her do some digging. What was her name?"

"Eveline," Loren said softly. "Eveline Connors."

"She might not have known what you were. If Connors made her leave the territory, she would have no choice but to follow him." He made it sound as if their relationship had been more of hunter and hunted than anything romantic.

"You, however, have lupine blood," he insisted. "In fact, your father must be a pureblood, most likely someone belonging to a nearby pack."

"Is that why you wanted me to go to Lukka?" She found the strength to ask. "So that I could be with a pack?"

He nodded, but kept his gaze on the window rather than look at her. "Isolation is *unnatural for* us. The need to belong to a pack is too strong—some go insane from it. Connors should have taken you to them the moment he sensed the blood in you. To keep you out here was unnecessarily cruel. Some might say criminal."

"What makes you think he knew?" She thought of the way her father treated her—cold and distant. Had he known all along that she might not have been his daughter? Was that why he hated her so much?

"It's obvious," McGoven said, facing her directly. "Maybe not right away, but…" He reached out, snagging a lock of hair. Before she could even flinch, he tucked it behind her ear.

"Anyone looking at you could tell that you are different."

He didn't make it sound like a compliment. Just fact.

"You belong with people *like* you, who can understand you. It sounds dramatic, I know, but once you feel for yourself what it's like to be in a pack... You will understand. You don't belong here."

Slowly, he pulled his hand away, but Loren couldn't ignore the trail of heat that lingered over her skin. Something lurched inside of her, making her chase the contact. Demand it. His fingertips brushed her shoulder as she inched closer.

He frowned. "Lukka could have given you that. Safety. Security. Everything you've never had."

Could have. She didn't miss his choice of words, but hope was a painful emotion to feel. It stabbed through her heart. Her eyes burned. "If it's so important, then why aren't you—"

He lurched to his feet gracefully, despite his injured leg.

"You asked why I left. I'll tell you. When you belong to a pack, loyalty is everything," he said in a low, gruff tone. "You should be ready to lay your life down for your Alpha at a moment's notice—I wasn't."

He entered the kitchen, swiping the remains of her sandwich into the trash before disappearing into another section of the house.

All Loren could do was sit there, watching the rain come down, and suffer the chill that replaced his heat.

28

It doesn't make sense. Bill seethed as he marched through the rain. He could smell the scent of fresh blood beneath the moisture and grudgingly acknowledged the source—him. His leg throbbed—one of those bastards had gotten him good with a knife hidden up his sleeve last night—but the pain barely even fazed him at this point.

Not when there were more important things to worry about. Kyle. Loren. The Eislanders. The whole thing didn't make any damn sense.

Eislander wolves were known to be ruthless, and fiercely protective of their territory—but it wasn't like them to attack strays on their land without provocation. Not without alerting their Alpha, at least.

Loreck Eislander may have been an overly aggressive prick, but he was honorable and fair—two words that could never apply to Lukka. Such a man wouldn't condone the murder of a young girl on his land. Not without his say so and certainly not without good reason.

Though, to be honest, that was the least of his worries.

The pack kept calling. They rang constantly, buzzing through the cell phone at his hip, a different number almost every time. He could guess the source without having to check the I.D. One of Lukka's many sycophants, or perhaps the bastard himself?

All to give him a half-hearted explanation as to how this had all been just some big misunderstanding. *Whoops!* They'd spew some shit apology and swear to come the next day to take the girl off his hands.

All nice and clean-like.

And all utter bullshit.

While he may not have been a brainiac like Lukka, Bill liked to believe that he wasn't stupid. Kyle hadn't taken a detour through enemy territory just to view the damn scenery. No—and the bastard wouldn't dare do *anything* without the go-ahead from his Alpha.

Only one conclusion fit the puzzle—they had abandoned her there on *purpose,* knowing full well what would happen.

It was a dangerous suspicion, borderline treason without any proof. Not to mention that he was breaking about fifty pack rules *alone* by ignoring the calls. In his mind, it was better not to answer at all, than cuss out the one man who held the keys to his freedom.

He loathed to admit it. The truth didn't matter in the face of his feelings. Lukka required just one excuse to revoke his exiled status and summon him for judgment.

One damn reason.

Though he would give them a hell of a lot more than that if Kyle had the nerve to step on his property after this. A showdown between the two of them had been a long time coming, anyway. Some might say it was fucking destiny.

Respect for Emma's memory was the sole reason he hadn't torn out his throat by now. As her brother, he deserved that much grace. But no more. Kyle could hate him all he wanted, but to use a young female as a pawn in his twisted revenge?

It was beyond cruel. Loren had no choice in becoming tethered to him. The thought of her made him pick up the pace, feeling the rain lash violently at his skin. He could still picture her, cornered and bruised in the center of that clearing. Her eyes had been wide with fear, and her heart pounded so hard he could practically taste her damn pulse in his throat.

The girl had lost so much already, only to be used as a pawn in some sick ploy—and to what end?

Bill had no idea.

At least now, he figured he wouldn't have to call her by that bastard's name anymore; wolves took the surnames of their father. If Connors wasn't a viable candidate, then…

Maybe *that* was the reason he'd been so damn eager to ship her off to Lukka? Wolves could sense family in a way humans couldn't. They wouldn't need a paternity test for the girl's sire to recognize her. Maybe he had hoped that if she'd gone to Lukka's pack, her real father would catch her scent.

And then what?

Claim the fully-grown daughter he'd never known? Accept her baggage with open arms? Like the fact that she had unintentionally mated a rogue?

Why don't you throw in sparkles, sunshine, and a happy ending, while you're at it? he thought sarcastically.

The point was that Loren was in pretty much the same boat he was—abandoned. Alone. Lukka had already failed her. Bill shuddered to think about what could have happened if he hadn't had the sense to follow her. Hell, it made him shudder to think what *he* might have done if—

He shook his head firmly, breaking off the thought, and headed for the trees. It was over and done with anyway. Only *he* could help Loren now. She needed a pack; she needed help. She needed…

Way more than he could give her. He might be able to help with the first two, not that it would matter much in the long run. There were things she should have learned almost a decade ago. Milestones she should have already reached.

And urges a female would need her mate to satisfy. He could feel it already. She was so damn innocent. Her arousal was so fresh. Sweet. Fragile. He doubted she even recognized the feeling for what it was—desire. Lust. Some sick part of him…*liked* that. His abdomen tightened, and he grunted, hating the physical reaction her nearness inspired within him. Sooner or later, she'd recognize the signs. His lingering touch. The way he couldn't keep his eyes off her. The erection straining the front of his pants.

No. Gritting his teeth, he shook his head. Loren wasn't his in that way. She couldn't be. Sooner or later, he would break their bond for her own good—once she became strong enough to hold her own, whatever path she decided. *First things first…*

With one hand, he yanked off his sweatpants, balled them in a fist, and tossed them in the direction of the house, cell phone and all. At the same time, he picked up speed, feeling his bare feet sink into the damp earth. Fresh blood dribbled harmlessly down his leg, not that the wound would plague him for much longer.

He inhaled the damp air, feeling his entire body thrum with the urge that preceded the shift. He had only a split-second's warning to throw his hands out in front of him before his body compacted, twisted, and transformed into the sleek form of a wolf.

He hit the ground running, barely losing momentum, and headed straight for the perimeter of his property. His land, while minuscule compared to Lukka's territory, was all he had. If that young pup had managed to walk right onto it without fear, then what was stopping someone like Kyle?

Or worse.

Justified or not, he had *killed* on another Alpha's territory. Offenses like that weren't just ignored—they couldn't be. Sooner or later, *they* would come knocking, demanding answers.

That makes two of us, Bill thought, as he began to scout, hunting for so much as a leaf out of place. Then, he pushed further into New Walsh, ensuring that Kyle and his cohorts hadn't infiltrated the town as well. He didn't like it. It was risky to venture beyond his property, especially with Loren there alone.

But therein lay the power of the mating bond. He could feel her despite the distance, always. Even if he hadn't followed her to Black Mountain, he would have known the instant she was in danger. If he were being honest with himself, he'd admit that from the second Kyle had arrived, she'd been afraid. That fear drew him like a moth to a flame, arguing with the logical part of him that knew she'd be better off with the pack. She was *his. His.* Even if he couldn't keep her here for long.

Regardless, if anyone dared to harm her, he'd come.

And ensure they never could again.

29

*T*hump!

Loren jolted awake with a wince. Her head was throbbing, her bottom lip stung, and the inside of her mouth tasted like copper. With one hand, she cradled her temple and tried to get her bearings.

For the first time since finding herself at Officer McGoven's, she wasn't in that large bed upstairs. She was on the couch instead, with a pile of schoolbooks on her lap and a pencil clutched in her fist.

Huh?

The last thing she remembered was attempting to tackle the work Naomi left. If she were going to stay in New Walsh a little longer, she might as well keep her academics on track. Plus, it gave her an excuse to stay up and wait for McGoven to come back—all while, trying *not* to be driven insane by the million thoughts crashing through her brain.

Dangerous thoughts. The main one being that the man who'd taken her in claimed to be able to shift into a wolf at will. Not to mention the bombshell that her father wasn't really her father after all.

She needed answers, and despite being obviously mentally unbalanced, Officer McGoven was the only person around. When he wasn't staying out all night, of course.

She guessed it to be a little after dawn, though not by much. A glance out the window revealed it had stopped raining, leaving the ground coated in a thick, silvery mist. Inside, the house was toasty warm and, despite wearing only a mud-splattered T-shirt, she felt comfortable. At least her ankle wasn't hurting anymore.

Yawning, she pulled herself upright, leaning against the couch for balance. It was only then that she realized that she hadn't woken up by coincidence. McGoven was back—she knew that as surely as her own name. And...he was angry. The emotion seeped into her in waves. It wasn't her rage. Her disgust. But his...

She could hear him. "Fuck!"

The sound sent her scrambling to her feet, and she raced through the house, stumbling onto the front porch. Icy daylight painted the landscape in muted shades of gray, creating a deceptively beautiful backdrop to the chaos awaiting her.

Blood flooded her nostrils first. Sharp. Pungent. But... It smelled different than hers or McGoven's. A heartbeat later, she spotted the source. Milky, large eyes stared up at her from the welcome mat, but they weren't human. They belonged to what once was a deer. Its head leaked a puddle of fresh blood that pooled over the wood.

A few paces away, propped against the steps, was its body.

"Get back!" She looked up to find McGoven racing down the path, his sweatpants caked in mud. "Get inside," he commanded.

She didn't even think to argue. Bile crawled up her throat as she turned away from the grisly sight. The smell haunted her, and the potential explanations weighed on her mind. Had the poor thing gotten lost? Had someone dropped off roadkill as a joke?

You know it wasn't a joke, that inner voice warned. *This is dangerous. Listen to him.*

She could hear him grunting, and curiosity made her peek out of the kitchen window. Already, he was halfway to the trees, the deer slung over his shoulder effortlessly. He moved with a grace that took her breath away—but his anger was glaringly apparent.

She tried to distract herself. She retreated into the shower and got dressed in the only clothing she could find—his shirt and a ragged pair of sweats. The second she entered the hall, her heart skipped a beat. Someone was in the house with her—in the kitchen, to be exact. Without bothering to be quiet, they rummaged through the cupboards, slamming several heavy objects down hard on the counter.

Thump! Bang! Slam!

The moment she crept to the doorway, the sounds stopped.

"Morning," Officer McGoven rasped. He stood frozen near the center island, holding a jar of mayonnaise in one hand and a slice of bread in the other. Slowly, he smeared the condiment onto the bread and slapped it on top of another already piled high with tuna.

"Are you okay?" His eyes scanned her face intently. He was hunting for something. Something that he didn't seem to find—and that relieved him. "Don't worry about… What happened earlier," he grumbled by way of apology. "Sometimes, the hunters around here choose to be generous with their bounty. I'm sorry you saw that."

He still wore that pair of sweatpants, which were damp and covered in mud. That dark hair was tangled in a way that made Loren wonder if he'd spent the night rolling around in the fields. Or *running* through them.

Suddenly, he closed the fridge with his hip and brought the sandwich to his mouth for a bite.

"Get washed up," he told her, before heading for the stairs. "I'll find you something to wear."

He took the steps two at a time, uncaringly tracking footprints across the floor. Had he really spent the night out in the wind and rain?

It sure smelled like it. His usual scent of pine was diluted by the earthy, musky scent of the woods. Rather than offensive, on him, the aroma seemed...wild. Untamed.

Feral.

Her heart pounded beneath his borrowed shirt, and suddenly the room felt way too small. Rather than mention that she had already showered, she stumbled into the bathroom and climbed into the shower for a second time without giving herself the chance to think about why.

The hot water pounded down—but, this time, every droplet felt...raw. Her skin was oversensitive, aware of every fluctuating temperature. His nearness. His smell. When she finally stepped into a towel, she shuddered at the feel of the terrycloth. Every fiber seemed to irritate her skin as if to tease her about a lack of something else. Something she craved, but couldn't name. Only images came to mind. Deep, golden skin. Calloused fingertips. Heat.

No! Terrified, she shook her head to clear it and saw that someone had placed a pile of folded clothes on the toilet seat for her, so quietly that she hadn't even heard them come in.

The thick flannel shirt and black sweatpants were about ten sizes too big, and she had to roll up the hems of both just to see her hands and feet. But they were warm and offered far more coverage than what she had on.

When she finally returned to the main room, McGoven wasn't there. From the sounds of rushing water coming from above, she guessed he too decided to shower. She had lived with her father for months, but the thought of a grown man showering—naked—in the same house *still* felt strange.

Especially when she could clearly picture his body—every taut, coiled bit of muscle. *No.* She bit her lip hard enough to sting and raced for the door. It wasn't the urge to escape driving her barefoot onto the porch.

No, it was something else.

Something that coiled in the base of her stomach like a snake waiting to strike. It taunted her, betraying just *how* much she remembered from earlier—dark skin and chiseled abs.

Not to mention the blood dripping from his mouth.

The thought made her shiver as she descended the porch steps. McGoven had worked fast. All traces of the deer were gone, and the landscape seemed as idyllic as usual as she crossed the field and headed straight for the barn.

Bunny greeted her as she slipped inside. Esther whinnied hello, and even Xavier seemed less shy. It could have been just another day, sneaking there to avoid her father—but it wasn't long before reality intruded.

The horses sensed him first. Esther shifted uneasily in her stall, while Xavier's dark head appeared over the mouth of his, nostrils flaring. Loren turned, unsurprised to find Officer McGoven in the doorway.

He held something—a dark shape that had her flinching back out of habit. There were two things, actually. Her pair of tan boots and his windbreaker tucked under his arm.

"It's freezing out." His tone was cautious, as if he expected her to bolt at any second.

Instead, she crept forward to take the clothes before darting back inside the safety of the barn. Thankfully, he kept his distance.

She wasn't *afraid* of him, she told herself. But, dressed in a thick polo, and a pair of jeans, he didn't look any less intimidating than he had in a pelt of fur. Even *more so*.

A shower had done him good. His hair was slicked back, his face cleaned of mud. The cleanliness made his gaze all the more piercing. He watched her as she pulled on her boots while leaning against Bunny's stall for balance. They were slightly damp and smelled like…

She sniffed and frowned. *Bleach?* They weren't the only odd-smelling item. This jacket seemed slightly older than the one he'd given her previously. Rather than pine, it reeked of laundry detergent. She zipped it up and waited for Officer McGoven to say something.

Order her back to the house?

All he *did*, was lean carefully against the doorway, arms crossed over his chest. Then, after a moment, he inclined his head toward the nearest stall, where she'd unconsciously gone back to stroking Bunny.

"You named them." It wasn't a question.

"I…I needed something to call them," Loren stammered, feeling her cheeks flame. "I couldn't find any names on their stalls."

"That one's Xavier?" He nodded toward the stallion.

"Yes."

"What about that one?"

"Bunny," she admitted.

"And the brown mare?"

"Esther."

The corner of McGoven's mouth twitched—barely perceptible, but still technically a smile. Though it only lasted a heartbeat.

Loren was mortified. "I'm probably not even close to their real names, am I?"

"Well…" McGoven's mouth returned to its usual frown. "They don't have any. When I…the person I acquired them from didn't tell me if they did or not."

"Oh," Loren said softly. She remembered the man Sonia mentioned. "Josiah Baker?"

He raised an eyebrow, surprised. "Yes. He was a good man. Cared for these animals himself for years, but let's just say talking wasn't his forte."

"He was a wolf, too? I mean a l-lycan."

"How do you... *Sonia*," he declared with a heavy sigh. Then he nodded. "A made. One of the few, if not the only, who I've ever known to leave the pack willingly. Not because he shunned our laws. I think he just preferred his solitude, and I couldn't blame him for that. He died not long after I was... After I left the pack. He'd just gotten the black one, in fact. And if I *had* named these horses, I don't think I'd have picked those names. The old swayback I probably would have called Whitey. The mare, Brownie, and the stallion..."

"Let me guess?" Loren asked before she could help herself. "Blackie?"

He nodded, but his expression was so serious she couldn't smother a laugh. Just a soft, trickling *ha, ha,* at first, but pretty soon, she was doubled over, gasping for air.

God, she couldn't remember the last time she'd laughed this hard—if ever. Once she started, she couldn't stop. It just kept coming, until she blinked to realize that tears were streaming down her face.

"I was never really creative," McGoven said softly, still watching her. "Feel free to call them whatever you want."

Loren felt the corner of her mouth twitch. Was that a smile? He seemed adept at drawing emotions from her, one after the other. "I don't know..." She turned back to the stall and dragged a hand through the mare's long mane. "Bunny just doesn't have quite the same ring to it as *Whitey*."

Had she just made a joke? She puzzled it over, still petting the horse. Suddenly, Bunny stiffened, shying back within her stall, her ears flat against her head. Esther reacted the same way, and Xavier shifted, prancing anxiously in his stall.

It wasn't until she felt a prickle over the back of her neck that she saw why. McGoven stood closer, fully inside the barn. His eyes flashed with confusion, as if he hadn't realized he'd moved at all. Awkwardly, he stumbled back until his toes toyed with the threshold once again.

Just like that, the horses quieted down.

"Is that...is that ah..." Loren trailed off. Hell, what did she mean to say? *Is that a wolf thing?*

He got the gist anyway.

"They can sense a predator nearby," he admitted, tucking his hands into his pockets. "It's instinct."

"But...*I* can touch them," she pointed out, trying not to let a note of "I told you so" slip into her voice. It did anyway.

"I know." His voice was that deep rumble again. "I've been thinking as to why..."

He never mentioned just what theories he'd come up with. He just watched her, until Loren felt the need to turn around. Her heart picked up speed, though she figured that it had already been pounding the moment he'd appeared in the doorway.

He felt too close—but not close *enough*. Everything running through her mind was conflicting. Her fingers shook as she dragged them through Bunny's mane over and over again.

What is wrong with me?

"I was going to clean out the barn," McGoven said.

"I can help," she offered. It was the least she could do after sneaking onto his property for nearly a year.

She turned to find him already holding two shovels, one of which he tossed to her. She caught it by the handle and had just a split-second's notice to set it aside before he grabbed a lead rope from the wall and tossed it to her as well.

"You can take them out to pasture if you want."

"S-Sure." Jerkily, Loren moved back to Bunny's stall and led the animal out.

McGoven wasn't anywhere in sight as she turned the nag loose in one of the paddocks. Confused, she went back in for Esther, who was almost too eager to get out into the fresh air, and finally Xavier, who nervously followed her out to join the others.

Afterward, she drifted back into the barn, only to find Officer McGoven standing casually in Bunny's open stall like he'd been there all along. He held a shovel, hefting soiled hay into a nearby wheelbarrow.

Without a word, Loren grabbed the other shovel and moved to help him.

They worked in silence for a long while, until Loren just lost herself in the busywork. She almost didn't notice the pair of eyes on the back of her neck. Not until she happened to turn and caught him staring.

Rather than look away, he held her gaze and cocked his head, demanding an answer to his next question. "What are you thinking? You seem distracted."

She would never understand how he could do that. Be so calm one minute. So authoritative the next.

"You knew my father?" The question slipped out before she could help it.

McGoven set the shovel aside and crossed his arms. "I knew Fred Connors."

Loren sucked in a deep breath, tipping her shovel to dump the last bit of soiled hay into the wheelbarrow. "What was he like? I mean...before...you said he broke the rules of the pack?"

Her heart swelled with a longing that caught her off guard. She just needed something...good? That he was kind once. Nice once. Life had ruined him—not her.

"I didn't know him well, but he did break the rules—at least from the outside looking in. Among us, any little infraction takes more effort than you might think. You must *willingly* go against the wishes of the Alpha. Such disobedience is never tolerated."

He said it the same, definitive way that someone might "You have to willingly go against the laws of gravity."

"What did he do?"

Again, McGoven shrugged, but his gaze turned to the wall behind her. "Nothing bad enough to die for, though, again, there are some who think that exile is worse."

The way he clenched his jaw told her that she wouldn't be getting anything else out of him on that subject.

"You said you were watching him? Why?"

The line of his jaw became tauter. "The pack sometimes sends rogues to watch other rogues. It keeps them... *Us* in line. Stray wolves can band together otherwise. Make trouble, by terrorizing humans or encroaching onto the territory of other packs. The presence of a stronger lycan helps them rethink those transgressions and adhere to the law."

"So you were like a parole officer?" At least that explained his role on the police force.

McGoven's mouth twisted into what could have been a grimace. "Something like that. More like an insurance policy. Unaffiliated rogues are dangerous, and exiles who wish to redeem themselves, or remain in good standing with the pack may sometimes watch another and report—" He broke off, frowning.

"Was that why?" Loren asked without thinking. "You stayed here."

She could read between the lines. Obviously, he wasn't "in good standing" with the pack either. Rather than answer, he took the handles of the wheelbarrow, and began carting the waste out into the field. A sharp jerk of his head was her only clue to follow.

She crept after him, sensing that his focus had shifted well beyond barnyard chores. Sure enough, he left the wheelbarrow near the front of the barn and just kept walking. When he reached the field opposite of the horse paddock, he turned, bent down…and twisted to throw something in her direction so swiftly she barely had time to catch it.

Dazed, she stared down to find a medium-sized rock clutched in her fist. Her palm smarted with the momentum of the blow, and she dropped it out of shock.

"You have good reflexes," he said, but his voice was devoid of any anger that might explain the unwarranted assault.

In one smooth motion, he advanced, capturing her chin before Loren even knew what was happening. "Your vision seems sharp," he commented, releasing her just as quickly. "Can you run?"

Loren glanced down at her still tender ankle before realizing that he probably meant in general.

"Kind of…" They ran laps in gym at the high school, and she kept up okay.

"What about endurance? Can you lift?"

She gave him what she hoped passed for a non-verbal answer by lifting her flabby arms, swallowed by the fabric of his clothes.

"These are skills you would have mastered, had you grown up in the pack," he explained. "Women and men are subjected to the same training. To master the change, one must hone both their body and mind."

Loren thought of Micha and Kyle, who all seemed to share his lean, muscular build. Even Sonia didn't have an ounce of fat on her.

"You don't seem *out* of shape," he said, eyeing her critically, but the words didn't seem like much of a compliment. "Unlike the myths surrounding 'werewolves'—" His voice held so much disdain that Loren half-expected him to put sarcastic air quotes around the word. "Our strength may be enhanced by our natural forms, but it doesn't come like magic. It is honed. Your body is a tool you must become accustomed to wielding."

Loren felt like she should nod, a student in the middle of an impromptu lecture.

"What about the full moon?" She found herself asking. "Does it—"

"We don't need it to shift if that's what you mean," he said, his tone mildly amused. "Think of it like this. You see better in the daylight, but that doesn't mean you have no vision at night. The full moon enhances our abilities, but we can shift without it."

Like right now.

He didn't say it, but he didn't have to. Primal energy practically radiated from every inch of him. His eyes told it all. He could shift at a moment's notice. Just rip off that dark shirt, sprout jet black fur all over and—

"But not on a whim."

"Oh." Loren looked away, fixating on the horses over in the muddy field. Her heart was still pounding, but not exactly because of the thought of him turning into a four-legged beast.

"The need to shift is instinctive," he said in a quieter tone that she barely heard over the wind. "Primal. Sacred. It's not something undertaken on a whim. It requires preparation. Respect. We embrace our other form with only the purest of intentions. Otherwise, it can be painful. You can cause injury to yourself or anyone who happens to get in the way."

He sounded uneasy about that, and she wondered just how much it had taken out of him to attack those men in the clearing. Though, he'd made it seem pretty easy in the moment.

"Why can't I?" She faced him, brushing the hair from her face, and sucked in a breath.

He had never looked more serious. His eyes practically glowed, his lips pursed in a hard line. "It's not that simple. It's like a muscle—the urge needs to be honed. Controlled. Exercised." He seemed to hesitate before adding, "Most learn those basics as children. You're older. You've grown up without learning the ways. You need—"

He broke off, jaw clenching shut.

Oh, no, you don't. He had taken her in and, so far, called all the shots with little explanation. It was about damn time she demanded some answers. "I need what? If I am what you say I am, why can't I shift?"

"It's not that simple," he grumbled.

"How?"

Too late did she realize her tone sounded challenging. Abruptly, he closed the distance between them and gently tapped the center of her chest with an outstretched finger.

"The instinct needs to be called forth," he murmured. "By an Alpha."

lpha. The word sounded different when uttered by him. Powerful.

But Loren couldn't understand how that factored into what he claimed was instinct. "What do you mean?"

"You've been on your own for too long," he went on. "The urge has remained dormant within you. It's not like in the movies. We aren't born with a mastery of the change. Our skill must be nurtured by the needs of the pack, the same way you learned your native language as a child. That constant interaction. That *pull.*"

Suddenly, he towered over her, his heat battering her in waves, easily cutting through the fabric of her borrowed windbreaker. The nearness conjured the strange sensation she'd felt earlier—that creeping, tingling warmth that pooled inexplicably in certain areas of her body. She was painfully aware of the fabric of his shirt, grazing her chest— her breasts. Her lips felt dry, and she desperately dragged her tongue along them, fighting to stay focused. It took twice the normal effort to breathe. Think.

His voice, however, was an anchor, too stern to overlook. "Proximity to an Alpha provides guidance. An example. Since Lukka isn't—" He broke off and seemed to try a different tactic. "You need a *pack*, Loren. I can help you, but I need you to trust me."

His earnest tone dislodged something at the back of her mind. A memory? Had he said something similar to her before? She couldn't remember. In fact, it was getting hard to remember a lot of things. Like the color of the grass or sky…

When he looked at her, all she could see was *silver*.

Until he turned and cut across the field, away from the barn. He didn't motion for her to follow. This time his body language seemed to convey less of a command and more of a question.

Trust me? Then come on.

Loren hesitated until he was halfway up the hill. Only then did she follow, and she wasn't surprised to find him waiting for her. Together, they neared the woods, with Loren only slightly behind.

Her mind raced as she struggled to keep pace with his long strides. Where on earth could he be taking her? The deeper within the forest they went, the taller the trees looming above became. The chilling wind didn't help calm her building anxiety.

Before any fear could truly set in, the underbrush thinned, and they stumbled into an open field where the tall grass had been mowed down.

There, Officer McGoven turned to face her. "You aren't like everyone else, Loren," he began, letting his voice carry on the wind. "That's your first lesson."

Lesson?

"You need to trust your instincts. Learn to rely on them."

Before she fully processed the advice, he lunged. The next second, she was lying on the ground, tasting dirt.

So much for instinct. Fear was a stronger impulse. *Don't move,* it told her. *Tuck. Curl into a ball—make yourself small. He'll get tired of hitting you eventually, as long as you don't move—*

"Loren."

Her hands were in front of her face. *Reflex,* she thought. Peeking through her fingers, she saw Officer McGoven standing over her. Not her father or any of the specters from her childhood. Rather than angry or aggressive, he looked...disappointed.

"Loren, get up. We can try again—" He paused with his hand outstretched, inches from her face. "I won't hurt you."

Shame flooded her cheeks. She could only imagine how pathetic she looked to trigger the concern in his voice. Warily, she took his hand, allowing him to pull her upright. The second she regained her balance, he let her go.

"You froze." His tone resonated with disapproval. "You didn't even see me coming, did you?"

She shook her head, wondering why he'd pushed her in the first place. He didn't even have the decency to look guilty.

"You hesitated." Confusing her further, his tone was softer, much like a teacher directing a student toward the right answer. "When I move, you watch me—don't think. Just react. Try again."

Though much slower, his arm swung out, giving her enough time to duck out of reach.

"Good." He watched her carefully, sizing her up with a single glance. "Watch where I am. Don't think. Let your body react."

Suddenly, he pivoted, aiming for her head. Loren obeyed his instruction and instinctively feinted to the left.

"Good," he praised. "You catch on quick. Maybe this isn't such a long shot after all—"

He broke off and let out a deep, heavy sigh.

"Look, we don't have the time for me to coddle you or hold your hand. This isn't a game. This is *real*, Loren. For whatever reason, there are people who want you dead, just to get to me. You have to be able to protect yourself, and I can only think of three ways for you to do that."

He held up his hand and began to tick off the options on his fingers one by one. "One, you get on a bus headed far from here and never look back. Two, you submit to your fate and don't put up a fight. Or three..." His voice deepened, almost into a growl.

"Three?" Loren pressed when he didn't speak.

He advanced step by step until it was way too late for her to run. "Three," he said finally when he was within arm's reach.

He was right; this wasn't a game. He caught her forearm in a bruising grip, forcing her to her knees. It hurt. Her free hand grasped at the muddy earth for leverage, and genuine fear ran down her spine. She tried to struggle, but he only tightened his hold. His strength was too much. She'd never overpower him. *No!* Her lips parted, readying for a scream.

But then another sound drowned out everything else. *Submit!* It was an order, echoing through her mind like a gunshot. His lips didn't even move, but it was his voice. Commanding her.

Submit. Give in. Obey. You are mine.

Confused, Loren could only stare up at him, her heart pounding so hard she could hear every beat. *Boom, boom, BOOM!*

"*Give in, Loren,*" his voice commanded inside her head. He crouched suddenly, still gripping her arm. His eyes were pure silver holding her captive—she couldn't even turn away.

Couldn't think.

"*Give in. Give up. I'm all you need. I can be your everything. Just give in to me.*"

Yes, a part of her whispered longingly. *He can take care of us. Help us. Protect us.*

Give in.

No! The fear came like a whip, cutting through the mindless drone. "No," she croaked out loud. "No, no, no, no—"

"Don't resist," he warned, raising his voice to combat hers. "Let me in. This is to help you—"

"No!"

She wrenched her gaze from his, and it was like an invisible chain tethering her to him snapped. With a sudden burst of strength, she was on her feet, running so fast she could barely feel the wind anymore. Just pure motion. Pushing her on, egging her forward.

Run, run, run!

Even still, there was a part of her that rebelled against the desire to flee. It sat, right *there* in the pit of her chest, and ached, no it *throbbed*, with the need to turn back. *Go back.*

Give in to him.

"No!" Slapping her hands over her ears, Loren kept moving.

She couldn't see, couldn't even think, to pick out a clear path. She just stumbled forward, feeling weeds and stray branches snag at her ankles, rip at her hair and slice into her cheek, drawing blood. The pain didn't even faze her.

He was coming. She could hear him on her trail. He was uncaringly loud, crashing over brambles and fallen leaves. Shouting…something.

Don't listen! Stupidly she squeezed her eyes shut, fighting the urge to scream just to block out the sound of his voice. It didn't work. She could hear him anyway, bellowing through her brain.

"Loren, watch out!"

Her eyes flew open just in time to catch sight of a rock-studded slope—but it was too late to change course. Her boot caught on a slick patch of mud, throwing her balance…

"Loren!"

Wham!

A solid force caught her from behind, knocking her down. She waited for the fall. Braced herself for the pain—but all she felt instead was heat and strength that encased her like a shell. A hand went around the back of her head, pulling her against a muscled chest that smelled like sweat and musk and pine…

She could sense motion around her—the thud and crunch of a body striking the ground. But the only thing she *felt* was sweltering heat and the breath being knocked from her chest as they finally came to a stop.

"Shhhh." The gentle murmur matched the concern her rescuer held her with. "It's okay. I've got you. You're alright—"

"Let me go." Loren didn't even recognize the sound of her own voice.

Stiffly, she pushed out with her hands—or at least as far as she could, considering they were restrained by an unmovable force. She still managed to glimpse their surroundings from over his shoulder—they were at the foot of the hill, with her body pinned against McGoven's. He held her so tightly that she could feel his breath ruffling her hair, basting her skin.

Even now, that overwhelming power radiated from him. *Give in.*

"Get off me!" She tried to kick him. Pinch him. Dig her fingers into the skin of his chest.

He resisted her easily and adjusted his weight to pin her to the ground. "Loren, wait. Breathe." His tone was insistent. Gentle. "Listen to me. You don't understand—"

"Get OFF me!" Was that her voice? Whoever it was sounded wild. Insane.

"Listen to me!" He held her tighter, growling each word against her throat. "Loren, please—"

She bit him.

She didn't know how. It was like a switch being flipped. Her mind went blank the second she lunged, teeth bared. Hard muscle gave beneath her teeth, and she tasted blood…

His blood.

Her vision flashed red. Everything congealed into scarlet as a dangerous voice picked up volume as if whispered in her ear. *Bite, tear, scratch. Fight!*

No one can hold you back.

"Loren!"

The pain in his voice startled her from the daze. She blinked to find McGoven hovering over her. For once—maybe for the first time, since she'd known him—he looked afraid. No, *terrified* in a way that he hadn't been, even when she'd gone off on Xavier or after fending off the men in the clearing.

"Are you okay?" he asked.

"Get off me," she whispered, horrified. This time her fear wasn't directed at *him* but the half-moon-shaped wound on his chest, right above the collar of his shirt. Scarlet liquid welled from it, dripping ceaselessly.

God, what had she done?

She was shaking. She couldn't catch her breath and panic had her teeth chattering together in a way that had nothing at all to do with the cold.

She had attacked a police officer. Not only that, but she'd *bitten* him like some wild animal. She'd be lucky to turn twenty-one after spending a long stint in jail.

Oh, God.

"Let me go, please!" She twisted, trying to crawl away from him, hands digging into the mud.

He dragged her back and wrenched her around to face him. "Listen to me," he commanded in a tone she couldn't ignore. "It's alright. Just listen—"

"No! I won't!" The moment the shout left her mouth, she knew it was a mistake. Fighting back against him would *always* be a mistake.

She would never win.

His gaze narrowed into slits of silver, piercing her down to the bone. He was angry. Her defiance annoyed him. Maybe, strangest of all, she'd surprised him.

She waited for him to yell. Hit her. Maybe *bite* her? Grow fangs, sprout fur, and...

She tensed as he leaned down, his teeth bared. Rather than go for her throat, he pressed his mouth against hers.

31

*I*t wasn't anything cute and romantic, like in the movies.

He kissed her *hard*, forcing her lips apart and stabbing his tongue deep before she even knew what was happening. Instantly, she realized that his previous actions had been child's play. This was a taste of his true power—his ability to turn physical contact into a weapon. Every motion was demanding. Taking. *Punishing.* Urging her to give in, *submit*, just like before.

Submit. The demand echoed inside her head, as loud as a shout. *Give in!* He didn't give her the chance to refuse. His weight pinned her in place against the wet earth as his free hand fisted in her hair. At the same time, he freed her mouth and pressed his lips to her throat.

Mine.

Sharp teeth nicked the column of skin, drawing blood. From far away, Loren heard herself gasp. He bit her. Really *bit* her.

She should have struggled. Screamed. Not... Tilt her throat to give him better access. She *shouldn't* have dug her fingers into the earth as his heat washed through her on a searing wave.

It was wrong. But, she couldn't ignore the part of her that insisted this was right. *This* was what she'd been unconsciously waiting for since the moment she faced him in the kitchen, wrapped in a blanket.

Contact. Acknowledgment. Claiming.

I'm his, some primal part of her purred—it was about damn time he proved it. As if sensing her thoughts, his touch turned possessive. One hand eased beneath her waist, crushing her against the hardness of his chest.

Her breaths feathered. This was...different. She could feel every inch of him, rippling with a strength that could easily tear her into pieces if he wanted. The thought made a part of her lurch, and suddenly she couldn't breathe at all. Her mind spun—dizzy. She couldn't think.

But maybe that was a good thing?

These days, it seemed like she thought way too much. This was so much better. Her body moved purely on instinct— ironically, just the way he taught her—and it wanted more. For all his strength, he wasn't doing enough. Touching her enough. Kissing her *enough.*

His mouth avoided hers on purpose, deliberately skirting the bruises on her throat and her swollen bottom lip. His fingers, flexing against her waist, never traveled any lower than that.

He was holding back.

Annoyed, Loren raked her fingers through his hair, forcing his head from the curve of her shoulder. His eyes locked onto hers, so damn molten they glowed.

Something unspoken passed between them, almost too quickly to track. A new challenge? This mattered more than her submission—his acknowledgment. Suddenly desperate for it, she arched her spine, seeking out his warmth.

He stiffened. A tortured grimace contorted his expression as if he were going to war within himself. In a second, something won out, and his posture shifted. He dropped the gallant act. His hips slammed into hers, driving the air from her lungs. That prickling heat returned, pulsing down her spine, between her legs... They parted to make room for him, and her eyes rolled at the sensation. His position applied pressure in dangerous ways. Too much to bear. Not enough...

This time, when she lurched up, forcing her lips against his, he didn't hesitate. He gave her what she wanted—needed.

Pain mingled with the harsh heat enveloping her like a blanket, so searing that it was a struggle to even remember what *cold* was. Her bruised lip ached, but his tongue was already there, caressing the wound before it really had the chance to smart. All before ramming his tongue between her lips and utterly stealing her breath away.

More.

Loren couldn't fight the violent urge that had her hands turning into claws, pressing against his back, forcing him against her, arching her hips to seek more contact.

Mine. More, more, more!

Suddenly, even kissing him, so harshly she could taste blood —his or hers?—wasn't enough. She needed him. All of him pressed against her so tightly it *hurt*.

He seemed to be thinking along those same lines. With a grunt, he rolled over, wrenching her upright, forcing her up to straddle his waist, mouth never losing contact.

His tongue battled hers, taking deep greedy pulls. Then, his fingers were dragging at the zipper to her windbreaker, tearing the whole thing from her shoulders, before tugging at her thermal. And then that was gone, too.

All that was left was her bra, which suddenly seemed irritating against her skin. She wanted it off—needed it off. *Now.*

Her hands flew up to the back-clasp, fumbling with the fastening, but a pair of thick fingers were there to impatiently bat hers away. In seconds, he had the clasp undone, and Loren sighed in relief as the pale straps slid down her shoulders. She lifted her arms, expecting him to make the fabric disappear along with the rest of her clothes—

Wait.

She was so dazed that she wasn't sure if the word had been spoken out loud or inside her head. Suddenly, McGoven bucked his hips, knocking her aside.

"Shit!" He was on his feet in an instant.

Loren landed on her back. Before she could blink, a tanned hand was there, holding her bunched-up thermal before her. She reacted out of habit, sitting up to slip the shirt on over her head, only to become uncomfortably aware of her dangerously loose bra, threatening to slide from her arms.

She glanced down, almost in shock, at the bared flesh of her stomach as she wrestled the thermal on. Her windbreaker was a few paces away, crumpled on the grass, and Officer McGoven…

His eyes were so wide she half-expected them to fall out of his head.

"Shit," he hissed again, raking a hand through that wild hair. In two steps, he snatched up her jacket and tossed it in her direction. "Get dressed."

The next second, he took off, marching across the field at a pace that forced her to run to keep up. They were closer to the house than she realized. Within seconds, she caught sight of the barn and…a bright pink car currently zooming up the driveway.

Oh shit, Loren thought. Suddenly McGoven's haste made sense.

But how had he known?

She never got the chance to ask. They reached the base of the porch steps the exact moment Naomi Tanner stepped from her car.

"Hey." Her eyes were sharp, darting from her to Officer McGoven and back. "Am I interrupting something?"

Loren's cheeks flamed. Her hair was a ragged mess. Mud splattered her clothes, her hands. It was all she could do to wrestle her other arm through the sleeve of her windbreaker and zip it up.

But, if Naomi reached any conclusions, she didn't mention them aloud.

"I brought your work," she said. "So, um…"

She glanced at Officer McGoven and then down—namely to the thick tanned fingers Loren could still feel entwined with her own.

"I'll let you two get to it." McGoven let her hand fall and turned, taking the porch steps two at a time. "I have something to take care of," he muttered, before disappearing through the screen door so quickly it was left swinging on its hinges.

"Damn," Naomi stage whispered. "What the hell happened to you two?"

Cheeks flaming, Loren shoved her hands into her pockets. "Nothing."

Something had happened. Something that made her dizzy and dazed to think on. Made her clothes feel too tight—not tight *enough*.

It was confusing. Men were a taboo subject—as was sex. She'd never had a boyfriend, and any mention of the topic in school had been through gossip or clinical descriptions from teachers regarding the mating behaviors of animals. She had no frame of reference to draw upon. Nothing to contextualize the strange feelings rampaging through her.

Or him.

"Earth to Connors," Naomi snapped. "What is wrong with you?"

"Let's get this over with," Loren muttered, mounting the porch steps in a rush.

Inside, Officer McGoven wasn't anywhere in sight. As they entered the living room, a door slammed, and a quick glance out of the kitchen window revealed a dark figure marching across the field, heading straight for that battered pick-up truck. Seconds later, it took off so fast mud sprayed from the wheels.

"What the hell did *you* do to piss him off?" Naomi's snarky tones were grating on Loren's already frayed nerves.

Rather than answer, she snatched a cup from the sink and gulped from the rim. She nearly spit the water back out.

The flavor was tainted—tinged with the tastes already on her tongue—mud and pine and a sharp metallic hint that made her belly twist into knots.

Images filled her mind before she could help it, each one more damning than the last. *Her. Officer McGoven. Heat. Her clothes being expertly torn off.*

Her throat went dry at the memory of the feel of his lips on her throat—his teeth. She reached up, fingering the flesh right beneath her collar. It burned, overly sensitive, painful to the touch.

"What the hell is wrong with you?" Naomi wondered.

Loren tried her hardest to ignore her.

"Whatever—" She blinked to find Naomi dragging a schoolbook from her bag. "When you're done being all psycho, I brought math, and social studies. Let's get this over with."

She couldn't agree more.

*T*he latest "study session" with Naomi could be politely described as torturous. Not only due to the antics of the evil blond.

It was *him*—namely, his absence.

Where did he go?

She couldn't make sense of it. Aside from the weird moments of physical contact, Officer McGoven didn't seem interested in her more than to fulfill his heroic civic duty—and perform whatever he seemed to think he owed her as a lycan.

But when he kissed her…

There hadn't been any sense of "heroics" at all. Just a pure, raw hunger that couldn't be denied. *Lust,* Loren thought, blushing at the word choice. Not exactly the redeeming quality of a kindly, but much older, benefactor.

What about you? a part of her demanded. She hadn't exactly been so sweet and innocent, either. After all, she did bite him first.

"Lincoln."

"Huh?" Loren blinked in confusion, coming face to face with a scowling Naomi.

"*Lincoln* freed the slaves," the blond snapped before scribbling the answer down on a piece of notebook paper. That's right, Loren recalled. They were studying for a final, reviewing a study guide. "If I'm forced to come all the way out here every damn night, the least you could do is pay fucking attention."

Loren didn't waste her breath explaining that she hadn't asked for Naomi, in particular, to deliver her work in the first place. Instead, like they had every minute since the blond had shown up, her eyes darted to the kitchen window.

Night had already fallen, and it was raining again. There was no sign of that battered pick-up truck, or an impossibly tall man wearing mud-stained jeans, pulling into the driveway.

How long would he stay away, this time?

Until midnight?

Morning?

Would he even come back at all…

"Hey!"

Loren jumped as a pair of pink-tipped fingernails were snapped right in front of her face.

"I'm calling it quits tonight," Naomi declared, gathering her books. "I'll just come back tomorrow."

Mentally, Loren kicked herself for giving the blond another reason to stick around. Maybe she should have taken McGoven up on his offer to have the school replace her with someone else? Before she could latch onto the thought, Naomi was already marching through the front door without so much as a "ta-ta."

Loren shrugged and went back to staring from the window, watching as Naomi struggled to her car through the rain. The minutes passed by like seconds, until a furious Naomi reemerged, heading straight for the house.

Loren barely made it to the entryway before the blond barged inside.

"My car won't start," she hissed. "Is there a phone?"

"I don't know," Loren admitted. "This isn't my house."

"Fine," Naomi snarled, "I guess I'll just have to *walk* home, then. Let me borrow this—"

Before Loren could reply, she snatched a blue windbreaker from the coat hook by the door.

"Wait! That's mine."

"So?" Naomi tossed back, raising a blond eyebrow. "It's raining out. Unless you *want* me to get soaking wet and catch fucking pneumonia?"

Loren bit her lip. *It's mine,* a part of her hissed. Not just hers, but Officer McGoven's.

Still, she wasn't exactly inclined to invite Naomi in to wait out the storm, either. Heart heavy, she just watched the blond drag the zipper up beneath her chin and walk out into the rain.

"Wait," she called reluctantly. "Maybe you should wait?" It was a long way back into town.

"Not on your life," Naomi tossed back, letting the front door slam after her.

Loren stayed near the door, convinced the blond would return any minute, and demand McGoven gives her a ride. When a cry finally pierced the hum of the storm, she sighed and prepared to open the door.

"I told you, you should have—"

Naomi wasn't standing on the porch—or anywhere in sight, for that matter. Still, Loren could sense her nearby. Then her nostrils flared, picking up a scent through the rain. Something sharp. Familiar. Blood? Her brain identified it hesitantly. Maybe Naomi had fallen and hurt herself?

She was already racing onto the porch when she heard the scream.

32

*B*ill drove mindlessly while rain lashed at the windshield. Each thud of moisture resonated like a million tiny punches—the imagery was poetic irony. He *needed* to be punched. In the face. Or, maybe somewhere else?

The bulge straining against the front of his jeans? At least then, he might be able to think of anything but her.

There were a million other issues to contend with—like what happened this morning. His heart panged as he recalled the present left on his doorstep. It served him right for venturing beyond his property. Though, he hadn't sensed another lycan in the area—whoever was behind the act must have used a human to deliver their message. Thankfully, Loren hadn't noticed. She'd even bought his lie, but sooner or later, she'd learn the truth. They—the bastards who sent that mangled deer—would come calling in person.

It was an old custom—the reckoning mark. To their kind, every animal's life was sacred. Killing a doe in such a brutal way was the biggest insult imaginable. A warning.

Someone wanted to pick a fight. The Eislanders? Lukka wasn't the sort to resort to such an archaic method of communication. No, he'd send one of his peons with a message instead. Obviously, the men from the woods had friends willing to avenge their cruelty.

But they could try. Loren was *his*...

He could still taste her. Sense her. Smell her. But the attraction went well beyond natural interest. It was one thing to have initiated the mating bond to *protect* Loren Connors—he didn't regret it—couldn't regret it.

But that didn't mean that he had to *maintain* it. Lukka or not, he should have broken the bond the moment she woke up and found some way to explain. Then he should have put her on a bus to a city far away, where she could live as a human and go on with her life.

She had no idea what was happening to her— what *had* happened to her. It made him sick just thinking of it. Or maybe that was just her memories crowding the back of his head? They were poison, though the girl seemed to have no idea what he'd taken from her that night in the woods—all the horror he'd just lifted off her mind like a telepathic vacuum.

The fear. The murder. The memories. *Especially* the memories. He never went through them, but they were dark

—he could tell that much. Seeing the scars on her wrist confirmed that suspicion.

Her file, tucked away in some back corner of the precinct, didn't contain much. Just a general list of the places she used to live, some mention of a mother's suicide, and some vague annotations to a child abuse case.

Even her mother's name, Eveline Connors, didn't ring a bell —and names held more meaning to lycans than humans. If she had belonged on Black Mountain, he would remember her. Every packmate held a place in his mind, even Fred Connors.

Loren, however, was an enigma. The funny thing was, even after nearly a week, he still couldn't bring himself to type her name into the damn database and research her in detail. Her past, and whatever horrors it contained, should come from her—nowhere else. He would wait until she was able to do so without the mating bond driving her emotions.

A pang of guilt stabbed through him as he realized how different things might have been if he'd taken the time to interact with her before this whole mess. At the time, he'd told himself that it was better to keep her at arm's length. As recently as a few days ago, he still held the belief that distance between them would make it easier when Lukka came to integrate her into the pack. After all, once she left for Black Mountain, it wasn't like he'd ever see her again.

But now…

There was a part of him that craved to learn everything about her. Good and bad. What made her tick? What made those hazel eyes widen in fear if he came too close to her? What haunted her nightmares?

Oh, he could guess that Fred Connors had something to do with it—but there was more to it. *Way* more. And every day, it was getting harder to maintain that boundary between them. Though, hell, he'd pretty much smashed that "boundary" anyway.

What happened in the field had been a mistake.

He meant only to help her. Stir up her instincts and give her a temporary Alpha to follow until he could puzzle out what to do next. It was a good idea in theory. He could coax her to shift, diminish the mating bond somewhat, and maybe finally be able to *think* without her damn thoughts in his head.

It should have been easy to force submission from one little female. Until she fought back—fuck, she *more* than fought back.

Frowning, he took one hand off the steering wheel to brush the bleeding wound on his chest. She'd bitten him deeply, and his heart thundered as he remembered the wild little sound she'd made, right before she had.

He may not have been a genius, but he knew it wasn't normal—*she* wasn't normal.

He could sense her at odds with herself. The meek little girl she presented to the world was struggling to resist something deep inside that couldn't be controlled. Something wild he could sometimes glimpse behind those hazel eyes.

And despite his years of mastery over his lycan side, Bill still couldn't ignore the part of him that had risen up in challenge at that. It was like the urge of a predator to give chase when prey turned tail and ran. Instinct so ingrained it was damn near impossible to resist, not that he would fall back on that stupid excuse.

He still shouldn't have kissed her. The mating bond was driving her, confusing her. She didn't know what she wanted.

And it was his fault.

Would she hate him for what he'd done, when she eventually learned the truth?

Probably.

But he couldn't bring himself to feel an ounce of guilt— everything he'd done had been entirely to save her. From Fred Connors. From herself.

Or at least, that was what he'd believed. Until he started having pesky little thoughts that proclaimed the exact opposite. Thoughts that whispered things like *mine*, whenever he caught sight of her, small and pale, with that brown hair falling down her shoulders.

Mine.

The thought was in his head now—his mind—craving her, when he should have tried to push her away. She wasn't the only one susceptible to the mating bond. It was changing *him* as well, making him think very dangerous things. Like, maybe it wasn't *so bad* if she stayed?

Lukka didn't want her, and even if the bastard did, there was no way in *hell* he'd let her go—

Suddenly, he slammed his foot against the brakes, coming to a stop in the middle of a country road.

Something was wrong. He could sense it in the air. Taste it in his throat. Without thinking, he wrenched the truck into reverse and sped toward his farm, pushing the battered pick-up to the limit. 70. 80. 90...

Impatience pulled at his gut, urging him on.

Loren. At the thought of her, he parked the car on the side of the road, leaving the keys in the ignition, and took off on foot, ripping off clothing as he went. He was working on removing his pants when he heard the first scream.

It was faint—he was about a mile off from his property— but the sound pierced him down to the bone.

On the spot, he invoked the shift with his jeans still entangled around his legs.

Son of a bitch... It hurt like hell. Muscle tore. Bones shattered and reformed. His legs strained against the confining fabric as they compacted and stretched into long lines of sinewy muscle.

But he didn't care. He took off racing through the fields, hating himself for ever leaving her alone in the first place.

33

*L*oren raced onto the porch.

She couldn't see Naomi anywhere. Not by her car, or down the path leading to the road. *She probably just broke a heel*, a part of her scoffed. But unease had her inching forward, regardless.

Something is wrong. The ominous feeling unfurled in her gut as she leaped from the porch without thinking. A few more steps carried her down the driveway. She didn't have her boots, and icy rain lashed at her hair, but that sinking feeling drove her forward, past the front yard and across the field.

"Naomi?" Her voice barely rose above the howl of the wind and rain. "Naomi!"

It was so dark. She could barely see a few feet in front of her while her eyes adjusted. Out here, surrounded by wilderness, she realized how stupid it had been for anyone to venture this far alone.

"Naomi!"

Loren's heart started to pound with dread.

Even before she saw *them*.

Four men stood in a line beyond the trees that edged the clearing. They faced the direction of the house, bodies shrouded in shadow, but...

Beside them was a wolf. Huge and hulking, it hunched a few paces away from the others, its fur a deep brown.

And even *that* wasn't what made her gasp as she skidded to a stop, heels dragging in the earth.

A body lay on the ground before them, so limp and motionless, it could have been part of the environment. Minus the dark navy windbreaker and hot pink miniskirt covering a pair of tanned legs.

No. Loren froze, feeling the back of her throat clench. "Naomi!"

The blond wasn't moving. But that wasn't even the worst part. Someone stood in front of her. Someone lean and wiry, with a head crowned by wild dark hair.

They were bleeding. The smell rode on the air—way too strong to have been just from a minor injury. It didn't take much of a stretch to realize that they had gone up against that massive wolf, and were dangerously close to having lost.

No. Fear washed over Loren like ice. It couldn't be him.

He couldn't be hurt.

Her heart fluttered as she ran, ignoring the danger. The closer she came, the more she realized that the man wasn't tall enough to be McGoven.

But she recognized him.

"This isn't the way," Micha called, in a voice that carried across the field. "This isn't right—"

"Don't talk about things you don't understand, pup," one of the men tossed back, arms crossed casually over his chest, while the wolf crouched in wait.

He had to be the leader, judging from how the others were grouped around him. Even the wolf seemed to be awaiting orders, growling low in the back of its throat.

"This has nothing to do with the old laws," the man went on, taking a step forward to reveal an angular face crowned by blood-red hair. "This is about retribution, plain and simple."

Retribution?

Loren gaped at Naomi. What could she have done to warrant being attacked in the middle of the woods?

Not her, some part of her whispered. *She's not the one they wanted.*

"The rogue killed one of our own," another man pitched in, his mouth twisted in a snarl. "The laws give us the right to recoup the loss. We followed protocol. Gave clear warning. The bastard sent a woman to face us instead."

"Though," the first man said with a shrug, "it seems as though we've *miscalculated*."

Loren could barely see him through the oppressive dark, but she could sense the exact moment his eyes locked onto *her*. His gaze was even colder than the icy breeze chilling her skin.

Glacial.

"L-leave her out of this," Micha stammered. He looked even worse the closer she came. His entire body was shaking, and his ragged sweatpants were filthy, and mud stained.

Or, bloodstained. Crimson liquid leaked from a gash in his left leg, and it seemed to take every ounce of strength he had just to stay on his feet. But he did. His gaze was steady, firmly fixed on all three men.

"This isn't about her," he said.

"It's not," the leader admitted with a shrug. "But *she* is the easiest way to get to *him*. Now stay back, pup. This has nothing to do with you." He moved to take a step, and everything seemed to happen at once.

Micha stumbled toward him. The wolf snarled, and Loren didn't think.

She reacted.

"No!" The cry was directed at Micha, who gaped as she shoved him back and positioned herself in front of him.

The four opposing figures were bulky, sporting varying degrees of muscle—and unlike the men from the clearing, she could tell that they weren't your average thugs.

They were organized. Dangerous. Should she have been afraid?

Probably—but, for some reason, she *wasn't.*

Not even when the wolf growled in warning, raising its haunches.

Silly little girl, she could picture them all thinking. *So damn naive.*

They don't matter, that inner voice warned, louder than ever. *This is about power. Focus on the leader, only him. He dictates their next move.*

For now, he seemed content to watch her. "This is nothing personal between you and me," he explained, sounding almost calm despite his previous threat. "Your mate killed one of our own—this is the law."

"This is stupid!" Micha snarled, appearing by her side. Loren could hear his ragged breathing, and she just hoped he wasn't stupid enough to try and fight. "She isn't a part of this! Those men were going to kill her!"

"Not correct," the leader said simply. "The man he killed was a trusted friend of Alpha Loreck—" His voice took on a lethal edge. "And he was *murdered* in cold blood."

"W-what?" Micha's confusion matched Loren's perfectly.

If this "trusted" friend was one of the men who'd attacked her in the clearing, there wasn't anything "innocent" about him. Still, these men didn't seem to be joking. Or lying. She could hear the honesty in their leader's voice.

"Alpha Loreck," he continued, "demands retribution. Which we are more than happy to act out on the rogue himself, if you desire. Where is he?"

"No." Loren didn't even realize that she'd spoken until the man's head swiveled in her direction.

Stupid girl! A part of her hissed. *What are you doing?*

What you should do, her inner voice murmured. *Assert your place. This is your land. Defend it!*

How? She had no clue. A cold sweat dripped down her spine. She couldn't breathe. The leader seemed aware of her weakness. He took her in with one skeptical gaze, raising a scarlet eyebrow.

"I'm guessing you're willing to suffer in his place?" He shrugged. "No matter—"

"Leave her out of this," Micha insisted, grappling for her shoulder. "She didn't do anything!"

As weak as he was, it was easy to shrug him off.

Completely devoid of emotion, Loren took a step, then another, crossing the short distance that separated her from the group of men. Her mind went blank. She didn't have time to process the fear.

"Leave," she told him in a voice she barely even recognized. It was cold. Hard. Icy. Nothing at all like the trademark Loren Connors' timid little whisper.

"I don't think so, pup," the red-haired man replied, with a shake of his head. "Your mate overstepped the boundaries. There must be consequences. Bill knows this."

Bill. Mate. The words bounced around the inside of her skull, but she pushed them away—*later.*

"*You* overstepped the boundaries," Loren insisted. Somehow, her voice didn't shake, easily rivaling his.

"Loren!" Micha sounded terrified in comparison. "Loren, get back—"

No. This time she didn't even waste her breath saying the word aloud. She just tilted her head back, ignoring the rain that slid down her forehead. With a confidence she couldn't explain, she met the red-haired man's mocking stare and held it.

Prove yourself, that voice in her head growled. *He is nothing to us. Nothing.*

He had brown eyes. Sharp and vibrant, they reflected the shadows and seemed to glow. *Animal eyes,* a part of her whispered.

But she didn't turn away—not that she could. Something deep inside forced her to keep the eye contact. *Don't back down now,* it warned. *Show no fear.*

"*You* are going to leave," she said, though her voice was even louder. A stranger's. "Now."

She heard Micha make a sound that could have been a groan. "Loren…"

The red-haired man didn't seem to mind the challenge. The corner of his mouth twitched like he wanted to laugh, but…

As time went on, his gaze narrowed, darkened, and as even more seconds passed, they widened again.

Then, he frowned.

The entire while, Loren never let her gaze slip. She kept it honed on him like a laser. This moment reminded her of middle school, where mental games of tug of war ran rampant. The strangest thing was that she wasn't the one struggling to stay upright in this little game.

He was.

It was like the reverse of her and McGoven. She could sense the fight in him. See his struggle in the way his mouth twitched almost imperceptibly. Then, slowly, but surely, a bead of sweat dripped down his forehead to mingle with the rain.

All of it added up to one conclusion that should have been *impossible.*

She was winning.

Of course, I am, some shadowy part of her insisted, almost bored. *He is no match.*

But the man didn't seem to accept the fact. He scowled, his upper lip pulling back from his teeth. It was like she could read his mind. She should have turned away, he assumed. Meekly submitted to die.

The hell I will. In a rush of determination, she took a step forward, not surprised a bit when the man took one step back.

He was close to breaking. She knew it. Relished in it.

Give in, she willed him, without ever saying it out loud.

She didn't have to.

The world around them faded away, leaving just the two of them locked in a battle for which he was no match. All at once, one word popped onto the tip of her tongue, and she found herself voicing it without any hesitation. "Submit—"

Grrrr...!

The sound cut through everything, as loud as the roar of a jet engine. Loren knew, even before the stocky body of a black wolf appeared over the crest of the hill, just who it belonged to.

34

McGoven growled again. Then, in a blur of shadow, he inserted himself between her and the intruders with one bounding leap.

Loren found herself pushed back by his bulk, and she stumbled, right into the hard chest of Micha, who maneuvered her behind him.

They waited.

The red-haired man watched them all—only he didn't look so smugly self-righteous anymore. He looked shaken. Loren didn't miss the way his eyes kept cutting to her. Partly confused. Partly…fearful?

Leave! In his current form, McGoven couldn't say the word aloud, so he just growled instead—but there was no missing what he meant.

"This isn't over," the red-haired man insisted. His tone kept it from seeming cliché. It was a promise. A statement of fact.

This isn't over.

"You killed a member on pack territory, rogue. Sooner or later, you will have to pay."

Like shadows, he and the three others turned and left.

But the ordeal was far from over.

It was like a switch had been flipped inside of her. In an instant, Loren deflated, sinking to the ground by Naomi's prone form.

"Naomi!"

There was blood. So much blood that she could smell it, thick and heavy and fresh.

"One of them bit her." The voice was Micha's, spoken from over her shoulder. "I tried to stop it…I—"

"She's not dead!" Somehow, Loren knew that even before she reached out for a pale throat and felt a pulse.

It wasn't very strong, though. While one side of her neck remained whole, the other side, hidden beneath a lank section of blond hair, was wet and dark…

"We need to get her to a hospital—"

Before she could even try to reason out *how*, a dark figure appeared beside her, gathering Naomi in his arms as easily as if she weighed nothing.

"Come on," Bill's voice was gruff. Loren didn't have to glance up to know that he was naked. All she did was lurch to her feet, too horrified by everything else to blush at the sight.

He took off, heading for the house, and Loren followed, croaking out to Micha, "Come on!"

He blinked and lurched into motion, heavily favoring his uninjured leg.

It seemed to take an eternity before they reached the house —though given the way McGoven moved, it could have only been minutes. He was already inside by the time she mounted the porch steps.

He had slung Naomi across the couch and began moving around the living room, flicking on the lights at random. With each one, Loren shuddered as the extent of the girl's injuries became apparent.

She'd been bitten in the neck. *More* than bitten—her throat seemed...

Torn.

Blood was everywhere. On him. On her. It even painted a scarlet trail out into the hall, staining the leather of the couch. Loren held her breath just to keep from gagging.

"Why?" she croaked. "Why would they do this?"

Of course, she already knew the answer. They had mistaken Naomi for *her*.

It was her fault.

"I tried to stop them—"

She turned to find Micha, hovering over the cusp of the living room, his eyes apologetically wide. At the sound of his voice, McGoven whipped around.

"What the hell are you doing here—"

"He tried to save her." Loren didn't even realize that she'd spoken out loud until McGoven cut his gaze in her direction. "He tried to save me."

The man didn't look convinced. "What the hell are you doing here?" he demanded of Micha, though his gaze never left her face.

"I told you," Micha insisted, "I'm not leaving until I've repaid my debt. And it's a good thing I was here, too. They weren't waiting for an invitation."

Bill's jaw tightened, and his eyes flashed with a mixture of rage and...guilt? When he spoke again, his tone was deeper. Cold. "They were Eislanders?"

Micha gave a sharp nod of his head. "I think so. They said you killed one of them—"

"I killed *four* of them," McGoven corrected without batting an eyelash. "But...they didn't seem like Loreck Eislander's type. What the hell did they want?"

"Revenge," Loren said, shuddering as the word left her mouth. "Either you or me, they didn't care."

"I wouldn't have let them touch her," Micha insisted heatedly. "I swear."

"Yeah," McGoven bellowed, "a lot of damn good you did. And you—" He turned to her again, his gaze demanding. "What the hell were you thinking? Do you know what he would have done to you? Ripped out your fucking throat!"

Loren faced his tirade without an explanation in mind. The truth "I mentally sparred with the man," didn't make sense.

Eventually, McGoven just sighed, raking his hand through his hair, as he glanced down at the motionless Naomi.

"Fuck."

Viewing the body in better lighting, Loren was sure a pulse had been entirely in her imagination.

"We need to call an ambulance," she said weakly. Deep down, she knew it wouldn't matter.

No one could survive a wound like that. The blank look McGoven gave her pretty much proved it.

"Loren…"

"No!" She backed away slowly, shaking her head. "We need to do something!"

It wasn't like she harbored any kind of love for Naomi, but no one deserved to die like this. In almost a week, Loren had already seen way too damn much of death.

No more.

"Do something." The words could have just been a pathetic form of denial—until she remembered… "You can save her, can't you?"

He could bite her.

"No!" McGoven's tone was firm, but that didn't keep Loren from stumbling across the room toward him.

"Please! You can save her! Do it! Please."

He looked away, his expression torn. "I can't."

"You know the rules," Micha said softly from the doorway, seeming to agree with him. "You turn a human without permission, and it's treason. Lukka won't like it."

"I know," McGoven hissed, but his gaze flashed as if that fact annoyed him. Then he sighed.

"If I do this… It won't be some simple good deed. Her life will be forever changed. There will be no going back."

A part of Loren stirred in acknowledgment, sensing exactly what he meant—and more. But… Her voice was small, "We can't just let her die."

"Turn around," McGoven snarled. "Close your eyes…don't look."

She scrambled to obey, eyeing the window and the storm raging outside. A second later, she heard a growl.

And then the snap of breaking bone and ripping flesh.

35

*L*oren woke up, frozen solid…except for the heat radiating from an arm slung across her waist. With a sigh, she relaxed into the embrace—until she realized her companion wasn't the man she'd become accustomed to waking up beside. They smelled wrong. Like smoke and rain instead of pine, along with a vague odor that reminded her of a wet dog.

Alarmed, she opened her eyes and rolled over—coming face to face with a boyish figure, their features half-hidden beneath a mop of curly hair. Micha. He was asleep, his chest rising and falling with gentle snores.

That's right, she remembered. They camped out in the living room to keep watch over Naomi. She and Micha had, anyway.

Bill left sometime before dawn. The dark glint in his eye warned against asking questions. Though, there were plenty that needed to be asked.

Enough secrecy. The need for answers loomed overhead like a storm cloud. She'd go insane without some kind of clarity. It had been hard enough keeping her mouth shut last night. All she'd done was watch.

And hear. Those horrific sounds still haunted her—the cracking of Naomi's bones being wrenched back into place —her neck had been broken during the attack, Bill explained afterward. He had to fix the fatal injury first...

Then, he bit her.

There wasn't any dramatic pause or fanfare. He merely hunched over that pale throat, teeth sinking deep. Then he cut himself, forcing his blood into Naomi's mouth with almost clinical precision.

A spoonful of sugar helps the medicine go down, a part of her snickered, though the situation wasn't funny in the least. After that, all they could do was wait. For what? Loren didn't know.

In the end, she and Micha must have passed out on the floor—though she distinctively remembered being on *opposite* sides of the room. *Not good,* a part of her whispered, cringing at the feel of him so close. *He shouldn't touch me.*

The fear itched at the back of her mind but, for now, she had bigger things to worry about. Sick with dread, she lifted her head and glanced over at Naomi. The blond still lay motionless on the couch.

In bits and pieces, the events of last night came flooding back. Naomi should have been dead—and the only reason she wasn't was because… Well, because a police officer, who just so happened to sprout four legs in his spare time, turned her into a werewolf.

How would she react? Even begin to understand? After all, it wasn't every day that you woke up in a stranger's house as something…

Else.

Tell me about it, Loren thought with a sigh, as she gingerly disentangled herself from Micha's grip and crawled to her feet. She just hoped that the blond's bitchy demeanor hadn't been just an act. After the events of last night, Naomi would need all the strength she could muster.

In the pale daylight streaming in from the bay window, she certainly didn't look any better. Dried blood splattered her designer ensemble. That expensively highlighted hair was a tangled mess. Her throat…

The wounds hadn't miraculously healed like in all the TV shows. They were still there. Still fresh. Still bleeding.

Loren's nostrils flared with the grisly stench, and she couldn't bear to look anymore. Eyeing the floor instead, she tried to rationalize her current reality. Relief and guilt went to war in the pit of her stomach. Within seconds, one emotion dominated. *My fault.*

This was all *her* fault.

What would happen to Naomi after this? She had no damn idea—

Thump. At the sudden noise, she realized that she hadn't woken up entirely by accident. Someone appeared in the entryway as she crept forward. Not an intruder. This man was painfully familiar, his shoulders hunched, his gray eyes glowing in the pale daylight.

Had he spent all night out in the fields again? It sure looked like it. He was barefoot, wearing another grungy pair of sweats. His gaze swept over her, then homed in on the still sleeping Micha.

His voice broke the silence barely louder than a whisper. "He touched you."

The low observation made her heart flutter. There was no point in denying it. Surprisingly enough, he grimaced, his nostrils flaring. There was a line he could have voiced but never did.

I'll break him. Destroy him. I'll kill him. With a hard swallow, he seemed to bite those threats back. Why? Because whatever happened between them in the fields was a mistake. He regretted it.

"You're starving." His voice fell flat as he changed the subject and headed into the kitchen before Loren's disappointment could fully resonate. "I'll make you something to eat."

Instead of fixing her a serving of tuna, he leaned against the center island, face in his hands. The sight pulled at something in her. Something that had her stumbling forward to the opposite side of the counter.

Once across from him, she couldn't bring herself to speak, let alone touch him.

He didn't acknowledge her, regardless. Didn't even move—but when he released a heavy sigh, she knew that his next words were directed at her.

"I'm not going to sugarcoat it," he began in a voice that rumbled with exhaustion. "This is *bad*, Loren." He withdrew his hand from his face, meeting her gaze. "You can't even *begin* to understand how serious. I've broken about fifty unspoken rules by doing what I did. I've put you in danger. Naomi…"

"You couldn't let her die," Loren whispered. "You couldn't just—"

"I *should* have." His tone was brutally frank. Honest. "You have *no idea* how hard life will be for her after this. She isn't like you—*mades* aren't entitled to the same status in a pack as a born lycan. They must earn their way in. Usually, their only chance is to be accepted by the pack of the wolf that originally bit them."

And it went without saying that wasn't an option in Naomi's case.

"Fuck… I should have let her die." His tone was cold, devoid of emotion.

"No!" Loren didn't know what possessed her to reach out, grabbing his free hand with her own. His fingers were cold and slightly damp—but they automatically tightened around hers with a strength that made something flutter deep inside.

"You couldn't just let her die," she insisted.

He didn't seem so sure, however. For a long minute, he watched her. Then he pulled himself to his full height. Loren didn't even have time to react before she found herself gently steered around the center island until she stood directly in front of him.

Her pulse raced. Up close, he looked even worse. Exhaustion dripped from him in waves, or maybe it was just rainwater? He was drenched, his hair plastered to his forehead. Still, he had never smelled more like pine. *Wild.*

She inhaled him deeply, drawing strength from his presence. Now more than ever, she felt convinced that he had done the right thing. Not for her, or even Naomi—but for *him.*

"You couldn't let her die," she insisted for the final time, voicing what she could sense through whatever invisible bond tethered them together. Like his anger, she was aware of something else lurking within him. An emotion he seemed determined to suppress.

Even if she hadn't begged him to intervene…he might have done so anyway.

"W-what's going to happen now?" she asked when he didn't speak. Her eyes darted over to the living room. "Will she—"

"It could happen slow." McGoven's hoarseness threw her off. He sounded drained. "It could take months—years. Her body and mind will change, but by the time the lycan blood takes full effect, she'll…be different. It could drive her insane. She'll be dangerous."

Loren winced. Naomi, sans claws, wasn't a pretty picture. The thought of her being capable of turning into a wolf, even *half* the size of McGoven was…

"There is another way," McGoven began carefully, but his tone had her stomach twisting into knots.

She glanced down to see that he still held her hand, and his grip tightened as if to make sure that—despite whatever he said next—she couldn't pull away.

"H-How?"

He sighed. "*Mades* need discipline; someone there to make sure they don't fall out of line."

He was dancing around the term, letting her fill in the blanks. *An Alpha*, she thought. As if reading her mind, McGoven nodded slowly, just once.

"But it isn't like I'm on good terms with too many of those. And…if *I* do this myself…I might as well jab a silver stake through my own chest right now—save someone else the trouble. There can be no turning back—" His eyes flickered a pale shade of gray. Again, Loren suspected he'd already made up his mind. "Out of everything I've done...this is the *one* thing that will serve as a direct challenge to Lukka. Something he won't be able to ignore."

"Why...why did those men—" She broke off. *You know the answer to that,* a part of her hissed. "Who were they?"

McGoven frowned. "Eislanders."

The name sounded familiar. Kyle had mentioned it, the night she'd been attacked.

"Loreck Eislander's pack has always rivaled ours," McGoven went on. "He's older, more inclined to fall back on the old laws. Lukka never really humored him; he's younger with less patience for the elders. But while their territory is roughly the same size, the Eislanders outnumber us two to one when it comes to fully grown males. Loreck doesn't tolerate any sign of aggression near his boundary."

Like four men being murdered on his doorstep. While she didn't know much about the "Lycan" way of life, she knew her father—and he'd gone ballistic at even the *thought* of having McGoven in his house. "What are we going to do?"

"We?" McGoven gave her an odd look. Suddenly, he released her hand and took a single step back. "*You* aren't going to do anything. This is *my* fight."

"No." Loren's cheeks flamed, but she didn't rush to apologize. Not even as he cocked his head, his gaze molten.

Disobeying him felt more weighty than just mouthing off. A corner of his mouth twitched. His eyelids lowered. Restraint alone was what kept him from snapping back with a command—she knew it in her soul. *You will listen to me.*

"I told you to do it," she added in a rush. "I should be involved in the consequences."

He didn't say anything for a long time. He just stood there. Close enough that his heat leached through her, as blazing as a furnace. Then, all at once, he sighed and turned for the back door, motioning with a jerk of his head for her to follow.

It was chilly out. Loren found herself shifting closer to McGoven—*because of his heat*, she told herself. Nothing more. On bare feet, she was clumsy, stumbling into him. He stiffened at the contact, but to her shock, he didn't recoil. His focus remained on the fields, scanning each one for any hint of danger.

"I have to make her submit to me," he said finally.

"H-how?" Though, she figured she already knew the answer. He'd chase her down. Pin her to the ground. And kiss her?

McGoven shrugged. "I tell her to. The growing lycan inside of her should recognize my strength and give in. If not, I could always use force."

"F-Force?" A tremor sank into her voice.

McGoven's head swiveled in her direction as if the mere hint of her unease distracted him from anything else. Even his own safety.

"Nothing that would harm her," he clarified. "The more heightened her emotions, the more susceptible she'll be to my compulsion. My will. Anything I do would *only* be to help her gain control of her lycan side before it could overwhelm her. That is all."

"Is that what you tried to do to me?"

"Yes." He looked away from her, his jaw tight. "It's easier to invoke the shift under the compulsion of an Alpha. It's how children are brought into lycan form for the first time. After that, it's a matter of practice and honing the skill to master it on their own."

"But it didn't work," she blurted. "I didn't...submit."

And that's the problem, a part of her whispered—even before she saw the odd look he gave her. His strength was obvious —undeniable. When he finally looked at her head-on, however, nothing in the world could have prepared her for the expression on his face.

He looked broken. A man at his wit's end. "Loren, I think you might be the exception in this equation. It might even be my fault. There... There is something you should know—"

"Sorry to interrupt!"

They both turned, springing apart, to find Micha in the doorway to the kitchen, leaning on his uninjured leg. The wound looked even worse than it had last night. For the moment, at least, his attention seemed to be somewhere else.

"Um...*she's* awake."

Sure enough, pained moans came from inside the house. Then a high-pitched curse promptly followed by a scream.

36

*E*ric Lanister had lived long enough—seen far
enough—that few things surprised him. Sworn to
the fiercest pack in the country, it took more than
bloodshed to turn his head. So was the life of a lycan.
Brutal. Predictable.

But... The sight of a little female—no bigger than his
shoulder—demanding submission from one of his men...

He couldn't shake it. It was more than an anomaly. It was
unheard of.

Her sex wasn't the sticking point—women were bred in the
same den of violence as men. At least under Loreck. No. It
was her youth that puzzled him. Her confidence. Rarely had
he seen a pup so young with such potential to lead. Not
since one man who belonged to a rival pack—and had since
failed to live up to his potential.

To be fair, Michael—the man she targeted—was an idiot.
An overconfident, egotistical, brain-dead *idiot*, but where he

379

lacked in smarts, the fool more than made up for in brute strength. Loreck had tasked him with leading the expedition to confront the rogue purely on a technicality— the man had been a close friend of Jamal's. It was custom, after all, to let the loved ones of those slain seek retribution on their behalf. Hurting for said vengeance, Michael may have gotten a little carried away. They were only supposed to confront the man, after all.

The female and the other rogue had been casualties of war —though, Eric wasn't ashamed to admit that he would have easily killed them all. An eye for an eye, it was their way. But, then that little female had stared them down without flinching.

Without betraying one damn ounce of fear.

Who the hell was she? Puzzled, he pictured those haunting eyes—a shade not quite green, or brown, with a hint of gold sprinkled in. A gaze that even *Eric*—whose position was second only to the Alpha—had been uneasy to face head-on. He couldn't escape the feeling that it was *familiar,* somehow. He had seen eyes like that before. A gaze just as fierce and unfaltering.

But where?

"Tell me again why you *didn't* kill him?"

Eric flinched at the disapproving tone. With a sigh, he respectfully inclined his head toward the man sitting across from an oak desk in the center of the room.

Eislanders weren't concerned with pomp and circumstance like other packs—Black Mountain paramount among them. The Alpha held court in an office off the main communal building, in a large space with very little decoration. Aside from the desk, some bookshelves, and a bearskin rug thrown across the wooden floor.

As far as he was concerned, there didn't need to be. A true leader spent more time out of any dwelling than inside it. This study more than sufficed as the base of operations for the Eislander territory. The man sitting behind the desk made the place seem just as regal as any King's throne room.

Dark brown hair, speckled with gray, framed a face that could have been chiseled from stone. The cold expression was a hallmark of the man in question—one of many traits that made him a force to be reckoned with.

"It was one against four," Loreck Eislander went on, voice deceptively calm, as he shuffled a stack of paperwork over the desk's surface. "Tell me again how that ends up in a retreat?"

"Four against *three*," Eric corrected. He may have been the man's Beta, but that didn't make him any less intimidated. Called here like a naughty child, he resisted the urge to wring his hands and fidget. "There was another rogue, and the female there with him as well. Not to mention a *human*. Besides," he added quickly. "The rogue would be driven to protect his mate."

Making him stronger than about *ten* wolves, but he had enough sense not to say it out loud.

Loreck, however, wasn't impressed. The Alpha didn't look up from his paperwork, but Eric could sense his annoyance, buzzing from him in waves.

"Fine," he said simply. "Then *you* can explain to Janelle and Robin why justice for Jamal was denied."

Eric went cold at the mention of Jamal's mate and child. The man had been found a couple days ago, near the boundary of the territory, attacked before he even had the chance to shift.

It just didn't make sense. Out of all the bastards deserving of being murdered, why *Jamal*? The man had never picked a battle with anyone he couldn't handle. Not to mention, what the hell was a rogue doing on their territory anyway?

Something doesn't make sense…

"That's the thing," Eric blurted, thinking on his feet. "The other rogue kept mentioning an attack. Said the murder was justified."

Which, again, just didn't make any damn sense—Jamal wouldn't harm a fly. But, there were bruises all over the girl, and *someone* would have had to get her mate riled enough to kill…

"Justified?" Suddenly, Loreck glanced up, gaze sharp. "Did you check into it?"

"Of-of course," Eric said, shifting uneasily on his feet. "Trevor and Lyla reported some strange noises by the west border the night of the murder, but a scout of the area revealed nothing out of the ordinary."

Nothing besides a trampled field and some strange scents—but at the time, he'd just assumed that some idiots from that fool Lukka's pack had decided to push the boundary too far.

Again.

But, now…

"Something doesn't seem right—if you don't mind me saying," he added hastily as Loreck's gaze narrowed. But, it was too late to clam up now. Taking a deep breath, he decided to lay it all on the table. "Why would that rogue kill Jamal? If he has a grudge against *anyone*, don't you think it would be Lukka?"

The man had exiled him, after all. Not to mention, that the asshole had already made more than his fair share of enemies, despite being Alpha for a few short years.

The corner of Loreck's mouth twitched up into something that could have been a smile if the dark emotion in those hazel eyes wasn't all wrong.

Fierce.

"Well, it's a good thing he's *here* so that we can ask him, isn't it?" Before Eric could react, the man stood and raised his voice. "Let him in."

The wooden double doors to the study opened from the outside. Then, as if, out of some bad television show drama, Lukka strolled in through the doorway, head held high.

Eric struggled to smother his disgust—at least out of the guise of politeness. Lukka would smell his dislike, regardless.

The man was young. He had an almost pretty face, set by two blue eyes and a mop of curly blond hair. Eric figured that he'd seen Barbie Dolls with more spunk, though rumors claimed the man could hold his own, despite his looks.

But he was young. *Too* young for Eric's liking. Even worse, he was arrogant and seemed to think that his youth entitled him to exert his will outside of his pack. To turn his back on the old ways. To steal.

Upstart little tyke, Eric thought as the man walked past him. In his day, arrogance like that got rewarded with a beating. To submission.

"Loreck," Lukka called by way of greeting, moving to clasp the older Alpha on the shoulder.

Loreck didn't return the favor. He only stood back, keeping the desk between the two of them to create a distance that spoke of the tension between them more than any words could.

"We have a problem," Loreck began, in a firm tone. "Not *only* is it your constant encroachment onto my land, or the way that pack of yours has been using our resources without permission…"

He let the words hang for a second—judging the young pup's reaction. In the years of the old Alpha, one might say that the Eislanders and Black Mountain wolves had existed…peacefully.

They still had their squabbles back then, but more importantly, there had been respect. Respect based on the old laws—which plainly said to keep your people on the right side of boundary lines or suffer the damn consequences.

Lukka changed all that. He constantly tested Loreck's patience and allowed his people to slip onto their territory unchecked. He had too many mouths to feed and not enough supplies with which to do so. Everyone knew it. Even worse, there were rumors that the bastard had sold off parts of his *own* territory—farmed them out for humans to develop for *money.*

It was a disgusting thought, one Eric doubted. No lycan could be so damn selfish. So greedy. So undeserving of the mantle of a leader.

But actions spoke louder than words. Why else would Black Mountain wolves be forced to fish in *their* rivers or hunt beyond their own forests?

Eric knew that it was only reluctance on Loreck's part to start a real conflict that the man didn't respond to the trespassing with vicious retaliation. But there was only so much patience in the world, and Loreck's was quickly running out.

But, if being confronted with the evidence of his own arrogance fazed Lukka any, the man didn't show it.

"Hmm," he murmured thoughtfully. "I hadn't heard."

The man had balls. Eric could give him that much. Though, he had even more respect for the fact that Loreck didn't reach across the table to smack the young pup on the ass like he so painfully deserved.

"Oh," Loreck replied in an equally casual tone. "And I'm sure that you didn't hear of the murder of one of my men, either?"

Lukka visibly flinched, blue eyes narrowing.

"I did," he said, nodding his head. "That's why I'm here—to offer my...condolences."

"Condolences." Loreck scoffed, running a hand over the gray-tinged brown stubble on his chin. "Then maybe you can tell me why one of *your* rogues killed him?"

Another emotion flashed across Lukka's gaze, too quickly for Eric to get a good read on it. Excitement. Fear? Satisfaction? Whatever it was faded in a flash.

"A chilling accusation," the pup said. "Do you have proof?"

Loreck snapped his fingers, and on cue, one of the men by the door came forward to drop a single object onto the table. Eric hissed, his nostrils wrinkling with the stench. It was a knife, smeared with blood, days old.

The insult couldn't be understated. To kill another lycan while in wolf form was one thing—grisly, but honorable. Accepted. To utilize a crude weapon and stealth? Despicable. At least Jamal's killer identified himself by leaving the blade behind. From it drifted a faint, musky odor as characteristic to any wolf as fingerprints were to humans.

"We think Jamal tried to fight back," Loreck explained gruffly. "He ultimately failed... However—" He reached down to trail a finger along the edge of the blade. "He still managed to draw his attacker's blood..."

So he wanted evidence? This was it—a scent trail was just as damning as a signed confession.

But Lukka seemed ready for it. The man didn't even have the decency to look shocked.

"McGoven's dangerous," he replied, recognizing the scent. "He took a mate without permission—forced her against her will and kept her hostage on his territory. She's a *blood* lycan," he added, making the crime so much worse. "You know the law—"

"She belongs with the pack of her father," Loreck said with a frown.

"Yes," Lukka agreed. "Only…when I sent my man out there to bring her to us, McGoven tracked them down, ambushed them, and took the girl back. I'm guessing that your man must have seen them, tried to help her and…"

Gotten his throat slit with a silver knife. It made sense. Jamal was a kindhearted soul. Seeing a crazed man, dragging some girl off into the woods would have incited his need to help.

And he paid the cost.

But…

Something didn't fit. While filthy and bruised, that girl didn't exactly look like she was being kept against her will. Though, if McGoven *had* mated her, that wouldn't mean much. Her desires would be entwined with his by now.

If murder was the worst crime a lycan could commit, mating an unwilling female would be a close second. Both deserved only one punishment—death.

But, something itched at the back of Eric's skull, demanding acknowledgment. Doubt.

"Why let her go in the first place?" he wondered, speaking out loud. "If he took her by force, why would he let your man take her? Let alone, allow them to get all the way out here before coming for her?"

And, while he was at it…

"What the hell was a full-blooded, unmated female doing so far from your territory anyway? Isn't it *your* job to keep your own wolves in line? And why didn't you go to welcome her personally? To send a beta for such a task, it's… It's unheard of."

Too late, did Eric realize that his tone came across harsher than intended. So much for politeness.

Loreck glanced at him in warning. But he could tell from his thoughtful expression that the Alpha had been thinking along those exact same lines.

Lukka shrugged. "We knew of her. She was supposedly the daughter of another rogue—a *made*. We didn't think there was a possibility she'd inherited the blood. But now…" He sighed, running a hand through his yellow hair. "We think that McGoven may have murdered the man to get to his daughter once he sensed the blood in her. Then he kept her heritage a secret. It was only when she murdered someone that he came clean. I'm sure you can see why."

Eric felt his eyes widen, but Loreck nodded. Just once.

"With a mate of his own, he could evade his rogue status. Challenge another Alpha on equal footing. Even start his own pack," he murmured. But suddenly, he tilted his head, raising a dark eyebrow. "Though, you've always been worried about him, haven't you? That's what you've feared. The day he might return and demand you *earn* your position the way an Alpha is meant to."

The question seemed aimed at Lukka like a dart—and it struck the bullseye. For a split second, the young pup dropped the friendly-neighbor routine. Those boyish blue eyes narrowed, so damn icy that even Eric suppressed the urge to shiver. Perhaps the wolf wasn't all talk after all.

"I *am* the Alpha," Lukka hissed. "I fear no one." But in the blink of an eye, his casual demeanor returned in full force, mouth quirking up in a faint smile. "But I can understand your concern. After all, without an heir, who knows what will happen to your pack should you meet your end before your time. A threat like the one McGoven presents must weigh heavily on your mind."

Son of a bitch. Low growls of warning echoed throughout the room. Eric felt himself take a step forward before he could help it—though Loreck managed to keep his composure.

It was a low blow, though the lack of an heir wasn't exactly a secret. Normally, an Alpha named a successor outright. Though there was no guarantee they would become the leader, the designation ensured stability. Direction. While childless, Loreck had held off on even naming a successor. If he died before he did so…

Eric didn't even want to think about the chaos that might ensue. Violence. Bloodshed. Civil War.

Loreck did have one benefit to withholding the name of an heir, blood or otherwise. It meant their pack ran smoothly. There were no political games. Everyone stood on equal footing, and he didn't need to worry about a challenge. Yet.

Lukka, on the other hand, wasn't so lucky. Rumors had swirled mere seconds after he claimed the title of leader.

Even outside packs weighed the risks of taking on Black Mountain and attempting a coup. He was on shaky ground, forced to defend his position at every turn. Paired with the obvious issues regarding feeding his enormous pack, you had a recipe for chaos.

"How ironic that you should mention heirs," Loreck replied, once the anger in the chamber died down somewhat, "when your own father named another man as his successor over *you*. It seems, an Alpha's will isn't always realized after death."

This time, Lukka couldn't have hidden the reaction if he tried. Pure, raw loathing crossed those handsome features—twisting them. It took way longer than a second for him to wrestle himself back under control.

"McGoven's *dangerous*," he insisted. "He's killed once, and he'll kill again. Do whatever you have to do to ensure justice for your own—"

"Wait," Eric said, ignoring the rival Alpha's glare. "What about the girl? I say we leave her out of this. She's full-blooded. If she's grown up in human territory…"

He didn't even want to think of what that meant. The mental damage that might be done, let alone physical, was horrifying. Especially if her first entry to lycan life was being mated against her will. Eric cringed as he thought of his own sister. That female deserved justice just as much as Jamal.

"She's an innocent," Loreck agreed. "If he mated her against her will, that just adds onto his crime."

"She's of no use to me. Just use her to get to him," Lukka suggested. "I never accepted her. She's not one of mine—"

Bang! At first, Eric thought someone had shot off a gun in the room, before he realized that the monstrous sound had come from Loreck slamming his fist onto the desk. A crack appeared within the wood, and Eric winced. It was an antique.

"You would *dare* leave one of your own? One of us? To fend for herself out there, pack-less? Have you no honor? No shame?"

His voice bellowed across the room. The territory, even. If the whole pack wasn't aware of this outburst, Eric would resign from his position on the spot. He doubted he had ever seen the Alpha so angry, without invoking the shift at least. Those hazel eyes flashed—emerald, brown...gold.

Wait a minute...

"No," Lukka admitted on a sigh. For the first time, he seemed to realize that he'd stepped too far. He shifted uneasily on his feet and cleared his throat. "But, I have a...liaison whose close to McGoven. I'll try to see if she can convince him to give up the girl."

"You do that. Or *we* will take her in. I will see to it personally," Loreck said.

Eric couldn't tell if he meant the threat, though he didn't feel the need to argue. A new female would be welcomed among them, as she should.

"There will be no need," Lukka said thickly. "She will be accepted into Black Mountain. Once she arrives."

"And after that," Loreck continued, his gaze electric, "we will have our justice."

Eric barely heard him. He was too busy trying his hardest to convince himself that it couldn't be—*she* couldn't be…

The girl's father was dead.

As he stared into his Alpha's hazel eyes, he knew that there was no damn way. Obviously, what he'd seen had been a trick of the light.

37

They entered the living room to find Naomi sitting upright, with one hand braced against the back of the couch, and the other clutching her throat. She looked entirely different from the confident, smirking figure Loren had become accustomed to avoiding. She was pale. That signature blond hair hung limply down her shoulders, dirty and clumped with mud.

"Where…where the hell am I?" she croaked, though Loren wasn't sure how she managed to speak at all.

Her throat…

Looking at her in the harsh light of morning, the futility of what they'd done hit Loren like a punch to the chest. All of it. Camping out, waiting for a miracle, had been foolish. A childish exercise. Forget McGoven's spiel on *lycans* and magic—Naomi needed a hospital.

Now.

She scanned the room, looking for a phone to do just that, but before she could so much as blink, McGoven moved...and every single shred of common sense just left her mind in an instant.

She could only watch him.

His exhaustion seemed to vanish. So did the guilt and hesitation she'd witnessed while on the porch. Now, only grim determination shined in those silver eyes.

Even covered in dirt and grime and streaks of blood, he looked one hundred percent... She couldn't seem to come up with a word *strong* enough, but one popped in her mind, unbidden—like an *Alpha*.

"Naomi." His voice was deep, silencing the blond's cries instantly. "Listen to me now. Get up." He didn't raise his voice, but he didn't have to.

Even Loren flinched, rocking on the balls of her toes. Despite her injuries, Naomi scrambled upright, leaning against the couch for balance. Those green eyes were wide, trailing from the bay window to the half-naked police officer facing her from across the coffee table.

"Wh...Where am I?"

"Follow me." McGoven turned, heading for the door without explaining.

And, for the first time, probably in her whole life, Naomi Tanner obeyed without so much as a snarky word in edgewise. Loren could only stare. It was strange—like watching every interaction she'd had with this same man, though from the outside looking in.

His knack for controlling people was...*eerie,* to say the least. *When he says jump, you don't even have the time to ask how high,* a part of her remarked in awe.

As if reading her mind, he cut his eyes to her. For a heartbeat, some of that icy strength softened. *Trust me,* he seemed to say. Just as quickly, his attention returned to Naomi. Her blood dripped onto the floor, leaving a trail of scarlet, as she struggled to follow.

"You—" McGoven eyed Micha, who stood near the doorway. "Help me."

Micha rushed forward, and together they took an arm on either side and manually steered Naomi outside. As they hastened out onto the porch, Loren's first thought was that they planned on getting her into the truck and taking her to the hospital after all. They should.

Instead...

They carried her down the steps and straight into the field beside the barn. There, in the grass, they released her.

Loren realized—as the wind pulled at her hair—that she had raced after them barefoot, with only her filthy flannel to protect her from the chill. Not that Naomi was any better off. Bleeding and dazed, the girl shivered, bracing her hands against the muddy earth. Panic filled her gaze as she eyed McGoven. Shockingly, she didn't scream or argue. She didn't seem able to.

"What now?" Micha stood back, serious for once. He had his arms crossed, his nostrils flared. Instantly, he looked older. Authoritative. "Are you sure about this? I've only seen one made successfully turned—with my dad's... The Alpha's guidance. It's not easy—"

"I know," McGoven said. Then he swallowed.

"And if it works," Micha added, "you know what that means, don't you?"

McGoven didn't reply, but his heavy sigh gave his answer away—*of course I do.*

"What are you doing?" Loren didn't know what made her step forward. After all, he'd already told her his plan. *Make Naomi submit.* But how?

"Stay back," Micha warned.

Both men didn't even look in her direction. McGoven, in particular, didn't seem willing to break eye contact with the blond curled up at his feet. Not even for a second. Suddenly, he squared his shoulders, and a low sound filled the air. A growl.

Loren felt it rumble through the earth. In her *bones.* The sensation was hair-raising, and she instantly pictured the black wolf who usually followed that sound. A wolf who could devour what remained of Naomi in one bite.

"No!" Blindly, Loren rushed forward, planting herself firmly in the middle of the fray. "Leave her alone!"

McGoven towered over her, and her heart sank. He wasn't like the man from the other day. There was no way on earth she could challenge him. But what was the alternative? Let Naomi die?

"She needs a hospital," she insisted, digging her toes into the wet earth as those silver eyes took on a darker shade. "Not...not *this!*"

"Loren—" She turned to find Micha at her side. Gingerly, he threw an arm over her shoulder and guided her a few paces away. "It's okay. Just wait. He's trying to help her. I know it looks scary, but it's not. She needs to trust him."

Loren couldn't imagine how bringing her out into the frigid cold air and dumping her on the ground was going to help anyone.

But then, she saw his eyes. He had turned to look at her, forsaking the blond for a painful second. *Trust me*, his gaze pleaded, before returning to Naomi.

Trust…

Loren wasn't sure if she even knew what that word meant. Could you trust someone when you didn't even know them? *Yes,* a part of her insisted without any hesitation. *You can. You will. You have to.*

Biting her lip, she waited… Though, nothing exciting seemed to be happening. McGoven just stared Naomi down and vice versa. On second thought, the eerie quiet settling in around them was an oddity. Despite the howling wind, the clearing was utterly silent. No animals. No birds. Nothing.

"She's weak," she heard Micha explain. He held her a little too close for her liking, but she was too engrossed by the unfolding scene to pull away. "I think he let her sleep to conserve her strength, though *I* wouldn't have. Changing sooner than later is her best bet. She needs to heal, and from a wound that bad, the only way to do so is to…"

"Shift," the word came from Officer McGoven as a growl, so damn compelling that Loren felt something deep inside of her shudder in response.

But the full brunt of the command was meant for Naomi. The blond trembled from head to toe, breaking the eye contact with a whimper.

See? The logical side of Loren whispered. *This is stupid.* But another part of her wasn't so sure. *Wait.*

Naomi didn't lurch up like she had, or turn tail and run. She didn't bite him. She didn't fight back.

She just…whimpered, pressing her body to the ground, and Loren knew instantly that this was what he'd wanted from her as well—*submission.* Triumphant, McGoven crouched and placed a hand on Naomi's shoulder, forcing her to face him again.

With Micha holding her back, Loren couldn't see what he did or hear what he said, but the next moment he bolted to his feet—dragging Naomi upright along with him. She whined, the cries harrowing.

"Stop!" Loren struggled against Micha's grip. "What are you doing—"

Before she could even get the words out, he turned, shoving Naomi in the direction of the trees so hard she went sailing to the ground.

Only when she landed...

The slender teenage girl disappeared.

And a wolf took her place.

38

*I*t was the smallest one yet. Lithe and delicate. Not even half the size of the black wolf, though still larger than any version Loren figured you would find in the wild. If there were any question as to its identity, a coat of golden fur glinted in the daylight, as it rolled onto its feet and took off.

It was fast, darting between the trees and out of sight. Left behind were the scattered remains of Naomi's outfit—a tattered blouse, a broken heel, and the fabric of a mini skirt ruffling in the wind.

"I need to go after her," McGoven muttered, tugging down the waistband of his sweatpants. His voice was still that deep, commanding tone, but beneath it all, he sounded relieved. Satisfied.

He glanced back at Micha and nodded to his injured leg. "You should shift too. I might need the help. You can corral her away from the town—"

"Sure thing." Wincing, Micha released Loren and began to remove his clothing. "I'll cover you."

Loren gaped as both men stripped naked, before common decency made her turn away, cheeks flaming. Next came the soft hiss of clothing hitting the ground, and then the heavier thud of two bodies lumbering into motion.

When she finally gathered the nerve to peek over her shoulder, she only just managed to catch sight of two giant wolves—one brown, and the other black—bolting for the woods. She didn't know how long she stood there after that, just staring.

It could have been minutes. An hour.

By the time she finally forced herself to move, her only action was to stoop for a pair of ratty, mud-stained sweats, which she tossed over her shoulder. She did the same to another pair, and then the torn remains of a pink blouse and mini skirt.

How thoughtful of you, a part of her hissed sarcastically. *Three people just change into wolves right in front of you—what do you do?*

Gather up the laundry.

You should be there, that same voice insisted. *Out there, with him…*

Her eyes seemed pulled to the forest against their will, scanning the shadows beyond the branches. But it wasn't like she could just sprout claws and fur anytime soon.

Why was that? If she was what he claimed, then why couldn't she shift? He said the urge was like a muscle that needed honing. Or perhaps, a switch you could just flick inside yourself, and voila? *Presto chango.*

I think my switch is broken, she thought as a halfhearted mental search revealed nothing out of the ordinary. No magic lever marked "lycan button." It seemed like the only thing she *could* do was the one thing she seemed to be best at. Cleaning up the mess.

The dirty clothes she left in a pile by the front door. Then, she entered the kitchen and stood near the window. Rain picked up again, dampening everything beneath a heavy sheet.

In the end…she didn't really know what made her go upstairs and tiptoe into that large bedroom. Boredom? A need to do *something?*

After a few minutes of rummaging through the closet, she found several clean pairs of sweats and a few oversized shirts. She showered and claimed one of the sweatpants for herself. The rest, she brought downstairs and set neatly folded by the door.

How damn thoughtful. *Why not go all out?* a part of her hissed. *Corrupting teenagers has got to be exhausting—why not make him dinner, too?*

As evening neared, she found herself in the kitchen, throwing open the fridge to do just that. *Old habit?* she guessed. A hold out from the days of living with her father, who demanded his meals be waiting for him. Whatever the reason, she dragged a loaf of bread from the counter and rummaged in the fridge for a carton of tuna.

As Sonia had joked, he didn't seem to have much else. A quick peek revealed some steaks in the freezer, and there was a carton of apple juice and some eggs on the shelf in the fridge. Though, maybe he just supplemented his diet with fresh meat?

A flicker of movement drew her gaze to the window, just in time to catch two dark shapes crossing the west field. Her heart lurched. The sun had already set, and the resulting shadow revealed just enough of tanned skin and long limbs for her to realize that both figures were fully human...and naked.

A desperate impulse kept her from blushing. Modesty wasn't important. She needed to see him... Boldly, her eyes went to the first figure, who just so happened to be the tallest.

He moved easily, black hair ruffled by the wind. The chiseled lines of his chest stood out as if etched in stone. It was only when he made it to the porch—close enough to have been fully illuminated by the house lights—that she finally turned away.

Fingers shaking, she slammed a piece of bread down to create the last sandwich. At the same time, the front door opened to a flood of footsteps. She waited until they had an adequate amount of time to notice the clothes before she finally peeked into the foyer.

She noticed Micha first. He stood fully upright on two uninjured legs as he wrestled a pair of pants on. The skin of his calf was merely smooth and tanned. Awe robbed her of some of her frustration. No wonder they'd been gone so long—if this was what shifting could do to them. Heal.

With renewed interest, she turned to McGoven. He ignored the T-shirts in favor of another pair of sweatpants which he already had on. Mud streaked him from head to toe, and he looked exhausted, but oddly...satisfied at the same time. The exercise of running obviously agreed with him.

But...

"Where's Naomi?"

The two men shared a look.

"She's home," Micha blurted finally.

"Home?" The remnants of the girl's clothes were right in front of her, by the door. Loren suspected there wasn't a *mall* out in the woods, stocked with clothing suitable for Naomi Tanner.

Considering he *wasn't* arrested, she figured that it was unlikely McGoven had marched the girl up her front walkway, completely butt naked, either.

"Home," McGoven insisted, tightening the drawstring to his pants. "She's safe."

"She's pretty, too," Micha gushed around a crooked grin. "You think I have a shot? You know, once she gets used to the whole *Teen wolf* thing."

McGoven ignored him. As the thrill of his change wore off, his frown returned. Those gray eyes found hers, and for the first time, she sensed an emotion in them that wasn't stern, or determined. Just…exhausted.

"Loren—" He sighed and nodded to the back door. "We need to talk."

"Okay." She followed him without hesitation.

As she slipped onto the porch, she could hear Micha shuffling into the kitchen. "Wow!" he exclaimed. "Is all this food for us?"

Loren felt too uneasy to answer him. It was freezing out, though before she really had the chance to feel it in full force, a fierce heat was there to displace the chill. *Pine.* He stood behind her, not quite touching, but when he spoke, she could practically feel his voice traveling right down her spine in a low, deep rumble.

"Let me explain…"

"What?" She whirled to face him, not knowing what to expect. What she *found* in his expression completely threw her off.

He looked…*vulnerable.* There was an aching softness to that stern jaw that she had never seen before. Unlike earlier, those eyes were a soft, wistful shade of gray that seemed hesitant to meet hers full-on.

"Ask me whatever you want," he said seriously. "I'll try to explain. I know it wasn't easy for you to see that. It looked violent. Barbaric, even."

Loren bit her lower lip. In hindsight, barbaric wasn't the word she'd use. Perhaps just...primal. "Where is Naomi?" she asked.

"She's *home*. I wasn't lying about that—" He broke off to run a hand through his hair. Then, he gestured for her to follow him over to the steps, where he sat down on the top one.

Loren shuddered. The stair wasn't all that large, and she had to sit close enough for her shoulder to brush his. Not that it was exactly a bad feeling...

She felt warm for a change. The icy, evening air barely affected her at all.

"So, Naomi's home?" She risked sneaking a glance at him.

"Yes," he said emphatically. "I swear. Her parents were there, but I managed to come up with a...plausible story to explain why she didn't come home last night."

Loren glanced at him sharply. "Naked?" Even now, he wasn't wearing a shirt, and he was the type of person who could draw notice wearing a sweater.

"That didn't matter, trust me." Something that could have been a frown tugged at the corner of his mouth. "I can be very...*persuasive* when I want to be. I was able to tell the Tanners a plausible story to explain why Naomi didn't come home last night—*after* Micha snuck into her room to get her clothes."

Loren felt a flicker of amusement. Despite his "powers of persuasion," he wasn't stupid.

"If you're curious," he added, "I told them she didn't want to risk driving in the storm. So, you suggested that she stay the night."

"So, what happens next?"

"I don't know," McGoven admitted. He scanned the horizon, eyes narrowing as they passed over the trees in the distance. "But, it won't be good. In fact…"

He faced her fully, and she sucked in a breath. Gone was the doubt. His eyes glittered through the darkness. "If you ask me, I should put you on a bus right now— one way—heading straight to some destination on the other side of the continent. You'd thank me in the long run."

It was impossible to meet his gaze. Nervously, Loren inspected her hands instead. "I appreciate everything you've done, but you don't have to keep making decisions for me. I'm eighteen."

In her world, at least, that age counted for something.

"I know." His tone threw her off, and she looked over to find him staring at the fields again. "I know."

"Maybe you should come with me?" she suggested. Even she wasn't sure if she was serious or making a joke. "You know, once Naomi tells the whole town that you turned her into a wolf."

"She won't."

He sounded so damn confident. Loren couldn't even find the strength to doubt him. "Why not?"

"Because I told her not to. Listen… By submitting to me, Naomi has accepted me as her Alpha—" She didn't miss how he seemed to cringe at the word, but he soldiered on anyway. "Among our kind, the Alpha's word is the *law*. If I told her to stay home tonight and say nothing to her parents, then she'll stay home and say nothing to her parents. It shouldn't cross her mind to disobey."

Loren's first instinct was to be skeptical. Then, she nodded. She knew firsthand the type of effect his voice could have.

"I want to know what you're thinking," he demanded.

She blinked, thrown again. "I think it sounds…"

"Like what? You can tell me."

"Like a dictatorship." Creepy on top of that. Having your thoughts and emotions decided for you? What kind of life was that?

McGoven nodded as if he fully expected her reaction. "It would to someone like you, who has grown up on the outside. To those of us within the pack, it's the complete opposite. We look to the Alpha for everything from strength to protection, and in return, we accept their leadership. Not out of fear. Out of love. We function as a family, of sorts, where everyone has a role to play. There is mutual respect," he insisted. "It's a two-sided relationship, one based solely on trust. Not violence. Not aggression."

"So, Naomi trusts *you?*" Loren asked, skeptical of that.

McGoven grimaced. "She will. Eventually."

"And...you'll trust her?"

He made a sound in the back of his throat that could have been a laugh if it weren't so strained. "I'll have to. She'll be my packmate. My family."

Don't like that, a part of Loren hissed. She flinched as something hot and prickly darted down her spine. Was that anger? Rage? Jealousy?

You should be jealous, some nasty part of her taunted. *After all, they don't wear clothing when they shift...*

"You're uncomfortable with the thought of me being so close to her."

Loren jumped for several reasons. One was that he seemed to be reading her mind again. The second was that he had reached for her hand while she'd been distracted. In frustration, she must have dug her nails into her palms, because the pad of his thumb gently trailed across the width of it, causing her fingers to loosen their grip.

"I-It's nothing," she stammered.

"You don't have to lie to me," he replied, scolding. His gaze trailed her face with concern, while his thumb continued to caress her hand. "I know what you're feeling. I've felt it too. It's instinct, nothing to be ashamed of."

He'd felt irritation because of Micha, she thought, her face hot. Desperate, she hunted for a change in topic. "It's just that…why didn't it work on me? Why didn't I s-submit to you?"

You know why, that snarky, shadowy part of her huffed. *We don't submit to anyone. Even him.*

"I'm not sure," McGoven admitted, his thumb left her palm, and he just wound up holding her fingers instead, locked within his. "I think… That there is some part of you that doesn't like being told what to do."

Loren had to snicker at that—she couldn't help it. Did "Turtle Girl" have a backbone all of a sudden? But when she thought of what happened in the field and the man from last night…

Suddenly, the thought wasn't so funny.

"Is that normal?" she croaked.

"No," he admitted. "There aren't many wolves who can resist the pull of a superior. Not because of my sex, either. I'm bigger. Stronger. Older. Your inner wolf should have sensed that and submitted within seconds. I've been questioning why you didn't, myself."

"Is it because I've been raised as a human?"

He shook his head. "I don't think so. But… One explanation is something we refer to as 'the calling.' When a young wolf resists the pull of an Alpha, not out of disobedience but instinct. It's rare, but it's happened."

Loren couldn't tell if he was merely trying to make her feel better. "Have you seen it happen?"

He seemed to tense. "Yes. It happened with me. I didn't submit to my Alpha the first time I was compelled to. I ran instead."

Shock rendered Loren silent. More questions buzzed her throat, aching to be asked, but she sensed it wasn't her place to rush this story. He needed to tell it in his own time.

"Such young wolves aren't seen as disobedient or flawed. They are nurtured and taken under their leader's wing. Lukas… He earned my trust, and then I submitted to him of my own free will."

There was something else. Something he wasn't saying.

"All this means is that I need to earn your trust. Your respect. I *also* think," McGoven added quietly before she had the chance to respond, "that we need to learn who your real father is. Soon."

"How?" Loren blurted, not understanding the urgency.

If Fred Connors really wasn't her father, she wasn't too heartbroken about that—but what did that say for her so-called "real" dad?

Was he any better? Considering that he had left her to be bounced from home to home after her mother's death, probably not.

"I need to know more about your mother," McGoven began warily.

"Like what?"

"Anything. Where she lived. Where she grew up. Her family, if any."

Loren squirmed. It shouldn't have been hard to respond. Children were supposed to know things about their parents, right? But, wracking her brain, all she could come up with were small details. Her smell. Her laugh. Her smile.

"I...I don't remember much of her," she admitted after a while.

"Tell me anything you can," McGoven urged. He didn't seem like the talkative, emotional type, so his encouragement shocked her enough into talking.

"She was p-pretty," she stammered, feeling like an idiot. "And funny, and that's all I really remember. Her name was Eveline, and we lived in Ridgerton. Before that? I don't know."

Her mother hadn't spoken much about her past life or where she'd come from. As to her real father, well, if Fred Connors wasn't it, she had no idea who it could be.

"Did she ever mention your father?" McGoven asked.

She shook her head. "Not to me, and I learned quickly that bringing up family around her wasn't a good idea."

She would get sad, Loren remembered. Clam up. Sometimes even crawl back into bed and stay there for the rest of the day.

"Does it hurt? To talk about her?"

Loren bit her bottom lip as she thought it over. "Yes. But in a way, it feels…good. She was a good person."

Unlike her father, the memories of her mother didn't sting and burn at the back of her mind.

"About my father…"

Beside her, she could feel McGoven stiffen as if knowing what she was going to say before the words even left her mouth.

"It's been almost a week, and I haven't been—" She broke off, trying to think of the right way to say it.

She hadn't been called for an interview. An autopsy report. To claim her father's body—legally, she was still his daughter after all. But some suspicious part of her couldn't help thinking that *he* had. He had done all of those things and didn't even think to include her in a single one.

Even weirder, he never mentioned the murder, or her father, or what she remembered from that night at all.

He's being polite, a part of her hissed. *Waiting for the right time.*

But would there ever *be* a right time to bring up something like this?

"I at least want to get some things from the house," she finished weakly.

That wasn't too much to ask, was it? But when she glanced at his face, it was carefully blank.

"I could arrange it with the station." He let go of her hand and stood. "If that's what you want."

Loren nodded. "I do."

He held out his hand, and she took it, allowing him to pull her to her feet. He was closer than she thought—she nearly ran right into him. But, seemingly out of reflex, his arm went around her waist before she had the chance to lose her balance.

Loren held her breath. Pressed against him, she could feel his heat. Her nostrils flared with his scent, and every cell in her body was tingly and alert.

She couldn't help but be flashed back to that incident in the field. The kiss…

At the thought, her throat went dry. She'd pushed the events from her mind out of concern for Naomi. But now…

She figured that she'd never really stopped thinking about it. It was always there at the back of her mind, far too dangerous to focus on.

"Did you… With Naomi? Did you…" She couldn't even form a coherent sentence.

Still, he knew exactly what she meant. "No. The bond between us—*our* situation is different."

"How?"

"I… Eventually, I will explain. I promise you that."

An awkward silence fell, and with every passing second her pulse raced, her cheeks warm. More than ever, she felt certain he was avoiding something. Something monumental. "Different" seemed to be an understatement when describing whatever lingered between them.

Intense, perhaps? Intimate. For instance, she could feel his uncertainty the same way she felt his anger—and more. He was worried. Restless. And… Something dangerous he seemed determined to smother. Hide, if not from her, then himself. It persisted regardless. Soon, he gave in with a low hiss that made her heart lurch.

A second later, he was smelling her, dragging her scent into his lungs with deep, greedy breaths.

She inhaled his scent in return, so rich it took her breath away. Suddenly, they were closer. Whether he had closed the distance, or she did, she didn't know. Only that she was the one who reached for him first.

Her hand landed flat against his bare chest, summoning a low sound that teased the air in response. His entire body vibrated with tension. No, this wasn't like the way he interacted with Naomi. Not even comparable.

But then, what was it?

Puzzled, she looked up, searching his expression. Any answer was elusive, hidden behind those gray eyes. They were darker than ever. Endless.

But she wanted to know more. For the first time since meeting him, she felt… Entitled to more. Entitled to touch him. Inch closer. Lower her gaze to his mouth and watch his lips twitch into a frown.

"Loren…" he was preparing to say something. Perhaps some variation of his usual request when it came to her. *Trust me. Listen to me. Obey.*

She wondered just what made him react to her in the woods. It hadn't been her nearness or even the heightened adrenaline from the chase. It had been this. Parting her lips, holding his stare and uttering just one word. "No."

His nostrils flared, his brows furrowing. Her skin tingled—she felt like someone on the verge of some great discovery. What made Bill McGoven tick? What could catch him off guard, make him react out of character?

It was more than disobedience, she sensed. *Oh yes,* that inner voice purred. It was whatever instinct had him lurching after her the second she started down the porch steps. She didn't dare go far—just beyond the circle of light cast by the porch lamp.

He was right on her heels. His hand caught her wrist, yanking her back. Her spine met the unyielding surface of his chest. And then…

They stood like that, breathing in tandem. His breath ruffled her hair, his pulse hammering through her skin. It should have been an awkward embrace. Instead, it felt...

Beyond natural. Right. He belonged here. He belonged with *her*.

But he didn't want to. He didn't want this. She could feel the second he wrestled his emotions under control.

"You should go eat," he murmured, pulling back.

"You should too," Loren countered breathlessly. If anyone needed food, it was him. But he shook his head, turning to face the trees.

"Need to scout," she thought she heard him murmur. "If those men really were Eislanders, they'll be back."

She could tell from the set to his shoulders that he intended to spend the night out in the fields again, patrolling for trouble.

"You should go inside," he added with his back facing her. "I'll keep watch."

His tone left no room for argument. *Go inside.* With a sigh, Loren turned, intending to head up the porch steps, when he called out behind her.

"Loren—" He was still turned away from her, but with every muscle in his body so tense, he could have been made from stone. "I'm sorry about what happened the other day. I...I got carried away. It...it won't happen again."

Before she could react, he lunged, taking off on foot beyond the shadows.

Carried away. Was that what they called it these days? Kissing someone so *hard* they could feel it all the way down to their toes? Absently, Loren reached up, trailing her fingers along her bottom lip.

"Hey!"

She spun around to find Micha leaning against the doorway to the kitchen, noisily chewing on a chunk of bread. He waved what she guessed to be the sole surviving sandwich through the air.

"Was I supposed to save some of these?"

She shook her head. "Knock yourself out."

Though, if it could help any at making sense of these past few days, maybe *she* was the one who needed a good tap on the head.

39

*B*ill scowled at the sky, hating himself for showing restraint almost as much as he was relieved to have lasted this long. Days with a warm, receptive female in his midst, and he hadn't gone further than a kiss—few men could say the same.

Not that he had a right to do a damn thing beyond that, of course. The logical arguments didn't matter. Biology and instinct didn't care about the morality of the situation. Add to it all that the female in question was his mate and…

There was no way they could go on like this for long. Already, he could sense her responding to the same urges plaguing him constantly. She craved his touch. His acceptance. More.

Breaking the bond now—with or without Lukka—could be the most humane decision in the long run. She would have to suffer her mental and emotional wounds alone, but she would have a sense of agency over her emotions again. Otherwise…

The longer the bond persisted, the more her unexamined memories weighed on his mind. Sooner or later, he wouldn't be able to keep himself from going through them and learning Loren Connors in and out. What haunted her at night when he could sense her fear and felt driven to comfort her?

A part of him didn't want to know. If he overstepped that boundary, there would be no turning back. He'd already lost one mate. He couldn't survive that pain again.

Not to mention, the threat of Lukka, Kyle, and now the Eislanders.

There were only a handful of ways both he and Loren could survive this mess unscathed—none of them appealing.

The first was to break the bond and prepare her to live as an unofficial rogue—at least until she could find a pack other than Black Mountain to take her in. It was a huge ask of an untrained lycan—assuming, of course, that she handled the revelation of their mating bond without…

Fireworks. Though she would have every right to be furious. Violated. Worse. Dropping that bomb on her and cutting her loose was cruelty he doubted he could go through with.

The second course of action was to try again to have her accepted into Black Mountain and go against every cell in his body, warning him not to trust Lukka farther than he could throw him.

But the third…

It was the option that lingered in his mind the most, feeding off every trace of Loren Connors he could still sense on the wind.

He could keep her here and accept the unofficial title thrust upon him as an Alpha. Going a step further, he could train her as a lycan. Educate her on their ways and prepare her fully for the dissolution of the mating bond. That, however, would require time—a luxury they didn't have.

Bill wasn't sure which decision he would be able to live with, let alone Loren.

But they would need to pick a course of action. Soon.

~ The story continues in Howl ~

A WORD FROM THE AUTHOR

Hey there!

Thank you so much for reading! If you enjoyed the story, please leave a review and recommend the book to any friend you think would love this twisted world. You'd have my eternal gratitude. Even a short sentence goes a long way!

Then, come join the rest of us dark romance lovers in my Facebook Group where you can get snippets, sneak peeks of upcoming books and even help vote on aspects of future novels.

Come to the dark side:
https://www.facebook.com/groups/lanasbeautifulmonsters/

WANT MORE STUFF TO READ?
Join my newsletter and get a **free book**! Plus, you get to stay updated with any new releases, random giveaways and exclusive sneak peeks!
https://www.lanaskybooks.com/newsletter

Other Novels: https://lanaskybooks.com/

FREE BOOK - JOIN MY NEWSLETTER

DARK, TWISTED ROMANCE

Join my newsletter and get a **free book**! Plus, you get to stay updated with any new releases, random giveaways and exclusive sneak peeks!

https://www.lanaskybooks.com/newsletter

ABOUT THE AUTHOR

Lana Sky is a reclusive writer in the United States who spends most of her time daydreaming about complex male characters and parenting her Cockapoo Joey. She writes dark, twisted romance across several genres. Her titles include everything from mafia romance to vampires.

facebook.com/AuthorLanaSky

twitter.com/lanasky101

amazon.com/author/lanasky

pinterest.com/lanasky101

goodreads.com/lanasky

instagram.com/lanasky101

bookbub.com/authors/lana-sky

tiktok.com/@author_lana_sky

www.ingramcontent.com/pod-product-compliance
Lightning Source LLC
Chambersburg PA
CBHW071430190726
48292CB00001B/185